LINES OF COURAGE

JENNIFER A. NIELSEN

LINES OF COURAGE

SCHOLASTIC PRESS · NEW YORK

Library of Congress Cataloging-in-Publication Data available

ISBN 978-1-338-62093-1

1 2021

Printed in the U.S.A.   23

First edition, March 2022

Book design by Christopher Stengel

To Sergeant Alvin C. York, a true hero

1914

FELIX

AUSTRIA-HUNGARY

The most terrible August in the history of the world.

—*Sir Arthur Conan Doyle (1914)*

CHAPTER
ONE

June 28, 1914

Deep inside, Felix knew something was wrong. A pinch had settled in his gut from the first moment he and his father stepped off the train in Sarajevo. It was the same feeling he'd had before his grandfather died last year.

"Are we safe here, Papa?" he asked.

But his father didn't answer. Instead, he was staring at a crowd that had gathered nearby. Felix arched his head in the same direction.

"Look there." Papa pointed to the man at the center of the crowd. "Remember this moment always, my son. Be proud of our empire."

Of course he was proud. Austria-Hungary was one of the largest and oldest empires in the world, and there, only meters away, was its future emperor.

Archduke Franz Ferdinand was square faced with brown

hair combed straight back and a wide mustache that turned up at the ends. He wore a high-collared light blue uniform decorated with more medals than Felix had ever seen before in one place. His wife was just as elegant, wearing a pale brown traveling coat, with her brown hair, the same color as Felix's mother had, swept up beneath a wide hat.

Papa leaned in close to Felix. "If our day begins with this much excitement, imagine how it may end! Shall we go now?"

The walk to their hotel would take less than an hour, though Felix was soon distracted by crowds of people lining the road, waiting for their own opportunity to see the Archduke and his wife.

The pinch in Felix's gut returned. He looked over at his father. "No one looks happy to be here."

Papa nodded. "They are not happy at all. They came to see their conqueror, not their future emperor."

Felix already understood that. Sarajevo was the capital city of Bosnia, which the empire had annexed into its territory six years ago. Bosnia had not come willingly.

Mama had warned them to postpone the trip. "Bosnia is not a safe place these days," she had said. "Sarajevo might be the most dangerous place in all of Europe right now!"

"The Archduke and his wife will be on the same train as us," Papa had said. "Do you really think they would go to Sarajevo if it was not safe?"

But Mama was insistent. "There are a lot of angry people

in the area. The Black Hand will be in Sarajevo! You should not be there too."

Those words replayed in Felix's mind as they continued walking. He looked up at his father. "What is the Black Hand?"

Papa glanced around them, then said, "Austria-Hungary is the finest empire in all of Europe, are we not? Yet Bosnia was not happy to be brought into the empire. Even angrier is its neighbor, Serbia. And why? Because Serbia wanted Bosnia for itself, to build their own empire. The Black Hand is a small group of Serbians who want to take Bosnia away from us, at any cost."

"Do you think they are here today?"

After a heavy sigh, Papa only said, "I did not think so before. But I do now. Come, let us hurry to our hotel."

Yet within another minute, they heard the rising sound of motors. Felix turned to see a black limousine slowly headed toward them, the first in a long line of fine automobiles.

"There is the Archduke again!" Felix pushed through the crowd to get a better look. The top was down on the limousine and the Archduke and his wife were waving at the people as they drove past.

Papa pulled Felix away from the side of the road so they could continue walking, following along with the limousine. "The Archduke is not wise to be so public. They would be honored in Vienna or even in Lemberg, but nobody here is celebrating." By that time, they had reached a bridge across a wide and shallow river.

Felix climbed onto the ledge of the bridge, where he could have a better view of the limousine. How happy the Archduke and his wife looked, so different from those who stood beside the road to watch them. Did the Archduke know how unwelcome his visit was? From where he sat, he couldn't have heard the way the people on the streets spoke his name, with sharp voices that dissolved into angry conversations. But surely he saw their expressions, the stiff wave of their hands as if a puppet master were lifting their arms on command.

That's when Felix saw the man with the grenade.

He was in a rumpled suit and wore an old cap over a head of thick black hair. The man pushed through the crowd, pulled the pin, and threw it at the Archduke's car.

The limousine driver must have seen the grenade too, for he sped up the car, although now the grenade headed directly for the Archduke. In one sharp, swift motion, the Archduke swatted it behind him just before it exploded.

The car that had been following the limousine was caught in the explosion. The force of the blast knocked Felix off his perch and he fell onto the bridge, even as others went running in all directions.

Papa gave Felix a quick glance before racing into the street to help those who had been injured. That's where he needed to be; Felix understood that. His father was a reserve soldier in the army, one of the rare people of the Jewish faith with the rank of Sergeant. Of course he needed to help in any emergency. Yet Felix was trembling so much, he wished

Papa had run to him instead. Wasn't he part of the emergency too?

Felix was still on the ground when his father finally returned. He helped Felix stand and brushed him off, then asked, "Is your leg all right?"

Felix looked down at his pants, now with a wide hole revealing his badly scraped knee. Until now, he hadn't even realized he was injured. He continued staring at it as he asked, "Where is the man who did this?"

Papa gestured to the river below the bridge. "He tried to jump in the water to escape, but as it's only a few centimeters deep, it was easy for the authorities to capture him."

"Was he part of the Black Hand?"

"He must have been, but he won't be a problem for us any longer."

Maybe. The pinch in Felix's gut was worse than ever. He knew this wasn't over and he wanted to say that, but Papa had never been wrong about anything before. So Felix nodded and quietly followed his father off the bridge.

Papa said, "We can be grateful that you are safe, that most of these people will be all right, and especially that the Archduke is safe. Can you imagine the consequences if that assassin had succeeded?"

Felix couldn't imagine anything. What was the point of imagining when his mind was already too full of reality?

They continued along the street in the same direction as the Archduke's car had gone after the explosion, Felix limping now to protect his scraped knee. He wished they were walking back to the train station instead. All he wanted was to go home.

Papa pointed across the street at a delicatessen. "I will go in and buy us a couple of pastries. Then you'll feel better."

No, he wouldn't. A few bites of *burek* didn't matter, not after what he'd just seen.

"It will all be forgotten in time," Papa said. "Our hotel is not much farther ahead. I'll finish my business tomorrow, then we can take the next train back to Lemberg, all right?"

Felix nodded because that's what he was supposed to do. But he didn't want a pastry—he didn't want anything except to go home.

"Do you think there are more assassins here?" he asked.

Papa only grunted, a quiet admission that yes, there had surely been more than one assassin. But he did say, "They had their chance, and that man failed. Besides, the Archduke and his wife are long gone by now."

He went inside the delicatessen while Felix stood outside and tried to tell himself that his father was right, because his father was always right.

Yet even as he did, he heard a familiar sound of a motor and looked toward the street. His jaw fell open as he saw the Archduke's black limousine driving toward him, headed back toward the bridge, where the grenade had exploded only an hour ago. Once again, the Archduke and his wife were in the back, still with the top down so they could wave at the people.

Papa hurried outside. He must have already seen the

limousine too, for he said to Felix, "Why would they come back here?"

The Archduke seemed to be wondering the same thing. He leaned forward and said something to the driver, who immediately turned onto a side road, stopping almost directly in front of Felix.

"There, see? He's turning around." Papa moved forward to hold the crowds back.

But Felix remained where he was, his eyes fixed on the royals directly ahead of him. He was so intent on them, he almost ignored the sudden movement in the corner of his vision. Sunlight reflected from a glint of metal and Felix turned, seeing a man hurrying toward the vehicle. He was young with dark hair and a short mustache and wore a dark suit jacket. He crossed between Felix and the Archduke, so close now, he could reach out and touch the limousine.

Scream, Felix thought. *Warn them!* But the words froze in his throat and the fear flooding through him made it impossible to move.

The limousine driver began to back up, his attention focused on the road rather than on the crowd around them.

He didn't see the man at the side of the limousine raise the gun in his hand. The man fired twice, killing the Archduke first and then his wife.

Horrified, Felix dropped to his knees. Papa and others in the crowd rushed at the man, but he had already pulled a vial of liquid from his mouth and swallowed its contents. If it was a poison he expected would kill him, then it did not seem to work. He was visibly ill but on his feet when the crowd dragged him away.

Minutes passed, or maybe seconds or hours, Felix wasn't sure. He only knew that at some point, his father pulled him back to his feet and told him to begin walking.

Somehow—Felix couldn't quite remember the details—his father got him back to the train station. He was sitting alone on a bench on the train platform when he jumped, hearing a sound beside him, then felt Papa's hand on his shoulder. "It's all right. You're all right." He held up two tickets. "Wherever the next train goes, we'll be on it."

Felix shrugged. "Then let's hope it does not go to Serbia."

Papa smiled grimly, then sat beside him. "I know that was an awful thing to witness today, but you're safe now."

Felix nodded, but deep inside, he wondered if it was possible for his father to be wrong a second time in a single day. Was he truly safe?

"I should have warned them," Felix said. He could have done it. He had known what was about to happen, almost before anyone else did.

But he hadn't made a sound. He'd only stood there, helpless, paralyzed with fear, watching everything happen in slow motion. If he had said something, anything at all, maybe he could have saved the man who would have been his next emperor.

"What happened back there wasn't your fault," Papa said. "You must not blame yourself."

Felix kicked at a pebble along the platform while mumbling, "The Archduke and his wife are dead, aren't they?"

"Yes," Papa answered. "And the entire world shall pay for it."

Felix lowered his head. He should have warned them.

July 1, 1914

The train journey home took three days, but even when they finally set foot in Lemberg, Felix still felt as if he were looking at the world through someone else's eyes. It was someone else who had seen the assassination, not him. Someone else who'd had the chance to warn the Archduke but only stood back, mute and helpless. Not him.

He felt relieved to live so far from Vienna, the empire's capital city. Surely the uproar over the assassination would be greater there.

Here in Lemberg, much farther east, things were quieter. The newspapers acknowledged the death of the crown prince, of course, but the headlines were smaller, and the mourning was as simple as flags flown at half-mast. Otherwise, people here were going on with their lives.

That was Felix's plan too: just try to pretend that everything was normal.

Mama seemed to have the same plan. As soon as they arrived home, she offered them warm hugs, then said, "Go upstairs and clean up from your journey. We have company arriving soon for supper."

"What company?" Papa asked. "Parties are inappropriate so soon after the Archduke's death."

"It's not a party, it's a quiet dinner with old friends. Major Dressler has been touring the area with his family while he is on military leave. They've come all the way from Germany. We cannot cancel on them now."

"No, I suppose not." Papa turned to Felix. "Do as your mother says, clean up. The Dresslers have a daughter a little younger than you, a girl named Elsa, I believe. I'm sure the two of you will get along fine while the adults talk."

Getting along with some girl Felix had never met before was the last thing he wanted. He would have much rather sat with the adults for supper to hear their thoughts about the assassination. It's all that anyone on the train had talked about on the way home. Several of them had mentioned war.

But there was nothing he could do. When evening came, there he was in the parlor room, staring at Elsa, an eleven-year-old girl with brown curls that bounced when she talked, and who was staring back at him with wide, curious eyes.

"We should be long-distance friends," she said. "We would have the most fun writing back and forth, don't you agree?"

Felix squinted back at her. "I don't even know you."

"Not yet." She twirled a curl of her hair around one finger. "What do you like to do?"

"I, uh . . ." He liked to read, but he hadn't read a single page in the last few days. He had been fascinated with automobiles once, but now he didn't care if he ever saw one again.

"I raise carrier pigeons," she said, apparently unaware that Felix hadn't answered. "I train them too."

"Oh." He truly didn't care. But they needed to have some conversation, so he asked, "Why?"

Elsa leaned forward. "Why? Because they are the most amazing animals. My father says they'll be most useful in the war."

Elsa said *most* a lot. Felix wondered about using the word too, as in "You are the *most* talkative girl I've ever met," or "You are making me the *most* annoyed."

But even if he had said something, she'd have just talked right over the top of his words. "Soldiers keep the pigeons in baskets and take them into battle. When they need to send a message back to the base, they simply attach it to the pigeon's leg, then release it. No matter where it is, the pigeon will find its way home. Even if the pigeon's home is moved to a different location, the pigeon will still find it. Isn't that the most amazing?"

It was a little amazing, Felix had to admit that.

"My father says our scientists have even developed a camera that the pigeon can wear. It can fly over enemy territory and take pictures. Now, that is the—"

"—most amazing, I agree," Felix said. "Anyway—"

"I brought you one of my birds," Elsa said. "My favorite bird, actually. I named him Wilhelm, after our Kaiser. Isn't that the most funny thing?"

No, it really wasn't. He asked, "What am I supposed to do with a homing pigeon?"

"I already told you, if we are friends, we should write letters to each other. So maybe in a few weeks, you could use Wilhelm to send me a letter. Unless you want to keep Wilhelm if you and your mother are ever in trouble. When your father goes off to war—"

Felix's heart leapt into his throat. "Why would he go to war?"

Elsa tilted her head as if the answer was obvious. "There must be a war, after the assassination. My father says you were there, that you saw the assassination yourself! Is that true?"

Felix's eyes shifted toward the doors of the dining room, wishing they were open so that he could escape through them. He searched his mind for any reason to leave, anything at all, but now his head was filled again with what he had seen back in Sarajevo. He shrugged and said, "I don't want to talk about it."

She clearly did. "How can you say that? That is probably the most amazing thing that will ever happen in your life!"

What if she was right? What if that horrible day turned out to be the biggest day of his life? Would the rest of his life be empty and boring by comparison?

Elsa wasn't finished. "If you *could* go to war, that would be the most wonderful thing you could do for Austria-Hungary. But, of course, the war should be over by Christmas, long before you're old enough to join."

That was interesting. Felix looked up. "I think the same way. Serbia barely shows up on a map compared to our empire. Of course the war won't last long."

Elsa shook her head. "That would change, of course, if Russia decides to fight with Serbia. Russia has the largest military in the world. But," she quickly added, "if war comes, Germany will join you." She leaned closer to him and whispered, "Truthfully, I think most of the German officers want war. Papa says we are ready and will have our victory."

Because Elsa's father was a major in the German army, she probably knew more than most about what might happen if a war began. That led Felix to another thought, one that brought that familiar pinch back in his gut.

Was Elsa right, that Papa would have to go to war? If so, he'd likely be sent to the front lines of the battle. Jews weren't given the ranks that kept them away from the fighting.

Felix added that to the list of things he never wanted to think about. He tried again to defend his empire. "Austria-Hungary is the strongest empire in all of Europe. We've lasted for hundreds of years already. We don't need Germany's help to defeat Serbia."

Elsa waved that idea away with one hand. "Just because your empire is old does not mean it is strong. See here. I'll show you how my mother explained it to me." She nodded at a game table in the far corner. "Do you have cards in there?"

He stood and retrieved a deck of cards from a drawer in the table, then gave them to Elsa. She divided the cards into four piles, which she set on the table.

She said, "Europe has always been a land of empires, no? Can you name the four empires in Europe now?"

He hesitated, not wanting to start with the obvious. So he began, "The British Empire."

Elsa nodded. She picked up four cards and laid them on their sides in a square, then placed other cards on top of the square, creating a small card house. "They'll be on Russia's side, and Serbia's, and they are strong, but mostly because for centuries, they've had the finest navy in the world. Germany has a navy too, but we also have airships that the world has never seen before. We have new weapons, enormous weapons. This will be a war beyond anyone's imagination!"

A shudder rose through Felix. Elsa spoke as if the idea of war was almost exciting to her.

"The second empire?" Elsa asked.

"The Russian Empire."

Elsa made another card house for Russia, though this one was twice as large as Britain's. As she worked, she said, "Russia has an enormous army, but their Tsar is unpopular, and his hold on the throne is not good. Now, do you know the third empire?"

"Your home. Germany."

Elsa built a third house of cards. "My father says that Germany has never been stronger. We are the only empire that is prepared to fight in this century while the others still live in the past. Do you know the fourth empire?"

The answer to this question was obvious. Felix said, "My own. Austria-Hungary."

"Yes. Now, you think you are strong enough to challenge Serbia in a war, but I will show you the problem." This time, the house of cards was different. Elsa built many smaller squares, all of them separate from one another, connected only by a single roof. "Your empire is made up of several small countries all controlled by one Kaiser. Each country has a different language and religion and culture. Worse still, all the countries hate one another. In fact, there is only one thing they agree on, and that is who they hate the most."

Felix frowned. "They hate our Kaiser. They hate that he rules over them." His mind drifted again to Bosnia, at the way the people had glared at the Archduke as he passed by. Did all of the countries within the empire feel the same way?

Elsa leaned in and gently blew on the many card houses. The first to fall was Austria-Hungary's. She glanced up at Felix. "If there is war, that is the most likely outcome for your empire. That is why you need Germany's help."

The door opened and Papa walked in. "Would you two like to join us? I'm sure you both have many questions."

"Yes, please!" Elsa jumped out of her seat.

But Felix remained where he was, staring at the cards flat on the table. It had taken so little for these houses to collapse. What if Elsa was right, and this was the future for Austria-Hungary? What if this was the future for all the empires?

All that remained was to wonder who would be left when the last card fell.

Elsa glanced back at the fallen cards, then looked over at Felix. "And *that* is why I am leaving one of my homing pigeons with you."

CHAPTER
THREE

July 28, 1914

The assassination had happened one month ago, though to Felix, it could have easily been only yesterday. His world was spinning faster and faster; each day seemed to pass in minutes, and every minute brought worse news than before.

Suppertime was the worst. The daily newspaper had become a guest at each meal, and Papa read from it as they ate. At first, it had seemed hopeful.

"The Kaiser has sent a list of ten demands to Serbia." That was what Papa had said last week. "Our requests are reasonable, considering that they assassinated the heir to the throne. Serbia would be foolish to reject them."

"But what if they do?" Felix had asked.

Papa just frowned back at him, not wanting to say the word that seemed to linger in the air, everywhere around them: *war.*

Only days later, Papa's news sounded even worse. "Russia

has chosen sides with Serbia. If we attack, Russia has promised to declare war on Austria-Hungary."

"Russia?" Mama looked around the room. "The first thing Russia would do is come here, to Lemberg. You know how much they want control of this city."

The Russians would come here? Felix gripped his fork tighter. "Maybe we should leave Lemberg now, go to Vienna."

"We are not at war, not yet." Papa smiled, the kind of smile that didn't reach his worried eyes. "All is not lost. The leaders of Russia and Germany are cousins. We must let them talk and work this out for all of us. Serbia has until the twenty-eighth to agree to the demands. War can still be avoided."

That was their conversation three days ago, and in the days since then, Felix had begun to lose hope. So had his parents. More than once, he had walked into the kitchen and caught his mother quickly brushing away tears, with a newspaper clutched in one hand. He saw the way Papa's shoulders were slumped over at the supper table; Papa always straightened up when he saw Felix watching, but within minutes, whatever weight he was bearing took its toll again.

They were afraid, so Felix was afraid. He realized he was slumped over too, nearly all the time.

On the evening of the twenty-eighth, Mama said to Papa, "Did I hear you received a telegram from Major Dressler today?"

"I did." His tone was grim, but he pulled the paper from his coat and passed it over to her. "Last night, Serbia sent a message to Germany. They agreed to nine of our ten demands."

Mama looked up from reading the telegram, smiling so wide that Felix couldn't help but smile too. "Then this is wonderful news! Surely there is no need for war if we are so close to an agreement."

"Serbia's message arrived in Germany last night," Papa continued. "It came in time to stop the war. But . . ." He paused, for a very long time. "According to that telegram, some of Germany's military leaders want war. So they hid Serbia's message. Their Kaiser did not see it until today, until it was too late. So now it is certain."

"Austria-Hungary is not prepared for war," Mama said. "Surely our Kaiser will do everything he can to keep the peace."

But Papa shook his head. "Earlier today, our Kaiser declared war on Serbia. Austria-Hungary just started the war."

"No." Mama exhaled the word, as if it took the last of her breath to speak. She put a hand to her heart. "What does this mean for us, Josef?"

"That depends on Russia now. We must hope they stay out of this. If they do, all this trouble will be over before the end of the year."

"What if Russia doesn't stay out?" Felix asked. "Elsa told me that if we declare war on Serbia, Russia will declare war on us."

Papa sighed and reached into his pocket, pulling out a second telegram. "The Kaiser fears the same thing. I am to report to Vienna at once. They are calling all reserve soldiers back into service."

Tears welled in Mama's eyes, and this time she didn't try to hide them. "When do you have to leave?"

A pause. Then, "Tomorrow."

With that single word, Felix's entire world caved in. Worry spilled out from the knot in his gut, flooding his entire body until he couldn't breathe or think, until he couldn't stay here a second longer. He slammed his spoon down, pushed back his chair so fast that it tipped over, then ran from the room. He didn't know where he was running, or why. He only knew that something in him had begun hurting in a way he'd never hurt before.

He ran out the back door and through the garden until he reached a thicker patch of woods. Blinded by his tears, he tripped over a log and fell. The sting from his fall echoed into his hands and knees, and he welcomed it. If nothing else, the physical pain was a distraction from the ache tearing at him inside.

"Felix?"

He turned and quickly wiped his eyes with the back of one hand, then sat up. "I'm here."

Papa walked closer, then sat on the same log over which Felix had just fallen. He leaned forward and clasped his hands together. "I suppose I could have broken that news in a better way."

Felix shrugged. What did it matter how he'd told them? The news was the same.

"My country needs me," Papa said. "I would be ashamed to stay at home when so many others are willing to make the sacrifice."

"What sacrifice?"

His father paused. "You're old enough now that I can speak to you like a man, because while I'm gone you must be the man about the house. This is war, Felix. Some of our soldiers will come home injured, and some won't come home at all, but I promise you this: I will do everything in my power to come back as quickly as possible."

"Will it be quick?"

Papa glanced away and wiped a tear from the corner of one eye. "No, I don't think so."

The ache in Felix's heart worsened. He had never seen his father cry before, never once. Until now.

Papa continued, "The truth is that we won't only be fighting Russia. France and Great Britain will join the war too, and maybe a great many other countries. Germany will be on our side, and perhaps we will gain some allies of our own. I think it is possible that the coming war may spread around the world before this is over."

New tears formed in Felix's eyes. Papa was the bravest man he knew, but what good was one person's courage against a war as big as the entire world?

Then a new thought entered his mind, one every bit as horrible as the idea of his father going to war.

"Papa, at what age would I have to serve in the military?"

His father sighed, as if he'd hoped not to hear that question. "Fifteen. That's three years away. Let us hope that this war will have ended by then."

"What if it hasn't?"

Papa's hand went to Felix's shoulder. "You have three years

to prepare. Learn to fight, to shoot, learn to be a good soldier now, and if you must go to war, be the best soldier the empire has ever seen."

Felix lowered his head, ashamed of himself. His father could not know him at all, to believe he was capable of such courage.

Papa reached into his pocket. "I brought this out here for you." In his hand was an old medal. It had a red cross set on a round gold background, hung from a bright red triangular cloth with a pin on the back. One edge of the cloth was torn, but otherwise it was still in perfect condition.

"Do you know what this is?" Papa asked.

Felix nodded. It was called the Golden Cross of Merit. Papa kept it in a display case in the dining room. When Elsa's family had come, Felix had even shown them the medal.

"Your grandfather earned this through his exceptional courage in the face of danger. He gave it to me before I joined the military, and now I wish to give it to you."

"I'm not a soldier."

"No, but it is possible that while I am gone, you will need to find your own exceptional courage."

Felix stared at the medal, but he could not take it. He hadn't earned something so precious and likely never would. Instead, he said, "I wish I were like you, Papa, but I'm not. I never will be."

Papa looked disappointed. "So you won't take the medal?"

"I won't accept what I haven't earned."

"*That* was a very courageous thing to say." Papa slid the medal into the pocket of his coat. "Sometimes we must grow into our bravery. It's there, Felix, even if you don't feel it yet. When you need your courage, trust that you will find it. Before I come home again, I believe you will have earned a medal of your own."

Papa hugged Felix close, but when it was time to return to the house, Felix walked beside his father, listening to the medal rustle in the pocket of Papa's coat. There it was, the second time his father had been wrong. Felix would never do anything worth a medal such as this.

CHAPTER
FOUR

September 3, 1914

Several weeks later, Mama rushed through the door, clutching three letters in her hand. "At last! We have mail."

Finally! Felix nearly tripped over his own feet running to her. "Is there anything from Papa?"

"Two letters! Also, a letter from your friend Elsa Dressler."

That was less exciting and Felix couldn't help but roll his eyes. Despite her insistence otherwise, Elsa was not his friend, nor could he think of any reason why she might have written him. But he did care deeply about the letters from his father. Papa had been gone for more than a month and they hadn't heard anything from him until now.

Felix followed his mother over to the sofa while she opened the envelopes. "I suggest we read the letters in order. Your father's first letter is from three weeks ago." She unfolded the letter and began to read:

To my darling wife and brave son:

We have arrived in Serbia, so many soldiers you would hardly
believe it. Some say there are nearly a half million of us.
We have moved quickly across the country and faced little
trouble thus far. Of course, it cannot always be so easy, but
for now, I am well, and proud to be part of this great empire.
I hope that when I write to you next, it will be from a hum-
bler Serbia, who will never again challenge our Kaiser.

All my love,

Josef (Papa)

Felix leaned over Mama's shoulder. After so long, there had
to be more. He *needed* there to be more. "That's all he wrote?"

"I'm sure he doesn't have much time, if they're in such a
hurry to get through Serbia." Mama held up the next letter.
"Would you like to read Elsa's letter now?"

Felix glanced over at Wilhelm, the carrier pigeon Elsa had
left with them two months ago. She thought it was so amazing, when really, the thing just ate a lot of seeds and scattered
them outside the cage for him to clean up each day. He had to
think about Elsa every time he saw the bird. Did he have to get
a letter from her too?

Felix shrugged and pointed to the other letter in Mama's
hand. "I'd rather hear more from Papa."

"Well, Elsa's is the next letter in order, so we'll read it together." She handed the letter to Felix. "Your turn."

He sighed and opened the letter. He could almost hear Elsa's cheery tone in the words as he read them.

To Felix,
I thought you might want to hear about our family since the night we left Lemberg.

This was painful. Felix glanced over at his mother, wondering if they could stop there. He hadn't wondered about her family even once since that night, and was certain he hadn't been interesting enough that she should have thought about him either. He continued reading.

As we traveled back to Germany, every place we went, all that people wanted to talk about was the coming war, especially when Papa was in his military uniform. But the most exciting time was after we arrived home. Every young man who is old enough has volunteered for the military (and even a few who are not quite old enough). They all want to be part of the great victories ahead.
Germany has already had one great victory in the east. Although we were out-numbered by the Russians, Papa said we surrounded them and now we have more

than 200,000 prisoners. What shall we do with them all?

Papa is off to war, of course. He is headed to northeastern France. I don't know the mission, but he did say something about how it would be German territory soon. That's probably a secret, so don't tell the Allies!

Yours in certain victory,
Elsa

Felix wrinkled his nose. "What does she mean by '*yours in certain victory*'?"

"It means she's been taught basic manners," Mama said. "You should write her back."

He groaned, wishing he had not asked. He decided right then that unless he had no other choice, he would never write her.

Mama opened Papa's second letter. She began at the top. "This one is dated August twentieth. Good news must travel quickly!" Then almost immediately, her hopeful expression fell. Felix leaned over her shoulder, worried about the sudden change in Mama's tone.

MY DEARESTS,

OUR FORTUNES HAVE CHANGED SINCE MY LAST LETTER, VERY MUCH FOR THE WORSE. THE REASON WE MOVED SO QUICKLY ACROSS THE SERBIAN FLATLANDS IS BECAUSE THEY WERE WAITING FOR US IN THE MOUNTAINS. WE HAVE LED FAR TOO MANY OF OUR SOLDIERS INTO A

TRAP, AND THOUGH THEY ARE FIGHTING BRAVELY, OUR NUMBERS OF
FALLEN SOLDIERS ARE ALREADY SO GREAT, I BARELY CAN BELIEVE IT.
I CANNOT SPEAK FOR THE SERBIANS, BUT OUR SIDE ALONE HAS THOU-
SANDS DEAD, WITH TWICE THE NUMBERS OF WOUNDED, AND SEVERAL
HUNDRED ALREADY TAKEN PRISONER.

OUR ORDERS ARE TO PRESS FORWARD, AND WE WILL, BUT IT IS
CLEAR THAT A LONG WAR IS NOW AHEAD. I WORRY THAT WE HAVE
MADE A TERRIBLE MISTAKE BY GOING TO WAR. INDEED, OUR SOLDIERS
ASK WHAT WE ARE FIGHTING FOR, AND I HAVE NO ANSWER TO GIVE
THEM. COULD THE LIFE OF ONE ARCHDUKE BE WORTH THE MILLIONS
WHO MAY YET FALL IN THIS WAR?

ALL MY LOVE,

JOSEF (PAPA)

Mama began to fold up the letter, but Felix grabbed the
paper. "Wait! There's more writing on the back!"
She turned it over and read.

P.S. I HAVE JUST HEARD MORE NEWS THAT CONCERNS ME. I WILL
DISPATCH A COURIER IN HOPES OF THIS LETTER ARRIVING QUICKLY AND
WITHOUT BEING PASSED THROUGH THE CENSORS. WE HAVE RECEIVED
WORD OF RUSSIAN SOLDIERS WHO ARE ADVANCING TOWARD LEMBERG.
WE HAVE ARMIES SURROUNDING THE CITY WITH ORDERS TO STOP THE
RUSSIANS, BUT THEIR ARMIES FAR OUTNUMBER OURS. AS SOON AS YOU

ARE ABLE TO PACK UP OUR THINGS AND ARRANGE FOR TRANSPORTATION
TO VIENNA, YOU SHOULD DO SO. I WILL WAIT TO SEND ANY MORE LETTERS
UNTIL YOU SEND ME POSTAL DIRECTIONS FOR VIENNA. UNTIL I WRITE
AGAIN, BE SAFE.

Mama folded up the letter, then sat in silence for so long that Felix felt worry building up in his chest, making it harder to breathe. When he couldn't stand it any longer, he asked, "Is it true? Are the Russians nearby?"

"I don't know, but if your father is right, we must leave Lemberg as soon as possible."

"We can leave this very minute!" Felix meant exactly what he had said, yet his mother continued to sit there, deep in thought. What was there to think about? If the Russians were coming, they needed to leave.

"We may have a little time," Mama said. "Our armies will defend Lemberg, which will slow the Russians down, or even stop them. I must speak to the Rabbi, so that we can organize to get all the Jews out of Lemberg. With their husbands and sons off to war, I must do what I can to make sure no one is left behind."

Felix clenched his fists in frustration. What if there wasn't time to speak to the Rabbi? What if she helped every family get out of Lemberg . . . and they were left behind?

But he knew his protests would do no good. Every day, Mama baked extra loaves of bread to help feed those who were struggling. She spent most afternoons visiting with families who had sent loved ones off to war, and who had heard bad news, or no news at all.

These were good things, Felix knew that, but the situation had changed. They had to think only of themselves now. "When can we leave?"

Mama grabbed her coat and hat. "I'll go see the Rabbi right now. While I am gone, pack up your room and anything of value. Then let us hope that our armies can stop the Russians before they enter the city."

The door hadn't even completely closed before Felix raced through the house, trying to decide what to bring and what to leave behind. They would need their candlesticks and the menorah that had been passed down for more generations than he could count. There were books to bring, changes of clothing for them both, and . . . he let out a groan. What to do with the pigeon?

Wilhelm wasn't coming with them, but he couldn't leave it behind either. Felix found a sheet of paper and wrote a note to Elsa, explaining that he was returning the bird now, as he was worried about whether they could escape from Lemberg before the Russians arrived. Then he rolled the note around Wilhelm's leg, fastened the note with some tape, and released the bird.

"That counts as my letter to you, Elsa," Felix mumbled.

Mama returned an hour later. "The news of the battle is worse than I thought. The Rabbi heard a report that the Russians have already broken through the lines. They could be here as soon as tonight. But"—she took Felix's hands in hers—"we should be fine. On my way home, I arranged for us to meet a driver in the town square at eight o'clock tonight. That should give us enough time to be out of Lemberg before the Russians arrive."

"Why can't we leave now?"

Mama frowned. "We are not the only ones trying to leave, and some people are much greater targets for the Russians than we are."

Felix's next question was interrupted by a loud commotion on the street. He ran to the window and saw rows of soldiers in gray uniforms with a red stripe down the side of each pant leg. Papa wore the very same uniform.

"Mama!" he called. When she came to the window, Felix asked, "Is Papa with them?"

"I don't think so," she said, scanning their lines. "But this is not a victory march. They must have retreated."

Felix looked up at his mother. "Are you sure the Russians won't be here until after eight o'clock?"

"Let us hope not," Mama said.

"What if they come early?"

The expression on his mother's face in that moment was instantly etched into Felix's memory. Her eyes had widened with a fear he had never before seen in her. She was terrified too.

"Eight o'clock," she mumbled. "That is not so many hours away. We cannot be here when the Russians come."

CHAPTER
FIVE

September 3, 1914

Once they were packed, Felix waited by the door, bags at his feet, watching the hand on the clock slowly tick forward.

"It will do no good to arrive early in the square," Mama said. "And it may put us at risk to be seen there with all our bags."

Maybe so, but that didn't lessen the feeling inside him that they were better off there, waiting for the driver, than being here at home.

Meanwhile, Mama swept the kitchen floor. And brought in cabbage from the garden. And wrote a letter to her sister.

The instant she stood with the letter in hand, Felix picked up the bags. "Now? Can we go now?"

"Yes, now."

The sun was sinking on the horizon when they stepped out the door. Felix carried one large bag with two hands, and Mama had two smaller bags in each hand. They had left behind nearly all their valuables and possessions, but Felix hardly cared. There was far more at stake than a set of silverware or a fine pair of shoes.

Here in the empire, the Kaiser treated the Jews well, but they'd heard different stories about Russia, awful stories. Felix didn't want to remain here to find out if they were true.

And it seemed that no one else wished to remain here either. The streets were full of people leaving Lemberg any way they could, some on foot, others with wagons and horses or bicycles, and a few even in automobiles.

"Lemberg will be empty by the time the Russians come," Felix said.

Mama looked around at the houses surrounding them. "I certainly hope so."

"Why couldn't our driver meet us by our home?"

"There are others traveling with us. It will be a central meeting place."

They passed markets and cafés and shops, all of which were empty or boarded up, and the city that normally bustled with activity in the evenings was strangely quiet.

"Can we walk faster?" Felix was so nervous, he hardly could breathe.

"If we went any faster, we'd be running," Mama replied.

"Then let's run. I'm afraid, Mama. I wish Papa were here."

She picked up speed. "Me too. But I will protect you, and you will protect me, yes?"

Felix shrugged. "You aren't strong like he is, and I'm not brave like he is."

"I am strong," Mama said. "In my own way. And you

must learn to be brave because the world will demand that of you now."

Felix knew he had lost the argument, but that didn't mean he was wrong. He began to hurry even faster until finally he saw a lone automobile on the street ahead.

"That's our driver," Mama said. "Run on ahead. Ask the car to wait until I can get there."

Felix hoisted his heavy bag even higher and began running. Mama wouldn't be far behind, but he worried that the driver had become impatient. He shouldn't have been. The bells had not yet rung eight o'clock. They were early.

Yet even before he reached the square, the automobile began to drive away.

"No!" Felix dropped his bag and ran forward until he crossed directly in front of the automobile. "We're here. We're ready to leave!"

The driver dimmed his lantern. "Get out of my way or I'll run you over."

"My mother is Frau Baum. She paid you to get us out of Lemberg."

The driver laughed. "Someone else paid me more."

Then he revved his motor and started forward, forcing Felix to step aside. He stared at the passengers' faces as they drove past, wondering who was sitting where he and his mother should have been.

What were they supposed to do now? There was nothing, no good option. No option at all.

"Oh," Mama said, when she reached his side a minute later. "I see."

"He took our money, but I don't think he ever intended to help us."

"No matter." Mama took a deep breath, then straightened up. "Retrieve your bag. If others can walk, so can we."

Felix did so and they turned to leave but had only taken a few steps when the sound of boots marching in perfect rhythm rounded the corner toward them. With each step, Felix's heart pounded harder against his chest.

"Mama?"

"Stand tall," Mama said, lowering her bags to the ground. "The Russians are here."

Already? Felix suddenly felt nauseous. He looked around, trying to think of where they might hide, or where they still had a chance to escape. "Let's run."

"Not now. We don't want them to think they must chase us. Be brave now, Felix."

He lowered his bag beside hers and tried to erase any sign of fear from his face. It wasn't working, he knew that, but at least he could try. He looked up at his mother and saw she was doing a much better job of it than he ever could, but it did give him some courage. If she could pretend not to be afraid, so could he.

The Russians came around a corner, led by their officers on horseback. Their uniforms were olive gray and belted at the waist with their trousers tucked into tall black boots. They marched in straight lines without a single soldier varying from the steps of those around him.

Felix grabbed his mother's hand as it became clear they were going to pass directly in front of them. "Please, let's just leave," he whispered.

"They have already seen us," Mama said. "It is all right for you to feel fear right now, but you must not *show* fear. Not now."

How was such a thing possible? His stomach felt worse than before and his hands were shaking. Mama seemed to realize that and gripped his hand tighter.

As the Russian soldiers passed by, one officer broke ranks to come to the side of the road. Mama stood even taller and the officer politely dipped his head, then continued onward. Next came the Russian infantry followed by other soldiers: their prisoners.

This final group of men were soldiers of the empire, Austro-Hungarian soldiers who had once roamed this city freely and with pride. These were not the soldiers from earlier that day who had safely retreated. Instead, these prisoners were being marched through the streets in humiliation, their heads down, their long coats open, showing that they had been stripped of their weapons.

"Where are the Russians taking them?" Felix asked.

"They will have to build a prison camp somewhere nearby." Mama huffed. "Imagine that, imprisoning these men on their own lands!"

Felix watched as row after row of men marched. He tried

counting them, twenty wide in the street, an endless line of slumped shoulders and vacant expressions. He searched each face, hoping not to see his father, though if he did, at least they would know he was still alive.

Mama must have known what he was doing. "Not to worry. Josef is fighting in Serbia."

A man's voice said, "Are you speaking of Sergeant Josef Baum?"

Felix jumped and turned to see the same officer who had dipped his head at them a minute ago. He was a little taller than Papa with very short dark hair, a square jaw, and a long mustache similar to the Archduke's. He must have circled back around on foot to be standing beside them now. In perfect German, he said, "My name is Captain Garinov. Would you happen to be Sergeant Baum's wife?"

Mama tilted her head. "How do you know my husband's name?"

"I make it my business to know as much as possible about a place before I bring my armies there. Josef Baum is a well-known businessman here in town, a sergeant in the military. Am I correct?"

"Yes."

"And your husband is a Jew, correct?"

Although the question was not addressed to him, Felix still felt its full meaning. He lowered his head, wishing this would all just go away.

But after a slight pause, Mama answered, "Yes, my family is Jewish. Do you have news of my husband?"

"No, other than from you just now, that he is fighting in Serbia. I'm sorry to hear that."

"Why?"

His tone became somber. "You see how easily we were able to conquer Lemberg, and it is the same with all cities in this area. We will conquer all soldiers who have invaded Serbia. I'm afraid there is little hope for your husband."

"My husband is a good soldier," Mama countered. "He and those who fight with him may yet prove you wrong."

Felix looked up in time to see Captain Garinov's smile, cold and arrogant, one side higher than the other. "Perhaps. But until then"—he gestured around the area—"Lemberg belongs to Russia now; this entire region is ours. We have endured much fighting and hardship along the way. Would you kindly host me and a few of my men for supper tomorrow evening? You can tell us more about this area, and perhaps we can tell you how the war is going in Serbia." He didn't wait for Mama to agree. "Shall we say six o'clock?"

She hesitated. "I, uh . . . we really don't—"

"Surely you were not leaving Lemberg? I assure you, it is safer to be in the city than to leave, where there is still active fighting."

"We haven't got much food, I'm afraid."

"I trust that you will be able to come up with a far better meal than we would eat on our own. Where is your home?"

Mama hesitated before giving in. "We're in the blue house just west of the cemetery."

"What a delightful invitation. Thank you." Captain

Garinov's eyes fell on Felix and he reached out to shake his hand. "You don't look like someone who'd ever want to go to war."

"No, sir." Felix felt his cheeks flush. Maybe that was the answer he was supposed to give, but it was also the truth, and that embarrassed him.

"Then you can be relieved. For it should be obvious now that this war will be over long before you're of age."

Felix shook the captain's hand because he had to, but he said nothing, as usual. He knew he'd just been insulted, but there was nothing he could do about it. He searched deep inside himself for the smallest spark of courage, anything really. And somewhere deep down, there was a spark, but that's all it was. Just a spark. He had no idea how to push back against the insult.

With that spark came a memory of the words Papa had spoken to him before leaving for the war, that courage was the kind of thing that had to grow.

He hoped Papa was right about this. If all Felix had was a spark, then that was a start. He had no idea how a person built up their courage, but if Papa said it was possible, then it was.

From that moment on, he vowed that once his courage grew enough, he would use it to get him and his mother to freedom.

This was not over yet.

CHAPTER
SIX

September 4, 1914

Captain Garinov brought two other soldiers to dine at Felix's home that evening, but rather than join him at the supper table, they each stood watch, one at the back of the house and one at the front.

Felix didn't like that. Suddenly, his home felt more like a prison. Because now it was. If there was a problem, he and his mother were trapped.

If Mama felt the same way, she hid those fears behind a polite smile as she set a bowl of cabbage soup in front of Captain Garinov. Felix couldn't even manage to directly look at the man.

While Mama and Captain Garinov made polite conversation, Felix quietly began to make plans. If this was a trap, he wouldn't stand back helpless and mute, like he had in Sarajevo.

He planned to be extra vigilant during the supper. If he saw the slightest sign of trouble, he would warn his mother to run and then attack Captain Garinov himself.

He would lose, of course, but at least Mama would have a chance to escape.

This was a terrible plan. Felix desperately hoped this was only a supper, nothing more.

"Felix, you haven't touched your soup," Mama prodded.

Reluctantly, Felix picked up his spoon. He didn't care about food. He cared that Captain Garinov had ruined Shabbat and still hadn't told them about Papa.

Mama must have remembered that too. After she had finally sat down, she said, "You mentioned the fighting in Serbia. So it is not going well?"

Captain Garinov's sigh was heavy. "Not for Austria-Hungary. We believe that you have more wounded and dead than soldiers still fighting."

Felix nearly dropped his spoon. How was that possible so soon in this war? He tried to do the math in his head. Papa had written that almost half a million soldiers were going into Serbia. If more had been lost than remained, that meant within only a few weeks, over two hundred and fifty thousand soldiers from the empire had been killed or wounded.

He closed his eyes and silently repeated to himself, *Papa wasn't one of them, Papa wasn't one of them.*

But Papa could have been. They had no way of knowing.

Mama somehow managed to keep her voice calm. "Do you have any news of my husband?"

"I do not know his fate, I'm sorry." Captain Garinov took a few more bites, then said, "But since Sergeant Baum has been so well-known here in Lemberg, I wonder if you could assist me in carrying out my orders."

Felix looked up. They weren't going to assist him with anything. He was the enemy! Felix quietly shook his head, hoping Mama would see. Even allowing a Russian to eat at their supper table seemed like a betrayal of Papa. They would not help him continue to conquer Lemberg.

"What help do you need?" Mama asked.

"This is Russian territory now, and when the war is over, it will become part of the Russian Empire."

"The war is not over yet."

"But it may be over *here*. My orders are to make this city look and feel more Russian. Thus, we must remove all undesirables from Lemberg."

Mama arched a brow. "Undesirables?"

"Obviously, no Gypsies. No Catholics, unless they convert to a Russian-approved faith." He lowered his spoon. "And I need your help in identifying the Jews of this city so that we can assist them with relocation."

Felix's gut had begun twisting yet again, not only for himself and Mama, but for their friends, other "undesirables."

"Relocation?" Mama's voice had risen in pitch. She was worried.

"They will be removed, sent to camps outside the city."

"Are they allowed to leave these camps if they choose?"

"I'm afraid not."

Mama was quiet for several seconds, then said, "Do you intend to transfer me and my son to these camps?"

Captain Garinov picked up his spoon again but held it in his hand. "I can only say that I have my orders. Some are less pleasant than others, but I must—"

"We won't help you," Felix said, staring down at the table.

"What was that?" Captain Garinov turned to him. "Speak up, boy."

Felix's heart was racing. He felt his mother's glare and knew she would not want him to say another word. But if Mama rejected Garinov's offer, she could be in terrible trouble. Felix was young. He had a better chance of escaping punishment.

Or at least, he hoped that would be how this worked.

So he looked up, barely able to hear anything but the beating of his heart. "That's not a relocation, it's an arrest. None of us have done anything wrong!"

"Felix, that's enough!" Mama scolded.

"At this very minute, my father is fighting you, trying to stop you. We will do the same."

"Russia did not start this war!" Captain Garinov thundered. "If you want to blame someone for your troubles, look to your own Kaiser. Did he care that he was sending soldiers to fight an army of our superior size and strength? Does he care, even now, that nearly three hundred thousand of his own soldiers have fallen already and that more will yet fall?"

"What of Russia?" Mama asked. "Are your numbers any better?"

"They are awful," Garinov said quietly. "Just not as bad as yours. And I will tell you now that I doubt whether our Tsar cares. Mark my words. This war will destroy your empire. It will destroy mine as well."

"Then we both lose the war," Felix said.

To Felix's surprise, Captain Garinov shook his head. "Perhaps you love your empire, but I have no love for our Tsar. The sooner we are rid of him, the sooner we can rebuild a new and better Russia."

"Russia will never be half of what our empire is!" Felix said. "The sooner we are rid of *you*, the better!" Instantly, he knew he had gone too far.

Captain Garinov stood and grabbed his arm, yanking him out of his chair and pulling him up so high, he had to stand on the tips of his toes to reach the floor. One of the soldiers ran into the dining room. "Is there trouble, sir?"

Rather than answer, Garinov said to Felix, "There's a lot of anger in you, boy. That is good. Anger is the fuel of war and you will need plenty of it to survive. But you will not show anger against me."

"My son is only a child who misses his father." Mama had stood as well and had a hand outstretched toward Felix. "Please, as a guest in my home, do not punish my son for his disrespect. Let us continue with this supper and discuss what help you might need from me."

After a moment, Captain Garinov drew a breath and nodded. He dismissed his soldier, then released Felix's arm.

"Go up to your room," Mama said sharply.

"But—"

"You heard me, go to your room."

Felix sighed and marched from the room, but he paused in time to hear Mama say, "Perhaps we can offer Russian language classes to some of the women in the city. I could help with that much."

That was all he heard before closing his door. He spent the next hour pacing the floor, angry with his mother for agreeing to help the Russians. But he was even angrier with himself. His plan to protect her had failed, and instead it had forced her to compromise with Captain Garinov. What else could she do after he had spoken out that way?

Never before in his life had he been so bold, but it had felt good to finally say the words with as much force as he felt them. It had felt good to be angry.

Felix was still awake that night when Mama came into his room. She stopped in his doorway and folded her arms. "What made you speak to a Russian officer like that?"

Felix had prepared himself for whatever punishment she wanted to give him. Maybe he deserved it, but he wouldn't apologize because he'd only done it to protect her. So for now, he only shrugged.

Mama stepped into his room. "You might have gotten into serious trouble."

"I know."

"So you felt it then, that fire inside you?"

Felix pressed his brows together, confused. "What fire?"

Mama sat on the corner of his bed. "There is a fire within each of us. If you fuel that fire with anger, it will burn all your happiness. But if you fuel it with courage, then the fire will give you strength to do difficult things. Captain Garinov was wrong, Felix. Anger will not get us through this war. Anger *is* the war."

For the first time in hours, Felix felt the most intense worry drain from him. "Yes, Mama."

Her smile widened. "And though it may not have been the wisest start, I believe you did us a favor."

"Oh, how?"

"There are many Jewish families still here in Lemberg. We must find a way to keep them out of those camps that Captain Garinov described. So we must become useful to the Russians, all of us, until the empire finds a way to set us free."

Felix sat up straighter. "What if they never do?"

Mama leaned in very close to him to whisper, "Then we will find the courage to set ourselves free."

Now he grinned. Whatever she asked, Felix was ready for it.

CHAPTER
SEVEN

October–November 1914

The changes in Lemberg began slowly. At first, they were barely noticeable.

Russians were to be seated first at cafés, even when locals were waiting. If a Russian entered the market, locals were expected to give up their place in line. Shop signs had to be reprinted in the Russian language.

People adapted—they had to—but Felix was determined not to accept the rules as a normal way of life. He hated feeling that he had become a puppet of the Russians; every movement, every spoken word watched and controlled.

But that was only the beginning.

At school, most of the teachers were new, brought in from Russia with lessons designed to turn the students into proper Russian citizens.

"I just ignore the teacher," Felix ranted to his mother one evening. "We are Austrian!"

"We are also Jewish and they have not forgotten that." She whispered the words, even though they were safe within their home, making him wonder if their home truly was safe at all. "Let's not make trouble for ourselves. Trouble will find us soon enough on its own."

"What kind of trouble?" Felix asked.

"The camps," Mama whispered. "Look around us. Today a Jewish family has disappeared; yesterday it was a Roma family, or someone they suspect of being a spy. We must be careful, for who knows what tomorrow may bring."

Almost as if her words had been carried away on the wind, they returned only days later when Mama invited Felix to walk with her.

"How far?" He didn't like the idea of being out too close to curfew. The last thing he wanted was a confrontation with a soldier on patrol.

"We'll be back within an hour if we hurry," Mama said. "I'd feel safer if you were with me."

Felix stood taller. It hadn't occurred to him that Mama might be afraid too, and he definitely had never considered himself capable of protecting her. But if she needed him, he would do his best to keep her safe.

Mama had packed a bag full of bread she planned to deliver to some of the poorer families in town. They passed a Catholic church on the way but paused as they heard a woman shouting.

"Where is our priest?" she demanded.

"Let's move on, Felix," Mama said.

She tugged at his arm, but he had stopped, unable to believe what he was seeing. The woman was scolding a Russian soldier as if he were her own child. It was foolish, yes, but so brave.

"You exiled him to Siberia?" she continued. "For what crime?" Before the soldier could answer, she added, "Did you think we wouldn't notice that you've changed our priest, that you've changed our religion? We will not accept this!"

From down the street, other soldiers began to arrive.

"Felix, we must go," Mama said.

This time, her grip on his arm gave him no choice but to follow, but he looked back as they walked.

The woman shouted, "You control the language I speak, the food I eat, the things I must do in public. But you cannot control the God I pray to!" With that, she turned and lunged for the church door where a paper in Russian writing had been nailed. She managed to pull most of it off, but that was the last the soldiers would tolerate of her.

They grabbed her arms and began leading her away. Her angry shouts turned more fearful as they gradually faded in the distance.

"Where are they taking her?" Felix asked.

"I don't know," Mama mumbled. "Nowhere good."

"Should we have helped her?"

"If it would have made any difference, yes." Mama sighed. "I worry that if we do not defend her beliefs, then no one will be here when the Russians try to change our beliefs."

In the silence that followed, Felix began wondering if he would eventually be the one dragged off by Russian soldiers.

Of course he would. They wanted the Jews in camps and punished anyone who refused to obey their rules. Lemberg was no longer a safe place.

"I'm going to fight them one day," Felix whispered.

"Quiet, please," Mama said.

But he couldn't help himself. "Austria-Hungary is the most powerful empire in the world. I will fight, just like Papa does. I will defeat the Russians myself."

"Felix, you must be quiet!" Mama stopped walking and looked around the street. Nobody was there, but she still frowned at him. "You do not know who is listening. Do not speak these thoughts aloud, not anymore. Not here, or at home, not even in your whispers in bed at night."

They continued walking once again, but his mind had already shifted elsewhere. How much better life would be if they were in Vienna right now, strolling beside the grand fountains, sitting in the park viewing the autumn leaves up in the hills, perhaps stopping on the way home for a pastry.

Truly he wanted to be nearly anywhere but here. Because the Russians weren't finished with their changes. The books from the local bookstores were removed to make way for new Russian-language titles. Newspapers were shut down, and any letters coming to the families of Lemberg were censored, or never arrived at all.

That was more than he could bear. Surely Papa had continued to write letters. Where were they?

Then Felix remembered. Papa wasn't sending letters. He

said he would wait until they sent him a letter from Vienna. Which meant they didn't know where Papa was, and Papa didn't know they were still here, trapped.

As bad as that was, the worst of the changes came in November. Felix was hurrying home from school. Mama would be anxious.

"We must not be on the streets if we can avoid it," she had told him only that morning. "The Russians have begun to say that the Jews are spies, that we cannot be trusted."

Felix had rolled his eyes. Surely nobody believed such a foolish thing.

But Mama continued, "Wherever these 'camps' are, they must be able to hold a great many people. Three Jewish families were taken this week alone."

He had noticed that very thing during school. Every day, another Jewish classmate disappeared. Felix's question was always the same: "Where are they?" The teacher's answer was always the same too: "They are no longer attending this school."

Felix's feeling that one day he would disappear too was a pinch in his gut that never went away. Today it felt worse than usual. Felix began walking faster.

"What is the hurry?" The deep voice interrupted his thoughts.

Felix had come around the corner so fast, he had nearly bumped into Captain Garinov, the same man who had intruded on their supper two months ago. By now, everyone in town knew who Captain Garinov was. If someone spoke his name, their voice always seemed to echo with fear.

Two Russian soldiers stood behind the Captain, and one spoke to Felix in Russian. Felix shook his head, unable to understand the words, which they seemed to take as an offense, based on their glares.

Captain Garinov shifted to speaking in German. "You've grown taller since that evening at supper."

Felix glanced down but didn't say a word. The last time he had spoken to Captain Garinov, it had ended badly. He wouldn't make that mistake again.

Captain Garinov continued, "At that supper, I asked your mother to help me collect the names of Jewish families who may need to be relocated outside of Lemberg. So far, she has not provided those names. Perhaps you could help me."

Felix didn't answer, and he wouldn't. How could he, when he knew what would happen to any families he reported?

Captain Garinov folded his arms. "Do you think I have forgotten our last conversation, the disrespect you showed to me? Give me the information I want; otherwise, I just might send you and your mother to those camps."

Felix's heart raced as he debated what to do. How could he refuse the Captain's request and still protect his mother? But she had refused to give the Captain any names, so he could not give up those names either.

Still looking at the ground, Felix mumbled, "I cannot help you."

"What? Speak up."

He raised his head, forcing himself to look directly at the

Captain. "I cannot help you. I will not help you. Lemberg is not yours and the fight here is not over."

Felix knew that he would pay for those words, but he didn't regret saying them. Papa would have done the very same thing. Felix had told his father he wanted to earn his own medal of courage. Perhaps he just had. He was afraid, absolutely afraid. But he was also proud of himself. Better still, he knew Papa would be proud of him too.

So when one of the soldiers stepped toward him, hands out, Felix turned to swing his bag of Russian-language books. He connected with one soldier's arm, but it didn't have nearly the effect he'd wanted, and the second soldier shoved him to the ground, pressing his face against the hard cobblestone road.

Within seconds, they had dragged Felix to a fence post and wrapped his arms around it, then chained his wrists together and fastened a lock on the chain.

Captain Garinov crouched down to his level. "One day, you might be a very good soldier. Since I cannot allow that to happen, I must send you and your mother to the camps."

"I will be a great soldier one day," Felix said. "I will become strong enough to defeat you!"

Garinov's face tightened, then he stood tall again. "When I come back, I want those names. Sit here and think about what will happen if you refuse me again."

A soldier posted a note above Felix, warning that he was not to be released, then he and the second soldier followed Captain Garinov away, leaving him alone.

Felix heaved a few deep breaths, trying to hold himself together, even as snowflakes began to fall around him. He was in the worst trouble of his life, but so was Mama now and she didn't even know it.

He didn't know how things could get any worse, but he had no doubt that before morning, he would find out.

CHAPTER
EIGHT

November 26, 1914

Felix must have fallen asleep at some point, and when he awoke, he was covered in a thin dusting of snow. It was dark outside and he was shivering.

His arms ached terribly. How long had he been sitting here? Probably several hours if it was this dark. Mama would be terribly worried. He needed to do something, to find some way of telling her where he was. But how?

Felix needed to think, but so many ideas were crowding his mind, no single thought broke through. At first, he had been certain that Papa would be proud of him for standing up to Captain Garinov, but now, it felt like the most foolish thing he'd ever done. He wondered what he should do next, if anything could get him out of this mess, and above all, he thought of what might happen when Captain Garinov returned. He would take Felix away, no doubt. By morning, the new empty chair in the classroom would be his.

Felix craned his head, hoping to read the note that the Russians had posted there. Above the warning not to help him was a single word: *Spy.*

The absurdity of it made the anger rise in him again. He was only twelve years old! Nobody would use him for a spy.

He leaned his head against the post and tried not to cry. He couldn't cry because it had taken a great deal of effort to find his courage. He couldn't let go of it now. He had to be strong.

Except that he wasn't strong, not really. Nor was he smart enough to know when to keep his mouth closed. Felix had not gone to war, but the war had come to him.

Now that it had, how much longer did he have left? Minutes? An hour? Or would Captain Garinov wait to come for him in the morning?

If he did have until morning, then there was still time for him to be rescued. Mama could come and—

Why hadn't she come?

Surely when he was late in coming home, she would have gone out looking for him, retracing his steps to school. She should have been here a long time ago.

But she hadn't come.

Which meant she could not come.

The Russians had probably arrested her too.

Panic surged through him. Felix tugged on the chain, hoping his wrists would be small enough to slide out, but that didn't work. He considered calling out for help, but he didn't. It was after curfew. If anyone came running, it would be a Russian.

Felix wished his coat were tighter around him, but maybe it would do no good anyway. The cold was already inside him, just as fear and doubt were also already inside him, so much louder than the courage he had once felt.

Maybe what he had felt before wasn't courage at all. Maybe it was just a terrible decision he had made, and one with consequences he couldn't bear to think about.

His thoughts were interrupted by a strange movement at the end of the street, like someone had darted out from behind a building, then hidden again behind a lamppost. It looked like a girl, far too young to be out past curfew.

Felix squinted, and after a few seconds, the girl ran from the lamppost directly toward him. She was in a dress, and her brown curls bounced when she ran.

Felix shook his head, certain he was imagining this. Because it was a *most* impossible idea.

The figure dashed straight toward him.

He hissed, "Elsa?"

"Shh."

"What are you—"

"Shh."

She had brought a small handsaw and began sawing at the fence post beside his hands. He twisted around to see what she was doing. "You're going to cut me."

"No, I won't. Oops!" Felix felt a sting on his wrist. Elsa said, "Sorry, I cut you."

"What are you doing here?"

"Obviously, your mother couldn't be out here, that's too

suspicious, and of course my father would have come himself, but he is in France. Mother and I were able to get false papers for ourselves though. Look!" Elsa widened her coat to show a folded paper. "It says I live here in Lemberg. This is the most clever plan, don't you think?"

Felix shook his head. He still didn't understand.

Elsa only smiled. "If I got caught, I'd just have to say I was lost, and I nearly did get lost a few times. Now that Lemberg has Russian signs, this has become a most confusing city, and with the snow and the darkness—"

"But how did you know?"

"Wilhelm, of course! You sent that note with him."

Now Felix tilted his head. Yes, he had sent her homing pigeon away with a note, but he had never intended for Elsa to come on a rescue mission. Honestly, he had never expected that Wilhelm would even return to her.

He whispered, "I don't wish to sound rude, but how can you and your mother help us escape an occupied city?"

Elsa frowned back at him. "That was a little rude, actually. Ah, there's the last cut! One more minute . . ." She wiggled out a slice of the fence post and Felix felt the chain go slack on his wrists.

"How can I get the chain off?" he asked.

"We have bolt cutters in the wagon. It's in the southern part of the city, but I don't know the best way to get there."

Felix could at least get them started. "Come on."

He led Elsa through the lesser-used roads, as much as

possible keeping to the shadows. A Russian patrol could show up anywhere.

Then they did. On a nearby street, he heard footsteps. Marching.

"Soldiers!" Felix flattened himself against a wall and Elsa did the same. The moon was still low enough in the sky that the entire street was in shadow, but it sounded as if the soldiers were going to pass the street directly in front of them. All it would take was for one soldier to simply turn his head.

"Felix?" Elsa whispered.

"Hush!"

Two soldiers appeared on the street ahead of them. One aimed a flashlight to look down the road. Felix saw its beam, only centimeters away from where they stood. He sucked in a breath and refused to release it. Three, four, five seconds passed, then the soldiers moved on.

Finally, Felix allowed himself to breathe. "Where did you say that wagon was?"

"South."

"South" could be a lot of places. But they continued in that direction, only choosing streets with so many footprints that theirs wouldn't stand out. Finally, Elsa said, "Wait! This is familiar. Follow me!"

She took him down a side road to the very edge of the city. Only a few homes were here, lined up on one side of the dirt road, and the other side was a ditch with a field behind it. There, in the field, was a wagon.

"Felix?"

Mama was standing at the edge of the road, craning her head to look for them. Now she motioned them over, gave each one a quick hug, then Elsa said, "Come, we must hurry."

Felix followed them through the ditch into the field, where Elsa's mother was in the driver's seat of the wagon. The back was loaded with hay.

"This won't work," Felix whispered.

"It's got to work," Mama replied.

Elsa's mother gestured to the back of the wagon. "You two will hide in there. Elsa and I will drive up front."

"This is just as dangerous for the two of you," Mama said.

Elsa's mother frowned. "No, it's different for us."

Felix understood that. He and Mama were Jewish. Elsa and her mother were not.

His mother climbed into the wagon first while Elsa spread straw over her. Then she picked up the bolt cutters. "You'll ride more comfortably if we cut off that chain."

Felix nodded and turned his back to Elsa, bending forward and lifting his wrists behind him for an easier cut. She snapped off one link, then stopped and breathed out, "Oh no."

Felix straightened up, his heart sinking as he saw Captain Garinov approaching them. The Captain said, "I was polite, I was respectful. I gave you every chance to save yourselves."

"We are saving ourselves now," Felix said. "You cannot stop us."

Captain Garinov laughed and took a step closer. "Is that so?"

"Elsa, get in the wagon," Felix muttered.

As soon as she did, Felix turned and shouted to Elsa's mother, "Go!"

She lifted the reins and Felix tried to leap into the back of the wagon, but Captain Garinov caught the loose end of his chain and yanked him back.

"We're not leaving without you!" Elsa cried.

"Then none of you will leave at all." Captain Garinov gave another hard tug on Felix's chain, but Elsa jumped down from the wagon with the bolt cutters in her hand.

Felix tried to break free, but Captain Garinov pulled harder on the chain. "We'll make an example of you for this!"

"No, you won't!" Elsa pressed the bolt cutter against Felix's wrist. The chain was cut free and instantly snapped toward Captain Garinov, hitting him in the eye. He howled with pain and fumbled backward with one hand over half his face.

This was their chance. Felix and Elsa raced to the wagon and jumped into the back, then Elsa's mother immediately drove them away. They looked back to see Garinov stumbling toward the road.

"You need to hide," Elsa said. "That officer might call his soldiers to find you."

Felix lay flat on the bottom of the wagon, where his mother took his hand and Elsa covered him with straw. But as the wagon continued on, he realized something. It might have seemed unimportant, but it wasn't, not to him. Mama's hand was shaking. His was not.

They rode for nearly an hour before the wagon finally stopped and Elsa said, "It's all right. You can come out now."

Felix and his mother sat up, brushing the straw from their hair and clothes, taking in clean breaths from the cool night air.

"No other problems?" Mama asked.

"No," Elsa said. "We were able to stay far off the roads. No one saw us."

Her mother passed back two train tickets. "Vienna," she said. "Your train will depart first thing in the morning."

Mama smiled and gratefully accepted the tickets. "Perhaps one day we can repay you for this."

Elsa shrugged. "I hope my life will be easy enough that I never need repayment."

Felix liked the idea of that and hoped the same for himself. Then he remembered his decision from many weeks ago, to do what he could to defeat Russia in this war.

In another three years, he would be old enough to volunteer for the war and he intended to do it. Until then, he needed to become as smart and strong and confident as possible.

"Well, thank you," Felix said, offering his hand for her to shake.

Elsa only smiled back at him. "If you must thank me, then would you finally write me a letter?"

Felix chuckled. "I could do that too."

1915

KARA

GREAT BRITAIN

There is hardly a form of human misery that has not come our way and wrung our hearts with the longing to do more and give more.

—Edith Wharton, Red Cross Volunteer Nurse (1915)

CHAPTER
NINE

January 19, 1915

The bright light tore Kara from her sleep. She sat up after the first flash, breathless, her heart pounding like a drum. It was immediately followed by a loud boom and the bed shook beneath her.

She threw back her blankets and raced into the hall, where she nearly collided with her mother. They grabbed each other and instinctively lowered their heads in time for a second explosion. Dust fell from the roof overhead, and Kara heard a second loud noise from outside, different from the last, like something big had collapsed.

"What is this?" she cried. "What is happening?"

Mother sounded just as anxious. "I think we're being bombed. Come, put on your shoes and I'll get my medical bag. We must find someplace safe!"

Bombed? Kara knew the war was growing fiercer each week, but they lived in a fishing town on Britain's coast. The biggest event of the day might be four o'clock tea. Why would anyone target them?

At the sound of another explosion, Kara and her mother raced outside, where hundreds of others had left their homes too. If the night was cold, she barely noticed. Instead, she stopped in the street and simply looked up.

In all her life, Kara had never seen anything like the ship that floated above the town. This was no regular airplane—she had seen several of those. This looked more like something from another world, an enormous floating tube, white and round. Then doors opened beneath it, dropping a much smaller tube.

A bomb.

Mother grabbed Kara's hand and together they began running away from the bomb's target area. It must have landed closer than she'd realized, because when it exploded, the rumble of the earth knocked her off her feet.

"Kara!" Mother pulled her up again and they continued to run, but Kara had no idea where they could go to be safe. Maybe there was no safe place.

Kara's mind raced. "They're bombing the port—our ships!"

Those were the military targets in town. Which meant the aircraft overhead was probably German. Austria-Hungary wouldn't have come all this way, but Britain was an easy distance from Germany.

Her country had faced attacks on land and sea before—everyone knew what to do there, but never before had they been attacked from the skies. Kara looked around at others who had run into the streets, parents with children in their arms or holding their hands, couples staring up at the sky in horror. Nobody had any idea what to do.

"Here, let's hide here." Mother opened the door of an automobile parked at the side of the road. Its hard roof might offer some protection from above.

Except that Kara had only barely entered the automobile when on the street a woman cried, "Can someone help me?" She was kneeling on the ground, cradling her husband on her lap. He was bleeding on the side of his head, but everyone around them ran past, almost without taking notice of her.

Kara's heart leapt into her throat. She knew what that meant.

"Stay here," Mother said. "I must—"

"I know." Kara whispered a silent prayer for her mother's safety. She understood her mother would have to go. She always did.

Britain had joined the war last August, in hopes of helping France protect itself from Germany. Yet the war was not going well for the Allies. Kara's mother had been kept busy in the hospitals tending to the wounded soldiers who seemed to arrive every day from the battlefields in France and Belgium.

But until tonight, the war had not been here, *in Britain*, and the wounded were only soldiers, not women and children and boys too young to fight, or elderly men who no longer could. When had they become military targets?

Kara watched from inside the car, fascinated by the way

her mother cared for the injured man, even while speaking words that comforted his wife.

Mother was an excellent nurse, everyone said so, but Kara had never seen her work in an emergency before. She was brilliant.

Somewhere farther on, Kara heard another cry for help and her spine stiffened. Mother would finish with the injured man, but rather than return to safety, she would tend to the next call for help, and the next after that. She couldn't do all of this alone.

Which left Kara with an awful decision, and no time at all to think about it. If she didn't help her mother, who would?

For the past six months, rather than returning to their flat after school, Kara went to the hospital to be near her mother. An entire new world had opened up to her there, this place where people could go in some of the hardest moments of their lives, and where a nurse helped them get through it.

Kara wanted to be a nurse one day, just like her mother. But if that was her plan, then she couldn't stay here.

Kara's heart pounded while her hand gripped the handle of the car door. "Stay here," Mother had said.

But Kara already knew she was going to ignore the rule. She just needed enough courage to pull on the handle.

"This is for you, Father," she muttered, then opened the door and ran back into the chaos. The young woman who had called for help was seated on the sidewalk with a baby in her arms. So far, no one had stopped for her or even seemed aware of her.

Kara put her arms over her head, hoping that would offer

some protection from any hazards above, then ran to the woman's side. "What do you need? I can help you."

"Get my baby to safety!" She held the infant up to Kara. "I twisted my foot. I can't walk."

Kara pulled the baby into her arms, but then balanced him on one hip and offered her other hand to the young woman. "Lean on me. I'm stronger than I look."

The woman pressed her lips together, then nodded and took Kara's hand to stand up and leaned heavily on her. Kara struggled to keep her balance, but even if they walked slowly, they would gradually make their way across the road. Mother noticed them and gestured to a place nearby where the young woman could sit.

Once there, Kara returned the baby while Mother handed her a roll of bandages. "You'll need to keep the ankle straight and wrap it tight. Can you do that?"

Kara nodded. Although she'd never attempted this, she'd seen her mother do it several times before. While she began to wrap the ankle, the young woman glanced up and let out a relieved sigh. "Oh. The bombing has ended, hasn't it?"

Kara followed her gaze upward and saw the airship was indeed gone. She'd been so intent in her work, she hadn't noticed.

Beside her, Mother began treating a child with a long cut on his arm. She was speaking to him calmly and even made him smile once or twice. That was Mother's secret, Kara realized. Kindness and humor were tools of nursing, as much as a bandage or a brace. She cared for their injuries, but she was healing their hearts too.

"Why did you leave the automobile?" Mother's tone wasn't unkind. She sounded genuinely curious. "Aren't you afraid?"

Kara thought about that. Yes, she had been afraid. She still was afraid, but one single thought finally made her leave the automobile.

"I think Father was afraid that night," Kara said. "But he didn't let that stop him, did he?"

She looked back down at her work, feeling her eyes grow hot. Father had been one of the first British casualties of the war. When his ship was attacked, he had gotten onto a life raft and would've been safe. But other sailors needed help, so he left the life raft. Her father had saved fifty-eight lives, but not his own.

"Your father was a hero," Mother said tenderly. "You are so much like him."

Kara brightened at that thought and finished wrapping the bandage before turning to look for another patient. Instead, she paused to watch her mother help a man lower his wife flat on the ground. She seemed to be having trouble breathing. Her hand was clutched to her chest and her eyes were wild with panic.

Mother said to the woman, "Close your mouth now, and trust me." When the woman did, Mother pressed her thumb against one nostril, forcing the woman to breathe through the other nostril. Almost immediately, her breaths began to slow and deepen, and within a few seconds, Mother moved her hand away. "Better now?"

The woman nodded, though she remained on the ground. "You knew just what to do," she said.

"I'm sure they could use someone like you in the war," her husband added. "Have you heard of the Red Cross?"

"They asked me to join them," Mother said. "They are desperate for nurses."

Kara's ears perked up. Mother hadn't mentioned that to her.

Her mother continued, "But, of course, I told them no." She gestured at Kara. "I could never leave my daughter."

By then, Kara had begun wrapping the arm of another small girl with a cut on her arm. The man pointed to her and said, "Your daughter seems to have your talent for nursing."

"She certainly does," Mother said.

The man helped his wife to her feet and offered his thanks while Kara finished knotting the girl's bandage. By the time the girl's father took her away, the streets had finally begun to quiet down.

Once they were alone, Kara turned to her mother. "The Red Cross asked you to join them? Did they want you to go to war?"

"Oh no. They asked me to work on the ambulance trains. Remember the one we saw in London last month?"

Of course Kara remembered. They had gone to London for the very purpose of seeing a new ambulance train before it was put into service. Some trains were half a kilometer long, bringing the wounded home from the war. They were entire hospitals on wheels.

Mother continued, "I didn't tell you because it didn't matter. Or so I thought . . . until tonight. Shall we go back home?"

For the first time, Kara felt the chill in the night air, though her mind was still full of questions. What did her mother mean by *until tonight*?

As they walked, Mother said, "I had another visit from the Red Cross earlier today, with a suggestion for how I could work on the trains. I had planned to tell them no again, but I was watching you just now, the way you cared for that young mother and the little girl."

"Oh?"

"Because there are so few nurses, the trains need orderlies. Usually, these are men because they are needed to lift the wounded in and out of the train. But they also need orderlies to—"

Kara stopped and grabbed her mother's arm. "Did they ask me to come as well?"

Mother's expression gave no hint of her answer. "Don't look so eager. It is difficult work, Kara, and there is plenty of it. The orderlies change bedsheets, deliver meals, run messages."

"I could do that!"

"You would be on your feet from the time your work begins until long after it should have ended. No matter how tired you are, or hungry, or afraid, the injured soldiers must come first."

An energy began to spread inside Kara, something she had not felt since the awful news about her father. "I'm not afraid of doing hard things. I'm afraid of a life where I do nothing!"

"I know that about you," Mother said. "But this is also dangerous work. We'll be in France, at the very heart of the war. They'll keep us away from the battles themselves, but there is no guarantee of our safety."

"There's no guarantee of it here!" Kara gestured around the area as proof.

"You must also realize that life on an ambulance train will show you the ugliness of war. The injuries you'll see there are far worse than what you've just seen here."

"If that's true, then they need your help." Kara hesitated for a very long time before adding, "Before he left for war, Father asked us to promise to do whatever we could for the war effort. Ever since he . . . has been gone, I've felt that I failed him because I've done nothing to keep that promise. Maybe I can't do much, but I want to do this, for Father."

Mother smiled. "That gentleman was right. You do seem to have a talent for nursing."

"Then let me use it. Let me help!"

Mother took Kara's hand and continued walking. "The Red Cross may have wanted me on their train, but I think it will not be long before they will realize that *you* are their true prize."

CHAPTER
TEN

March 20, 1915

Kara stared down the railway lines in both directions. Where was the train?

In many ways, Kara felt that she had been waiting her entire life for an opportunity like this. While other girls knitted socks for the soldiers, Kara made bandages. They read *Sketch* magazine for fashion advice. She read her mother's old medical books.

The train would be here at any minute, and Kara reviewed her plans in her head. Before they'd trust her with any real responsibilities, she had to do the simple jobs. Eventually, they'd make her an orderly. Then she'd earn her Red Cross pin and with it, she could begin work as a nurse. Her life had never seemed so clear.

"Mum, it's here!" she cried as the train finally approached in the distance. They were at the station in Étaples, on the west coast of France. A large Allied military base was here, the final stop for many ambulance trains after collecting wounded soldiers from deeper in France.

"Stop bouncing, dear."

That was Mother's second reminder for Kara to be still, but she could hardly help it. This was the most exciting moment of her life. It was impossible not to bounce just a little. She felt like the train itself, made to move forward, built for adventures ahead.

At her side, Kara's mother wore the full Red Cross uniform: a long-sleeved blue dress covered by a white apron with a red cross across the chest. A white hat covered her hair, pulled back into a bun, and on a high collar around the neck, she wore a round Red Cross pin.

The pin was Kara's favorite, gold and red around the edges, and in the center, a white shield with the red cross on it.

"Will they ever give me a pin like that?" Kara asked.

For now, she simply had the blue dress and white apron. But Mother answered, "They will not *give* you anything. If you wish to *earn* this pin, you must learn to obey every rule while on the train, follow every order given."

"Of course I will."

Her mother smiled. "You say that now, but I know how you are with rules. You haven't even stopped bouncing, despite *my* warnings!"

Kara laughed, though her heels flattened to the ground as the train slowed to a stop. A swell of nerves sent a chill through her and she shivered. This was real now. Despite all her studies, Kara realized how little she actually knew about medical care, at least the kind of care these soldiers might need. How would she ever earn that pin for herself?

Mother glanced over at Kara. "Take a deep breath. And don't go about rushing ahead when the doors open. Remember that we don't board until the wounded have been unloaded."

"There can't be that many." Kara expected to see five or six perhaps, and most of them able to walk on their own. After all, those who were very bad off wouldn't be fit for travel on a swaying, rumbling train.

But within seconds of the train rolling to a stop, the doors of every car opened and orderlies began carrying out the stretchers, laying them in rows along the platform. Five were carried out, then ten, and then twenty, and then Kara lost count.

"Mum," Kara whispered, "are these the usual numbers?"

"No." Which made Kara feel a little better until her mother added, "I think it is usually much worse."

How could that be? Yes, some of the soldiers did walk off the train with one arm in a splint or with a limp that could have been caused by severe trench foot. But they were only a few when compared to the greater numbers with amputated arms or legs, or with bandages wrapped over their heads, sometimes covering an eye or the side of a face. Still more came, a few of them so bandaged and broken that Kara wondered how they'd survived this far.

Before the orderlies finished, nearly two hundred men were laid out in rows on the platform, waiting to be picked up by ambulances for their next rounds of treatment at the base hospital.

And her mother thought that it was usually much worse.

Kara stepped back, unable to look at them all. It had been a mistake to come here. At her best, she could never help with needs as great as this. What did a drink of water or a fresh bedsheet matter to a soldier who had lost so much?

Finally, Kara understood her mother's warnings: Nothing about war was exciting, or glamorous, nor could she ever be fully prepared for whatever was coming next.

But what struck her most was the expressions on the faces of the soldiers. "Do you see them, Mum?" Kara asked. "They're all the same."

No matter the injury, every soldier's expression seemed to mirror the man's next to him: with exhaustion in their smiles; some awful blend of happiness to be returning home and sadness to be returning home this way.

"That is the very reason you are needed," Mother said. "Read them their letters from home, remind them of how lucky they are to be alive. Smile. Give help where you can."

Kara nodded, feeling hopeful again. She could do this. She could do this.

They needed her to be able to do this.

"It's not too late to walk away," Mother said. "If it's too much for you."

Maybe it was too much, but Kara knew it would be even worse at home, with little to do but listen to the silence outside, waiting for it to be broken once again by a German airship, or to think about her father, and her last promise to him that she would help win this war.

With him in mind, she smiled and tried to pretend she felt confident. "I believe that Father would be proud of us today."

Mama wrapped an arm around Kara's shoulders. "I know he is."

And for that brief moment, those few remaining seconds on the platform, Kara was certain they were right to have come here. She had seen the broken and the injured, and despite that, or maybe because of that, she made her final decision. She planned to be the best almost-an-orderly that the Red Cross had ever seen.

"You're Sister Webb, our new nurse?"

Kara turned to see an orderly approaching but looking only at Mother. He was thin with narrow eyes and was starting to bald, making him look older than he probably was. "My name is Corporal Bryant. I work mostly in the D ward—that's where you'll be too." Now he glanced at Kara and his expression immediately cooled. "This must be your daughter. She won't be in the way, I hope?"

"I'm here to help." Kara had been prepared to defend her presence here. She just hadn't expected the need for it so soon. "I'm ready to help, Mr. Bryant."

"*Corporal* Bryant." He chuckled and Kara immediately recognized her mistake. Heat rushed to her face and she knew she was blushing, which only made the embarrassment worse. She didn't appreciate being laughed at when she had only been trying to explain herself.

Corporal Bryant's laugh turned to an instant frown. "Nobody has time to hold anyone's hand and show them what to do. You'll be expected to work as long and hard as any of us."

Kara wanted to tell him that maybe *he* would have to keep up with her, but as it was only her first day on duty, she simply answered, "I came here to work."

He scratched his jaw. "There won't be much for someone your age. Just don't make anything worse. We have enough difficulties on the job as it is."

"Don't worry about him," Mother said as they followed Bryant toward the train. "Goodness knows we have enough enemies. He is not one of them."

Kara wasn't entirely sure about that. It was true that he looked tired, and his eyes had a faint echo of the same despair she had seen in the expressions of the injured soldiers. A better person might've felt sympathy for Corporal Bryant, but she was still irritated, still determined to prove that she deserved to be here as much as he did.

Though first, Kara would have to prove that to herself.

She tightened her grip on her bag, then boarded the train. Just like the train she had seen before, the first car she entered was lined with hospital beds stacked three high, one of several ward cars that made up most of the train's length. This particular car was half full and a medical officer was making rounds to each man in preparation for a stop at the next army base.

Bryant stepped in behind them. "We're an entire hospital on wheels. Sixteen cars in total, nearly half a kilometer. We can take up to five hundred wounded, so it's all really quite brilliant." He gestured to his right. "Operating room is that way, when necessary, and one kitchen, which is always necessary. You'll find the ward for the officers that way as well, near the infectious disease patients. Can't let the officers have all the luxuries." He laughed at what was supposed to be a joke, but neither Mother nor Kara smiled. He gestured to his left, obviously deflated. "More wards that way, our pharmacy ward, another kitchen, and storage is at the end."

"How many workers are on board?" Kara asked.

"Staff," he corrected. "The *staff* are led by three medical officers. You'll follow every order they give. Also three nurses, forty-seven orderlies, and you." He turned back to Kara's mother. "You are needed right away. Perhaps your daughter can carry your bags to your bunks while you start to work."

Kara wanted to object. She was here to work with the patients, but a stern glance from Mother told her to do as Bryant had suggested. She picked up her mother's bag and heard him say from behind, "It'll be the train car after the kitchen. Do you think you can find it?"

"Is anything required to get there other than to walk straight?" Kara glanced back. "I can manage that."

"The other nurses reserved a shared compartment for you and your mother. It's bog standard, but you'll know which one it is."

Kara sighed and began to walk forward, passing rows of soldiers who were headed to a different stop ahead. She knew it was rude to stare, but they were certainly staring at her, as if she was as much an outsider here as she already thought herself to be. Others lay on their beds with eyes closed, their only sign of life in the gentle rise and fall of the blanket covering their chests.

In every car she passed through, someone was moaning in pain, and more than one soldier asked for her help, but Kara merely apologized and continued walking. She still didn't have permission to help the soldiers directly. If Bryant had his way, she never would.

A whistle sounded, and seconds later, the train lurched forward, nearly causing Kara to lose her balance. She dropped her bags as she reached out to protect herself from falling, but her hand accidentally bumped a man's arm, wrapped with bandages.

He cried out in pain and another orderly came running. He glared at Kara. "What did you do?"

"Nothing! I just bumped him, only a little."

"You bumped an arm burned by a German flamethrower. Get on with you now!"

Kara turned and picked up her bags again, but even as the man settled down, tears welled in her eyes. She had never meant to cause anyone pain. That was the very opposite of why she had come.

Kara left that ward, feeling worse than useless. If she couldn't turn things around, she would be exactly what Bryant thought: a burden the rest of the staff would have to tolerate until they could be rid of her.

Finally, Kara reached the quarters for the nurses, and as Bryant had suggested, it was simple but suitable. She peered into a tiny room with an upper and lower bunk, and a small counter and washbasin. This must be it. She gave her mother the lower bed and took the upper one for herself. After setting down the bags, she leaned against the wall, utterly discouraged. She had not yet begun and was already making mistakes.

As Kara sat there, a single thought ran through her mind: that if she stayed here, she really would be useless. She needed to get out there, though doing so felt almost as difficult as pulling the automobile's door handle on the night of the bombing.

With a long, slow breath, Kara left the nurses' compartment. She paused as she entered the ward where she had bumped the man's arm. There, just inside the transom doors, was a pitcher of water with a few cups set out. She poured a glass half full, then walked it back to the same man.

He was breathing easier now, though he seemed to tense up with every larger bump of the train.

Kara looked over his chart, as Mother had taught her to do, and saw that he was allowed to have water. Most of the men were.

"Thirsty?" she asked.

He turned his head and made an attempt at smiling. "You're the girl who—"

Kara's spirits fell. So he did remember her, how clumsy she had been. "I'm so sorry about that."

But his smile only widened. "You're the girl who's come to help us here on the train. That is brave of you."

Now Kara found herself smiling too. "Water?"

"Yes, please."

She helped him to drink it, and when he finished, she said, "They told me your arm was injured by a flamethrower."

"My arm got the worst of it. I was one of the lucky ones."

Kara sucked in a short breath, wondering how awful the battle must have been if he considered himself lucky. But she wasn't here for her own thoughts now. She was here for the wounded.

"Would you like to talk about it?" Kara asked. "When my father went to war, my mum said it always helps to talk about it."

He slowly shook his head. "There is nothing from the battlefield that I ever want to talk about." He briefly closed his eyes, then opened them again. "But if you're interested, I'll tell you about my family and my home."

"They must be excited to have you come back."

"If they are, it is nothing compared to how I feel. I should be happiest if I never left home again."

"And I'd be miserable if they sent me home now." She looked at the train around her. "I am exactly where I belong."

CHAPTER
ELEVEN

May 1, 1915

It had taken some time, but Kara had finally begun to feel as if she understood her work. Since she wasn't officially part of the Red Cross, her tasks were only those that could cause no harm. She delivered food and returned empty plates to the kitchen. She read letters to the soldiers who couldn't do so for themselves, notified the nurses of any complaints, and carried messages from one ward to another. In her spare time—which meant the hours in which she would have otherwise been sleeping—Kara refilled water, restocked supplies, and changed the bed linens.

The work was difficult, but she also knew how much it mattered. Even if all she had done was listen to a soldier talk for a few minutes, his smile when she left brightened her day.

The soldiers on the trains came from all over. Most were British and French, but soldiers from other Allied countries were here too, including Canada, India, Australia, and more.

On rare occasions, they had soldiers from the Central Powers—
a German or Bulgarian or someone from the Ottoman Empire.

Kara helped them all, fed them all, and quickly learned
that nothing she did mattered more than showing kindness.
Especially to those whose wounds went deeper than bandages
could heal.

However, Kara's duties were nothing compared to the
nurses'. Whenever possible, she studied the nurses as they
worked, then tried to find them in a free moment and ask questions. In the first few weeks, they complained to her mother
nearly every evening about it.

"You mustn't bother them," Mother would say. "They
have enough work as it is."

"But if they answer my questions, then I can help," Kara
would reply.

The conversation always ended with Mother's long sigh.
"Ask me your questions instead."

So Kara did, because a hundred were stored in her brain,
just waiting to be asked. The more she learned, the more she
had to know. After a few weeks of Kara's questions, the other
nurses finally began inviting her closer to watch them work.

"Would you help me, Kara?" Sister Mary had a needle in
one hand and was bent over a soldier who was swatting at her.

Kara set down the tray of dishes she had been carrying and
hurried over to the nurse's side. "How can I help?"

"He doesn't understand what I'm doing," she said.

Kara looked at the markings of his uniform, gray with let-
tering different from any alphabet she had ever seen.

"Russian." Sister Mary ducked to avoid one of his flailing arms. "Try to calm him down so I can give him this shot. But be careful with this one."

He was sputtering out a language completely unfamiliar to Kara. How was she supposed to calm him when they couldn't communicate?

Or maybe they could.

Kara pressed between him and Sister Mary, then began to sing the first song that came to her mind. It was a bedtime tune her mother used to sing many years ago. She felt rather daft for choosing it, but after only a few lines, he began to relax and even smiled a little, as if the tune had triggered a memory in him. His eyes fixed on her, carrying the same haunted expression that so many other soldiers had on this train. Maybe a nursery song was exactly the thing he needed.

Gradually, his smile faded, his eyes closed, and by the final note, he was asleep.

Sister Mary tapped Kara's shoulder. "That's a bit of magic, eh?"

Kara turned. "My singing?"

The nurse held up the empty needle. "Modern medicine. Put him straight off to sleep."

Kara smiled to herself, then asked, "Can you show me how to use a needle?"

Sister Mary considered that, then gestured with her head. "Come with me."

Kara followed, asking, "Why did you warn me to be careful around that soldier? Because of the way he was fighting you?"

"Oh no. I can take a swat or two at my arms when they're afraid; that doesn't mean a thing to me. But did you see the red star on his hat? That man was a Red."

"A Red?" Kara blinked back at Sister Mary. "What does that mean?"

"Red is their nickname. They call themselves Bolsheviks and they are enemies of the Tsar—the Russian king. Do you remember the assassination of the Archduke in Bosnia?"

"Of course!"

"I think there are more than a few Bolsheviks who'd try assassinating their own Tsar in the same way."

Kara glanced at the Russian, sleeping peacefully now. "If he's dangerous, then why did we bring him on board?"

Sister Mary turned to her, as if shocked at her words. "The Red Cross has no business deciding who is worthy of care and who is not. Our only job is to save lives. Let God and the generals decide the rest."

Kara nodded, and she decided in that instant to adopt the same attitude. Her only job was to save lives.

"Besides, the Russians are on our side in this war," Sister Mary added. "It is not this man's fault that their Tsar does not know how to lead them. Russia's best days of the war are already behind them."

"Already?" Kara's brows pressed low. "How is that possible, with such a large army?"

"That large army is shrinking fast. They lose hundreds, or even thousands, of soldiers every day." She sighed. "So do we. I suppose the war will only end when everyone runs out of soldiers."

That was a somber thought. Kara knew how many soldiers they carried on each trip away from the battlefield, and
their train was only one of several. Every day, the wounded
kept coming and the war pressed on.

"Enough of our whinging now." Sister Mary stood taller.
"Let's teach you about using needles."

"Sister Mary!" Corporal Bryant ducked into the ward.
"You are needed at once."

She frowned at Kara. "Another time, I suppose." Then she
hurried away, leaving Kara alone in E ward.

Kara was disappointed, of course, but there was still other
work to be done. She had no sooner picked up the tray of dishes
than a soldier farther down the ward began loudly gasping for
air. Kara lowered the tray and rushed over to the man. He was
half sitting up, his eyes wide and panicked, and he was drawing in huge gulps of air, as if unable to stop himself.

Kara pushed him down by his shoulders and said, "Trust
me." Then she covered his mouth with one hand and pinched
one nostril closed with the other, forcing him to breathe through
the second nostril. He fought Kara at first, much as the Russian
had fought Sister Mary, but Kara remembered her words, that
she could take a swat or two when the soldier is afraid.

After only a few forced breaths, he began to calm down
and lower his arms. Once his breathing slowed, Kara removed
her hands from his face.

"Thank you," he mumbled. "I don't know what happened.
I suddenly couldn't get enough air."

"It's called hyperventilation and it happens to people

sometimes." Kara smiled at him. "Will you be all right until I return? I need to call for a nurse."

"Why didn't you before?" a voice behind her asked.

Kara turned and saw one of the medical officers standing behind her, Captain Stout, whose name perfectly fit his appearance. She had seen him many times during her work, but he was always too busy to pay her any notice. From the tone of his voice, she wasn't sure she wanted his attention now.

He folded his arms. "Miss Webb, is it? I asked why you did not call for a nurse to help that man."

Kara wanted to shrink away to nothing, but since that was impossible, she tried to hold herself together long enough to reply, "It wasn't necessary, sir. I knew what to do."

"At your age? Where would you have learned that?"

"From my mum. I've seen her do it before."

"Hmmm." He stepped closer. "You were informed of your duties on board this train, were you not?"

"Yes, sir."

"Were you ever told that your duties included emergency medical treatment?"

"No, sir."

He frowned and took another step closer. "Tell me one early sign that a wound has become infected."

Kara was confused by his question, but he was waiting for an answer, so she said, "Fever, sir. If the infection is in a wound, the area will look red and feel warm."

"What if a patient suddenly awakens screaming, or reacts with fear at the sound of a slamming door?"

"Shell shock," Kara replied. "I don't know the actual name, but that's what the nurses call it."

"I've heard you often watch the nurses when they work." Kara nodded and he said, "Miss Webb, if a soldier ever needs emergency care, you will call an orderly or a nurse to help. That is the rule, understood?"

She lowered her eyes. "Yes, sir."

He turned to leave, then glanced back. "However, if you continue to learn at this rate, I have no doubt that one day very soon, you will be the one others call on when they need help. I am impressed."

Kara thanked him but kept her head lowered. Not in humility. It's only that she wondered if it was also against the rules to smile as wide as she now was.

TWELVE

June 1, 1915

One month later, Kara was retrieving food plates to return to the kitchen when Corporal Bryant pulled her aside. "Captain Stout has ordered everyone to remain on duty," he said. "We've just got word that there is heavy fighting up north. We're on our way there, but he warned us to prepare for what he called *different* soldiers."

Kara's nose wrinkled. "What does that mean?"

He had already begun to walk away but turned back to answer. "It seems the Germans have found an even deadlier weapon: poison gas. This is a new war now, one the world has never seen before, and mind you, it'll be more terrible than you can imagine."

"Poison gas?" Kara took a deep breath, then caught it in her throat, horrified by the idea that even the act of breathing was now considered dangerous.

Bryant gestured to the dishes in her hands. "Get those back

to the kitchen, then help us make up beds. When we arrive at this next Clearing Station, it is likely that we will find more wounded than we can carry."

Casualty Clearing Stations were the first stop for medical care off the front lines and often little more than patchwork repair buildings when the wounded began arriving by wagon-loads from the heat of battle. Many of the soldiers had no chance of surviving unless an ambulance train carried them to a base hospital. Now Bryant was telling her there wouldn't be enough room for everyone?

Kara followed Bryant down the aisle. "Surely we won't leave anyone behind."

He had already picked up a patient's chart but sighed heavily. "When the beds are full, they are full."

"Someone can use my bunk." Maybe it was only one more bed she could offer, but that would be one more life they could save.

Bryant replaced the chart, then frowned over at her. "I don't question Captain Stout's orders. Don't you question mine. We have less than two hours and nearly five hundred bunks in need of new bedding."

Kara pressed her lips together, then turned sharply toward the kitchen. She came back with her arms full of fresh linens, determined to work faster than any of the orderlies. She moved from one bed to another to another, working more efficiently each time. Finally, Bryant returned to her ward and asked, "How many do you still have in this ward?"

Kara climbed down from the bunk where she had just tucked in the linen. "None, Corporal."

"And in the cars behind you?"

Kara forced herself not to smile. "None, Corporal."

"None?" He nodded back at her. "Very well, then. I'll let the others know."

Only when Bryant left her car did Kara slump into the nearest chair and lean her head against the wall. She had just closed her eyes when a new orderly entered, saying, "Let's be sure all the supplies are restocked."

Kara muffled a groan as she stood again, but she had not even taken three steps when the brakes on the train squealed and she lurched forward, nearly losing her balance. On the shelves behind her, medicine bottles and bandage packages toppled over or fell into the aisles. The few patients still with them groaned at the sudden change in speed, and orders began to be shouted for everyone on staff to report any problems to their senior officer.

Who for Kara, unfortunately, was Corporal Bryant.

After ensuring that the soldiers in her ward were safe, Kara peered out the window, framing her face with her hands to block out any light inside.

She couldn't see much that was different from any other battle zone: The ground was uprooted and trampled, with only an occasional tree or bush left standing as evidence that this had once been a living place. It was so late at night, she shouldn't have been able to see even that much, except that streaks of red and yellow were dancing along the horizon, ending in bright flashes of light as they fell.

"That'll be the war," Mother said as she entered Kara's ward. "The sky will be this way all night, or until they run out of shells, but that doesn't seem likely, does it? And when it does stop, some officer too eager to earn himself a medal will send his men over the top, and then we'll really start to see wounded."

Kara's brows pressed low. "Over the top?"

Mother pointed out the window. "Look carefully. You'll see a long, jagged tunnel dug into the earth. See it there?"

Kara squinted and could barely make out the tunnel her mother was describing. "Are those the trenches the soldiers talk about?"

"Yes. It's where they live, where they stand to fire their weapons at the enemy trench, and where they hope they will find protection when the enemy fires back. But if their commander orders them over the top, then they climb up and out onto the field of battle in hopes of capturing the enemy's trench. A commander would have to be off his trolley to send valuable soldiers over the top, in my opinion, but then, I'm not the one giving orders."

Kara peered outside again, with new respect for the wounded soldiers they had treated. Maybe she thought she was brave, but it was nothing compared to any of them.

"Come now," Mother prompted. "Let's see what this hullaballoo is about."

Kara followed her into the next ward and, to her surprise,

saw Captain Stout there with two other nurses and at least twenty orderlies, including Corporal Bryant.

"This same message is being given to all staff members on this train," Stout said. "The reason we are stopped is because the rail lines ahead are gone. A battle must have come through here that we weren't warned about, or perhaps some artillery misfired. But we still have hundreds of men waiting for us. The stretcher bearers will need our help to bring the wounded here."

"How far away is the next Casualty Clearing Station?" Mother asked.

"More than a kilometer. Four hundred and six beds are still available on this train and we can expect to fill every one. At the moment, we have a crew of fifty people. If we work in pairs to carry the stretchers, and if enough stretcher bearers are available, we can still expect about eight trips to and from the battle lines for every one of us. Remember too that this is an active war zone, and in the darkness, nobody will know or care that you are Red Cross. Does everyone know what they need to do?"

"I can help," Kara said.

Stout turned to her. "No, obviously not—"

Kara wouldn't accept that. "I am strong, and I can help with the medical care. You need all the help you can get!"

"You're too young," Mother said. "I'm sorry, love. I know how you feel, but you will be a great help once the wounded arrive."

Kara clamped her mouth shut and quietly fumed. Anyone could give the soldiers a drink of water or an extra blanket. They had to get the wounded here first.

Captain Stout sighed. "Then it's settled. Everyone, dress for a long night and make sure your red crosses are visible. I don't want any of you becoming one of our wounded."

The others brushed past Kara as they walked to their quarters, but Stout remained where he was, staring at her with a frown. "I saw the faces of the nurses when I told them what we must do tonight. Not one of them wants to leave this train. Why did you volunteer?"

Kara looked back at him. "Last year, my father's ship was hit by a German torpedo. He wasn't a senior officer, and he had every right to save himself first, but he didn't. In that moment, he knew he could save a lot of lives, even if it put him at risk. Sir, if you'll let me go out there, I can save lives too. It would honor my father's memory."

Stout's eyes seemed to soften and he nodded at her with something that almost looked like respect. In a gentler tone, he said, "You have a courageous heart, but your mother was right. This is too dangerous for you."

"Then it's too dangerous for all of us. A missile won't ask your age before it lands."

His frown deepened. "Let us hope that none of us have to learn that for ourselves."

As the nurses began to leave the train, Mother paused by Kara's side. "It could be more than an hour before the first of us return. Prepare the wards to receive our soldiers."

The beds were made, the pitchers were filled, and they had plenty of supplies already. There was nothing for her to do here but wait.

Finally, Kara was left alone, or nearly so, in the train car. She sat on the steps of the open doors and watched the others scramble over fallen trees and wood fences, beneath a red sky lit with missile fire. She closed her eyes, whispering a prayer for everyone's safety, but for her mother most of all.

When the last of them had disappeared, she walked from one mostly empty ward car to the other, looking for anything she might do to better prepare for when the wounded arrived. Kara straightened medical tools, delivered water to the soldiers already on board, and tried not to think about her mother and everyone else who had gone to help.

It felt to Kara that many hours had passed before the first load of wounded arrived. Eight orderlies in pairs carried stretchers onto the trains to begin loading men into the beds. They were accompanied by about thirty injured men who were capable of walking here on their own. This group looked to be among the less serious—with broken bones or shallow wounds on their arms or legs. No sooner had they set the soldiers down in their beds than the orderlies returned to begin their next round.

Finally, Kara had some work to do. She began checking on each soldier and taking down notes about his condition, something she would never be allowed to do under normal circumstances. Yet she was less than halfway through when from outside, a familiar voice called, "Help, please!"

Kara darted to the door and saw Corporal Bryant desperately waving to get her attention. She hurried down the steps, then raced into the field. The orderly who had been his partner was on the ground, holding his foot.

"I didn't see the hole," he said. "I think I've broken my ankle."

"Can you get back to the train on your own?" Kara asked.

He nodded and she turned her attention to the soldier on the stretcher they had been carrying. A bandage was wrapped around his middle, so Kara knew he needed to get inside the train as quickly as possible.

She picked up one end of the stretcher, but Bryant was still watching her. "Are you sure you can carry this? We can't risk dropping this man a second time."

"I won't drop him," Kara assured Bryant, though when he picked up his half of the stretcher, the weight pulled at her shoulders and she nearly lost her hold. She tightened her grip on the handles and tried to convince herself that this wasn't any heavier than the bundles of laundry she managed on the train.

That wasn't true, of course, but this soldier could die if he were left out here much longer. He needed her to be strong enough to get him to the train.

By the time Bryant and Kara got the soldier settled into a bed, the second orderly had made it inside too. He sighed and stared at them. "I can't go back out there, not with my ankle like this. But I can stay and care for those who are already here."

Bryant grunted. "If I don't have a partner, I can't bring anyone else back."

Kara drew in a deep breath, thinking of how furious Mother would be, but there was no other choice. She grabbed a medical bag and slung it over one shoulder, then said to Bryant, "Let's go. I'm your partner now."

CHAPTER
THIRTEEN

June 1, 1915

If the moon was anywhere overhead, Kara couldn't see it. Instead, her path was guided by creases of light from the missiles that streamed through the sky, or by the fires of homes that must have been part of a small village only earlier this evening. And she kept close to Corporal Bryant, who said, "Careful to step only where I do. This area could have been mined."

A rush of fear spread over Kara. His steps were wider than hers, so she couldn't follow them exactly. All she could do was to take his same route and hope that was good enough.

On their way, they passed several stretcher bearers in their bright red vests, along with other orderlies and nurses, but Kara never saw her mother. Why not?

Bryant caught Kara staring as a nurse passed them by. He said, "Don't you worry yourself. They probably kept your mother at the Clearing Station to tend to the wounded as they come in. They're overwhelmed with patients now."

"Is it far away?"

"No. You'll see it ahead, the next time the battle gives us some light." Almost on cue, an explosion ahead of them lit the smoky horizon. Kara was close enough now to hear the cracking of trees as they fell, dulled only by the shouts and cries of soldiers in the distance. She saw the medics with their stretchers running toward the explosion and smelled the gunpowder in the air, so thick she tasted it.

Kara stopped walking, stopped any movement at all. How had the other nurses and orderlies done this? Surely they were seeing the same things as she was. The war was all around her now, pressing in far too close.

Bryant turned back. His tone wasn't harsh, but it was firm as he said, "You're in the same danger whether standing still or moving. You may as well move."

Kara blinked back at him, and as his words sank in, she began walking again, faster than before. The Casualty Clearing Station was sure to be safer than out here. Yet when they arrived, Kara instantly changed her mind. This wasn't a secure, brightly marked building for the enemy to see and avoid. It was only a long tent with large prints of the Red Cross on it. Hardly comforting.

Kara asked, "Is it true that the enemy won't target medical workers?"

Bryant *humphed* and looked away. "If we're on the battlefield or in the trenches, be sure that we're a target, same as any other soldier. Once we're away from the front lines, we're mostly left alone. But we're never safe. Something can misfire, we can be exposed to disease and infections, and the poison gasses don't care if we wear a red cross or not."

Kara frowned over at him. Most of the time, she respected his honesty, but she wouldn't have minded discussing something else right now. At least they were nearly to the station. He turned to her again. "Brace yourself. The soldiers you'll see in here are fresh off the battlefield, some of them only from an hour or two ago."

She had already begun to notice the differences. Aside from the occasional nightmare, or groans when the train bumped more than usual, the soldiers on the ambulance train were mostly quiet. However, even from out here, she heard the echoes inside the tent of moans for help and cries of pain.

It only became louder once Kara entered. This was a large tent, but hardly a centimeter existed that wasn't filled by an injured soldier, or by someone trying to help in his care. Tables on the far end of the tent were set up for the surgeons, who shouted for orderlies to bring them more light or to locate a medical tool.

Other nurses tended to the soldiers needing temporary bandages until they could be treated on the train, and far too many soldiers were seated or lying along the sides, waiting for their turn to be seen.

Kara shook her head. Were all of these wounded from only a single night of battle? How was that possible? Was anyone still left on the battlefield to fight?

For the first time, Bryant's tone was gentle. "They need your help, Kara. You came to help."

She drew in a breath, balled her hands into fists, then

followed him deeper inside toward a sea of stretchers, though many men were lying on only bare ground. Kara still didn't see her mother, but how could she in all this chaos?

A doctor brushed by Kara, calling for the orderlies. He pointed to a man who had just been carried in. "Take him to the moribund ward."

Kara looked over at Bryant. "The moribund ward?"

"He won't live," Bryant said. "They'll try to make him as comfortable as possible."

"And who's that man with the doctor?"

"The Grave Registration Officer." Bryant gestured toward the battlefield. "His job is to record where each man is buried, as best he can. One day, the families will want to know where to come to mourn."

Kara's heart sank. She was here to save lives. They needed her to be strong. With refreshened courage, she said, "We should get moving again. Who shall we take?"

"The next in line." Bryant stepped around a few soldiers on stretchers and picked up the handles near one man's head. He had bandages wrapped around his chest and wasn't conscious, but Kara watched the bandages rise and fall as he breathed. Then she picked up the lower half of the stretcher and together, they walked back into the night.

Kara knew what to expect this time, which made it easier, but her arms were also sore from the last time she'd carried a stretcher, and that was only for a short distance. She genuinely didn't know if she could make it all the way back to the train.

At least this was a younger soldier than before, so he was lighter than the last man. Kara looked down at him, his eyes closed, his mouth set in a grimace of pain. She gritted her teeth and determined that she would get him to the train, and the next one after him and so on, until there were no more wounded, or until the train was full.

With that thought, her shoulders fell. She had just seen for herself how fast the wounded came in. The train would fill up long before the Clearing Station ran out of wounded.

Once this soldier was delivered, Bryant and Kara returned again into the night, but by now, a mist had begun to form. Maybe it would offer some protection from the enemy, or maybe it gave the enemy places to hide. If a German soldier leapt out in front of them, they had no way to defend themselves.

They were halfway to the Clearing Station when Kara paused, hearing a whistling sound in the air overhead.

"Get down!" Bryant cried.

For once, Kara didn't question his orders, or even stop to think about them. She immediately dropped to the ground, covering her head with her arms. She first felt the rush of air, then heard the explosion. Dirt and debris scattered all over them. Beneath her, the ground shook and she heard trees falling, which terrified her. What if one fell in their direction?

But that was followed by something far worse. Utter silence. There was so much of nothing at all that Kara became certain another shell would drop just to fill the void.

She finally looked over at Bryant. "I'm all right. You?"

He didn't respond, so she touched his hand. He groaned, then suddenly his head shot up and he let out a cry. No, he was not all right.

Kara scrambled over to him, and within a few steps, she understood the problem, and it was bad. A heavy tree branch had fallen directly onto his upper leg, trapping him beneath it.

"I can pull you out," Kara said, though she truly didn't know how she would do it.

He spoke between tightly gritted teeth. "I'm too heavy to pull, and the branch is too heavy to push. It doesn't matter anyway. I'm certain that fall has broken my femur."

Just like that, the bad news became nearly the worst possible. That was the long bone of his thigh, a serious injury in any circumstance, but even worse out here. They were still half a kilometer from the train. He couldn't walk on his own, and if Kara tried to drag him that far, the movement of his leg would put him into shock.

She tried to think through everything she had learned about what to do. Only last week, she had sat with the nurses at supper as they discussed new ideas on how to handle this very situation. One of the ideas came to mind. It wasn't great, and she was nervous to try it, but if she didn't, Bryant had little chance to live.

Bryant had been carrying their empty stretcher before the explosion. Kara picked it up and set it beside him. "Give me your helmet," she said.

He sighed but passed it over to her. "Why don't you have one?"

Kara arched her brows. "Because I'm not an orderly. I was

never meant to leave the train." She knelt on the ground and began using Bryant's helmet to dig into the ground beneath his leg. Thanks to a recent rainstorm, the dirt was soft, allowing her to clear out a few centimeters of space beneath his leg in only a few minutes. She continued to work until he could slide his leg out from beneath the branch, though every tiny movement caused him to stop and cry out in pain.

Once he was free, he lay down again, breathing heavily. "Thanks for that, but it will do no good. You can't bring me to the train on your own."

Kara ignored him and began feeling around for other branches that had fallen. She needed two branches as long as his leg and as straight as possible. When she had what she wanted, she knelt beside him again. "I'm going to brace your leg. It will hurt, but you've got to let me do it."

"How old are you?" he asked.

"Nearly fourteen."

He lifted his head. "No thirteen-year-old is going to set my leg!"

"I said that I'm nearly fourteen, and I'm not setting your leg, only bracing it. Now, stop whinging and let me work."

He nodded and she knelt beside his feet to begin working. Kara dug through her medical bag, but nothing in there was long enough. She reached to the bottom of her dress, already torn from where it had snagged on a branch earlier, and ripped off a long piece.

"Captain Stout won't like that you ruined your dress," Bryant said.

"Captain Stout will have bigger reasons than this to be angry with me." Kara slid the fabric beneath his leg and the branch, then began to bind them tightly together. He cried out at first, and she said, "Tell me about the shells. How did you know to tell me to get down?"

He gritted his teeth, breathing heavily until she asked the question again, more forcefully. "If it's a longer whistle, two or three seconds, then it still has a ways to go before it lands. Very short whistle, directly overhead. It's about to go off." He stopped to breathe again. "Enough!" he shouted. "This won't work."

"It will work!" Kara said. "Be angry if you want, but I'm going to do this before another shell lands!"

He drew in a sharp breath, then said, "The shrapnel from an exploding shell is dangerous, but what got me is the blast wave of air. You shouldn't be out here, Kara."

"If I wasn't, who'd be saving your life right now?" Kara smiled at him and finished the last knot on his leg. But the question she had intended to ask became lodged in her throat.

Because, overhead, she had just heard a very short whistle, followed by a thud as the shell hit the ground.

Kara whispered, "Bryant, what does that mean?"

CHAPTER
FOURTEEN

June 1, 1915

K ara threw herself to the ground, covering Bryant's legs with her body. The shell landed a short distance away, but this one didn't explode like the others. Instead, it began releasing a gas she faintly smelled from here.

"That's poison," Bryant said. "Get us out of here now!"

Fortunately, the wind was carrying most of the gas away from them, but if Kara could smell it, then she was already breathing in some of it. Her lungs felt prickly and tight.

Bryant rolled himself onto the stretcher, but Kara knew the most difficult challenge was still ahead. She had to drag the stretcher along the ground without jarring his leg while also moving away from the gas.

Kara grabbed the handles on one end, lifted him waist-high, and began to pull. He cried out in pain and had to hold the sides of the stretcher to keep himself from sliding off, but the brace on his leg seemed to be holding.

"Breathe as little as you must," she said, though she had to pull in great gulps of air just to continue to drag the Corporal along the ground. Her lungs burned fiercely but she was slowly getting them into fresher air, if the remnants of shell explosions and smoke from the fires around them could be called that.

"You're slowing down," Bryant said.

"I'm not."

"You are, and it's all right. Let me down."

"Why?" Kara turned back to him, still determined to press on. "So you can say that you were right all along, that I was too young, too weak to be on the train? Why have you never believed in me, or even liked me?"

"What?" Bryant looked genuinely confused. "Kara, I was only hard on you because I wanted you to become good enough to earn your Red Cross pin. If you had been nothing more than the child I accused you of being when we first met, I would have left you alone entirely."

"Then leave me alone now," Kara said. "I need my strength for pulling you, not arguing with you."

But she also knew he was right. She was getting tired.

"Oi!" a voice called out through the darkness.

Kara stopped, seeing vague shadows moving toward them, two of them.

"Over here!" she called.

A pair of orderlies emerged from the darkness. The first man to arrive took the handles from Kara while the other grabbed the lower end of the stretcher. She stood back to watch them, almost ready to collapse from exhaustion.

"You did well, Miss," one of them said. "We'll take him the rest of the way. Stay close to us, will you?"

Kara stumbled forward, though it was almost as difficult to make herself walk as it had been to pull Bryant. But she did brighten a little when one of the orderlies turned to her with a smile. "You made a splint. That might've saved the Corporal's life."

They reached the train, and though she would have liked to rest or declare herself off duty for the rest of the night, that could not be.

By now, the train was loaded with wounded soldiers. Every bed she saw in the first ward was full, and the ward after that, and after that.

Bryant was carried past her into yet another ward, but when he passed Sister Mary in the aisle, he said, "Give that girl water. Her throat must be burning."

"I can get it for myself." Kara had entered the train too dazed and exhausted to think about her throat, but now that she did, it almost felt like she was swallowing fire.

By the time Kara walked to the counter, Sister Mary already had water poured for her and said, "Keep sipping water and the worst of it should pass soon. When you're finished, go into the privy and wash off, change your clothes, then be back here in twenty minutes."

"I've made up the beds," Kara said.

"I'll be asking more of you tonight. I'm the only nurse here, and we have hundreds of wounded soldiers in need of help. You'll work on one side of the aisle, and I'll be on the other. Do you think you can do that?"

Despite her exhaustion, Kara couldn't help but smile. She was back, ready to work, in only fifteen minutes.

CHAPTER
FIFTEEN

October 4, 1915

Months had passed since that night, yet Kara still remembered how angry her mother had been when she returned from the Casualty Clearing Station. But that was nothing compared to Captain Stout. Even now, months after that incident, her ears still burned with the lecture they had both given her.

"You had orders," Stout had said.

"It wasn't safe," Mother had said.

"What if things had gone differently?" Both of them said that, almost at the very same time.

And Kara had responded, "If they had gone differently and I wasn't there, Corporal Bryant might not be alive today. He told me to come out from the train and help him." She'd looked directly at Captain Stout. "Didn't you say I was to always obey orders?"

His face had puckered into a grimace before he said, "I'll tell you this, never in my life have I met someone so young and so brave. You have talent, Miss Webb, and you are intelligent and strong and everything I could ever hope to find in a top-quality nurse. You saved someone's life tonight when most people might have given up. But"—now the stern look returned—"we have rules on this train for a reason. I will give you one last chance. Do you understand?"

"Yes, sir."

So for the past four months, she had done everything with perfect obedience. She worked harder than before, faster than before. Captain Stout seemed to respect her skills, but slowly, he was beginning to trust her judgment too.

"Keep this up, and I daresay you'll have that Red Cross pin by the end of the month," Mother told Kara one afternoon.

"Do you think so?" Kara asked.

"By now, you've surely proven to him that you can be of better use if he gives you real responsibilities."

Kara hoped so because she doubted there was anything more she could do. She was on her feet all day and fell asleep almost before her head hit her pillow between shifts. At every meal, she crammed her head full of school studies, nursing studies, and with making notes on what each patient might need for the short time they were on the train.

But she was particularly sleepy later that evening. She sat at a table in the dining car, trying to stay awake long enough to finish the day's French lesson. She couldn't allow herself to get behind. That was a condition Mother had insisted she agree to since she would be missing school back home.

Kara finished the chapter, then yawned as she reached for

the nursing manuals. There was so much to learn, so many questions begging to be answered. She opened to a page with the latest theories on how sickness could be transferred from one person to another, though her eyes were already glazing over, wanting to sleep.

She laid her head down on the book, just to rest. As she drifted off, she thought about a comment she'd heard Captain Stout say to her mother that morning.

"Kara will be a fine nurse one day," he'd said, then added, "What a pity she isn't a boy. She'd have made a wonderful doctor."

At that very moment, Kara had made up her mind to become a doctor, one of the first female doctors ever. Which meant she needed top marks with her studies.

But first, she needed to sleep.

Before she knew it, Kara jumped to attention at the sound of a bell, signaling that they were approaching their stop. They had been headed to a Casualty Clearing Station in northern France, a place they returned to often because of the intense fighting there.

As the train slowed to a stop, Kara retied her apron, checked to be sure her cap was straight on her head, and hurried outside, becoming part of the routine once again. At least one hundred injured soldiers were laid out in a double row along the concrete platform on the side of the train. The injuries seemed worse than usual, so whatever fighting had just happened here, it must have been brutal.

Orderlies bustled past her, carrying the wounded in as

quickly as they could get them settled. Kara wandered among them, moving farther down the lines, looking for anyone who might need immediate help.

Then, at the far end of the line, she noticed one soldier who had been passed over. At first she thought it must be a mistake, but then she saw one orderly point to him, and another orderly next to him shake his head, then they walked away.

Why were they ignoring this soldier?

"Pardon me," she asked a third orderly as he passed by. "Why isn't anyone bringing that man in?"

"He's one of *them*," the orderly said. "Austro-Hungarian. Our enemies don't get a bed until all of our own soldiers are loaded."

"You can see his injuries are severe. He'll die if he doesn't get help."

But there was no sympathy in the orderly's response. "He'll get on last, if he gets on at all."

Kara huffed, then marched back inside and crossed down to nearly the end of the train, to the ward where the nurses slept. She opened their carriage door, and when no one was watching, she darted outside and ran over to the soldier. He was very much alone now, with the orderlies carrying in men much farther away.

"English?" she asked. *"Française?"*

The man nodded. Kara didn't know how well he spoke French, but if it was their common language, it would have to do.

So in French, she asked, "Where are you injured?"

He shook his head and mumbled something about fighting the Russians. Kara lifted the corner of his uniform and saw a bandage wrapped around his side, but he had bled through it. He definitely needed help.

The name on his uniform was Baum and his rank was Sergeant. If he was Austro-Hungarian, then yes, he did belong to the enemy. It was his country that had started this war. He fought against the soldiers she worked so hard every day to save.

Sergeant Baum put his hand over Kara's and whispered only one word: "Please."

Kara's heart softened as she looked at him. This man was not his country, nor responsible for the decisions of his leaders. He needed her help.

She looked around the area. The orderlies were working even farther away now. At their distance, she hoped they wouldn't realize what she was doing.

"Sergeant Baum," Kara said. "I will help you, but you must walk into the train yourself. It's only five steps and two stairs. You must hurry."

He shook his head. "I cannot."

Kara wouldn't give up so easily. "Surely there are people at home who you love, who you promised to return to. Get up for them, sir. Five steps and two stairs, that's all."

"I have a son, Felix," he mumbled. "And the most beautiful wife in the world." He gritted his teeth as he sat up. With one hand over his wound and the other around Kara's shoulder, he leaned heavily on her to stumble inside the train. Kara brought him into the compartment she shared with her mother. He'd have to go on the lower bunk, which she knew would make her mother angry, but not half as angry as the fact that Kara had brought him in here at all. She would find a way to explain this, before she was found out. Kara knew she could make her mother understand.

The bigger question was whether she could make the rest of the staff understand. For that, she needed time. Time to help him, and time to think up a good enough answer for what she had done. But for now, she had other responsibilities to the rest of the soldiers who had just come on board.

Kara whispered to the Sergeant, "Stay here. I'll be back as soon as I can."

He closed his eyes, unable to keep himself from falling asleep. Of course he would stay here. He had barely been able to move on his own. He wasn't going anywhere.

Kara hoped. She was fully aware that she had just brought an enemy soldier on board the train. If she was wrong, every person on this train might pay for her mistake.

CHAPTER
SIXTEEN

October 4, 1915

No matter how hard Kara tried to get away, for the rest of the evening, she was kept busy with the other wounded. Ordinarily, she would have been glad to help with any need, but tonight, all she could think about was Sergeant Baum. Nobody was helping him.

"You're distracted tonight," Mother said. "Is everything all right?" Kara was helping her wrap a wound, but it seemed to be taking so long.

"It's fine, but—" Kara hesitated. She knew that she had to confess to what she had done, but it couldn't be here, in front of the other soldiers. Perhaps some of them were wounded *because* of Sergeant Baum.

Or . . . perhaps his wounds were because of them.

"I'm fine," Kara said, more firmly this time. "Maybe I need a few minutes to rest."

"I can see that. Be back here in fifteen minutes."

"I will!"

She knew she'd be alone in the nurses' quarters. It was likely that all the nurses would be required to work throughout the night. If Kara ignored her mother's request to return in fifteen minutes, then she might have five or six hours to figure out what to do with Sergeant Baum. Every bed on the train was full, so she couldn't transfer him, and likely she couldn't move him anyway without someone noticing.

"Kara," she mumbled to herself, "you've really dug yourself in deep this time."

She paused before entering her compartment. This really had been a mistake, to bring this man, this enemy of her country, on board the train. If there was a list of rules for Red Cross nurses, she had probably broken every single one of them.

With one exception. It was the rule Sister Mary had taught her, that every life mattered, regardless of where the person came from, their race, or their rank. This man's life mattered just as much as any other man's.

Didn't it?

Kara opened the door with great caution, peeking in first to be sure that it was safe. Sergeant Baum was awake and nodded when she entered, but he had gone more pale, and she could see that the bleeding on his side had gotten worse. She had brought more bandages with her, but the care he needed was far beyond what she could provide.

"My name is Kara," she whispered. "I'm too young to be a nurse, but I will do my best."

He smiled faintly, obviously trying to keep his eyes open. "My son . . . Felix . . . He would admire your courage."

Kara bit her lip, then began unrolling the bandage. Sergeant Baum grunted as she forced him to move so that she could roll the bandage beneath him, but she was able to place fresh gauze over the wound on his side. She had hoped that would be good enough, but it was obvious that the bleeding had not stopped. This was a far more serious injury than she had realized before.

When Kara rolled the Sergeant onto his back again, his eyes were closed and his breathing had become shallow. She dug into her bag and pulled out a blood pressure cuff, then wrapped it on his arm and hurried to take the reading.

The results were alarming. His blood pressure was low, and falling even as she tried to get an accurate reading. He was dying.

Kara raced from her compartment, through the kitchen car, and into the third car, where Captain Stout was giving instructions to Sister Mary.

"There's a patient with wound shock," she said.

They looked at each other. "Where?"

Kara knew how bad this would be once she told them, but there was no choice now. "Nurses' quarters."

Captain Stout's face turned almost plum colored, but he grabbed a medical bag and raced the way she had just come.

"Kara? What's happening?" Mother had just entered this train car. Kara wasn't sure how much she had overheard, but she clearly understood something was wrong.

She frowned back. "The other orderlies were just going to let him die, right on the platform. They didn't care."

"What are you talking about?"

Kara shrugged and led her mother to the nurses' quarters, where Captain Stout and Sister Mary had pulled Sergeant Baum out into the aisle. They were working on his injuries while an orderly behind them passed equipment as they asked for it.

Mother stared at Kara. "What have you done?"

"Nobody was allowing him onto the train," Kara said.

"He's the enemy," the orderly said.

"And we're the Red Cross," she countered. "We don't look at friends and enemies. We look at the wounded."

"Why do we have so many wounded? Because of him and others who fight on his side! How many of our own soldiers are being neglected right now so that we can care for him?"

Kara turned to her mother. "You wouldn't have left him out there to die."

"I wouldn't have made the decision on my own. I would have checked first with a superior officer. This is serious, Kara."

Kara closed her mouth tight, knowing if she didn't, she would likely say something to get herself into greater trouble, if that was possible. She had done the right thing, she was sure of it. But nobody else in this room seemed to agree.

Sister Mary briefly glanced up. "I spoke to this man back at the Clearing Station. He was just transferred into a German unit. He'd have fought with those who launch explosives at our boys, release poison gas for them to breathe in. And now you, Kara, want to reward him by saving his life."

Captain Stout sighed. "He was only following orders, just as our soldiers follow orders. I doubt he wants to be part of this war any more than we do."

They returned to their work and finally Kara asked, "Will he live?"

Stout said to the orderly, "Escort Miss Webb to the kitchen ward. She is to remain there until we are finished."

"I only wanted to help," Kara protested.

"*This* was not helpful." The orderly gestured toward the door. "You first."

Kara hung her head and left with the orderly, while Mother stayed behind to continue assisting.

"Don't forget the reason we're all here," the orderly said as they walked. "Austria-Hungary started this war."

"After Serbia killed their crown prince."

"Whatever their reasons, he is our enemy now."

Kara sank into a seat in the dining car, crossed her hands on the table, then rested her chin on them. "You don't have to childmind me," she said. "I'll wait here."

"Good, because I'll probably be the one having to clean up the mess you made."

Kara mumbled an apology as he left, but it was the only apology she intended to give. Sergeant Baum probably wouldn't be alive now unless she had brought him on board. That was the right thing.

But for now, it certainly didn't feel that way.

Nearly an hour later, the orderly and Sister Mary entered the dining car, and with only a passing glance at Kara, walked on by to the other wards. A few minutes later, Mother entered with Captain Stout behind her.

He was the one to speak. "Sergeant Baum is resting comfortably. A space will be made available for him by transferring an enlisted soldier into the officers' quarters. They won't like that, and when they ask me why I have done this, I will have to tell them about you."

That made Kara nervous. "Did I do some sort of military crime?"

"No, but it was a serious violation of our rules, and there must be consequences." He held out his hand. "Four months ago, I warned you that you were on your last chance. Give me your apron."

Kara's hand flew to her chest. "What? Why?"

"You cannot be associated with the Red Cross any longer."

"Why? Because I saved the wrong person's life?"

"Because you acted on your own, without authority. That cannot be tolerated."

"Sir, my daughter is young," Mother said. "It was a mistake of compassion."

"No, the mistake was ours, by allowing her to be here in the first place. You may choose to stay or leave, but your daughter has made her decision. From this point forward, she will not work with the patients, not even to deliver a glass of water. She will not read their letters nor offer them a blanket. She is to stay in the nurses' quarters or in the kitchen car only, and may not go outside when the wounded are being carried in or dropped off. Agree to those terms or she will be sent back to England on the very next ship."

Kara answered for her mother. "I agree to the terms." Captain Stout stared at her as if waiting for an apology, but he wouldn't get one, not while she remained certain that saving a human life was more important than some list of rules.

Yet that didn't make it any easier to remove the apron, and Kara fully understood that she had erased every hope of receiving the Red Cross pin that she had worked so hard for. Every dream she'd had for nearly a year was now lost.

Captain Stout folded the apron beneath his arm and frowned down at her. "I had high hopes for you, but if you cannot follow rules, you will never be one of us."

After he left, Kara turned to her mother, though she was unable to look directly at her. "I'm sorry if this will make things more difficult for you here."

Mother put her arms around Kara and let her softly cry. "I will defend what you did every day for the rest of my life. It was a bad rule that forced you to act. But it was a rule."

Kara hadn't expected the punishment to be so severe, but if she was mature enough to disregard a rule, then she had to be mature enough to bear the consequences.

"I won't cause any more trouble, I promise," Kara said. "Do you think there is any chance they will allow me to come back?"

Mother frowned. "I don't know. This is more serious than you may realize. What you have done will be placed on your nursing record, and that record will follow you into your future career. No one will hire a nurse who has broken the rules, even a young nurse."

"What if . . . what if I want to become a doctor instead?"

Mother hugged Kara even tighter than before. "Then do it, and hopefully one day you will be the person making the rules. Until then, I've got to return to work, but I want you to know that despite everything, I am proud of you."

That gave Kara some relief, to know that at least her mother understood her, but as she slumped back into the dining car seat, she wondered if that would be enough to get her through the next several months, or even years, however long her mother's service was needed here.

Only a few minutes later, two orderlies carried Sergeant Baum past on a stretcher.

The stretcher paused right in front of Kara long enough for the orderly to open the transom door. The Austrian turned his head to stare at her and offer a smile of gratitude. And somehow, despite having lost so much, perhaps having sacrificed every hope for her future dreams, that smile made everything she had done entirely worth it.

CHAPTER
SEVENTEEN

October 5, 1915

Mother never returned to their compartment that night. That wasn't unusual, not with a train of newly arrived casualties. But it was different tonight. Because until now, Kara had always been at her mother's side to help.

Now she was stuck in a compartment the size of a closet, and no matter how hard she tried, it was impossible to sleep. Besides, what did it matter if she slept now? For the rest of her days on this train, she'd have nothing to do other than to study or sleep.

Kara thought back to that first morning in the train station in Étaples, that moment when everything had seemed so clear for her life. What a mess she had made of those plans. She would never be a nurse, never get her Red Cross pin, maybe never even earn back the privilege of making up beds and delivering meals.

At some point, she must have drifted off because she awoke

to Mother's hand on her arm. "It's morning," she whispered. "But we have a problem."

Kara sat up, immediately worried. "Sergeant Baum, is he—" Kara couldn't finish the question, but she still had to know the answer.

"He's a little better, and certainly over the wound shock."

Kara rubbed her eyes. "What time is it?"

"Five thirty. Now get dressed. The Sergeant was awake all night, insisting he be allowed to see you. The other nurses feel he will be less of a disturbance if we give him what he wants."

With some eagerness, Kara started out of bed, but Mother quickly added, "You understand that you may not speak to the other soldiers, not even to ask how they are. If they ask for water, tell an orderly."

The reminder wasn't necessary. Kara had thought of nothing else all night but the details of her punishment. Still, she was excited to see Sergeant Baum again, so she hurried to dress, then followed her mother to the train car where he had been placed. It was a short walk. He had been given a lower bunk in the farthest train car back, as if the position was meant to remind him that he did not belong here.

Sergeant Baum began by thanking Kara in French, then he pointed to her plain dress. "I'm so sorry. They told me what you lost because of me."

Kara shrugged, trying to pretend it didn't matter. "How are you today?"

"Your Captain stitched up my side last night. I feel a little better now."

"Do you need anything?"

"I have my life. That is enough." He closed his eyes to rest a little, then said, "I promised Felix that I would do everything I can to come back home. I will keep my promise, but not as soon as I would hope."

"Where is your home?"

"Lemberg. In the eastern part of the empire."

Kara's eyes narrowed. "Didn't the Russians—"

"We defeated them in June; they are gone from Lemberg," he said, and again Kara was reminded that he was not on their side in this war. The Russians were. She had saved the life of someone who had fought against her country and its allies.

He continued, "Lemberg is still not a safe place though. My family is in Vienna now."

"Your injury should be enough to send you home," Kara said.

"Or to a prison camp." He shrugged. "Better one here in France or in Britain. I understand conditions are worse in the Russian camps."

"Oh." Kara wasn't sure what she ought to say to that. Sergeant Baum seemed like a decent man. Perhaps he fought for the enemy, but he wasn't her enemy.

The Sergeant remained quiet for some time, and his face became steadily more somber. Finally, he asked, "Do you know how many a million is?"

Kara wasn't sure that she had understood correctly. "It's . . . one million."

"Yes, but think about that number, because I've lived in

the trenches for weeks, with nothing to block out the sounds of war except a single thought: how big one million is." Before she could ask why the number mattered so much to him, he continued, "Do you know that one million hours is more than one hundred and fourteen years?"

"Yes, sir, it's a big number." But she still didn't understand why they were discussing it.

He sighed. "In less than one year of war, one million of my countrymen have died, or been wounded, or taken prisoner. One million, and now I am one of them. If we took only a single hour to mourn each man we have lost, our mourning would not end for one hundred and fourteen years."

"Oh." That was well into the next century, and they were only fifteen years into this one. Hoping to change the conversation to any other topic, Kara said, "Tell me about your son, about Felix."

Sergeant Baum smiled. "He is gentle in nature and kind to others, but he wants to go to war now, to fight against a Russian officer who was very hard on him in Lemberg. This war cannot possibly last two more years, but if it does, he will become a soldier too. By then I expect we will have lost our second or third million, if Austria-Hungary even still exists."

Kara listened to every word and felt sorry for him, and for his son, Felix. If only they were not on opposite sides of the war. Then she could write Felix a letter and tell him about meeting his father, and tell him that he should not want to go to war. But of course that was impossible. Felix was supposed to be her enemy too.

"Let us pray for a quick peace, then," Kara said.

Sergeant Baum shrugged. "I have forgotten what peace is. Do you know how the men fight each other?"

Kara knew very little about it, and even that was more than she wished to know. Most of the soldiers she had spoken to avoided any talk of what they had seen or experienced while in battle.

"On the seas, sailors board a ship whose sole purpose is to sink the ship of their enemy. With well-placed cannon fire, they will send a thousand men to a watery grave, but never see their faces. Or they climb aboard airships and drop bombs from a thousand kilometers aboveground. From that height, they'll see buildings fall, but not a single face of those who are running for their lives. The rest of us dig long tunnels into the earth—trenches. They are deeper than our tallest man and from there we fight, and try to live another day, all while knowing that a thousand meters away, another trench is filled with men who have become our enemies only because our Kaisers and Kings and Tsars wish for more power. Eventually, one side or the other will claim to have the last living soldier, and he alone will declare victory in this great and terrible war. But Austria-Hungary will not make that declaration. We have no chance of winning this war. Not with one million soldiers already lost."

Kara frowned. She had no idea what to say to Sergeant Baum. He looked so sad, and not only for his country's role in the war, but because war existed at all. "I'd . . . better go back to my quarters."

"Wait! Please forgive me." Sergeant Baum shook his head and then tried to offer a smile. "I am a miserable man lately, but I wasn't always. Will you do me one service, please? Can you offer me a single happy thought, something that I can carry with me until I am home again with my wife and my son?"

"I'll try." Kara thought for a while, glancing outside in hopes of getting an idea. Finally, in the early morning light, she spotted a pigeon flying in the distance, following almost the same path as the train. "Do you see that?"

He grunted as he turned his head. "The pigeon?"

"Yes, do you know what it is?"

"Tell me."

"It's a homing pigeon. A trained homing pigeon is amazing. Wrap a message around its leg, no matter where you are, and it will carry the message back to its home."

This time, Sergeant Baum's smile seemed genuine. "Felix was given the gift of a homing pigeon, named Wilhelm."

Kara wrinkled her nose. "Wilhelm? The German Kaiser's name?"

"In my defense, I did not name him. Last year, Wilhelm played a role in the rescue of my family."

Kara stood, struck by a sudden, wonderful idea. "One moment, please." She returned a minute later with a length of spare fabric bandage. On it she had written, "Sergeant Baum will come home to his family soon." Then she wrapped the bandage around his leg and fastened it with a strip of medical tape. "There," Kara said. "Now you are Wilhelm, *you* are the homing pigeon, and that is the message you will give to them yourself one day."

Sergeant Baum moved his leg to see what she had written, then nodded, clearly pleased. "Thank you. That does indeed make me smile. Again, I am sorry for all that you lost because of me."

Kara shrugged. "It doesn't matter."

"It does. I saw the hurt in your eyes just now when I mentioned it. I can't replace the loss, but I can give you this." He reached into a pocket of his uniform and pulled out a gold-and-red medal in the shape of a cross. "This is the Golden Cross of Merit, given by my country to honor acts of great courage during war. It should belong to you now."

Kara stepped back, overwhelmed. Sometimes the wounded soldiers offered her little gifts in appreciation for her service, and they were kind gestures, but no one had ever offered anything like this. "No, sir, I can't take that."

"But you must. I know the courage it took for you to sneak me on board this train, and to ask for help, even though you must have known the risks. For that matter, it takes great courage just to be on this train at all."

"I can't accept that medal. I know how valuable it must be."

"Until we spoke, I did not realize how the war had begun to poison my mind, and my spirit. You helped to heal me, in ways you may never understand."

Kara did understand that he was smiling now, and seemed more relaxed. But she had done nothing more than she would have for any injured soldier, certainly not enough to earn that medal.

Sergeant Baum added, "If you wish, perhaps one day you can share this medal with someone else. I like to think that it will become part of a journey that inspires courage in others. Until then, you have inspired me to do better."

"Thank you." This time, Kara took the medal and turned it over in her hands as she studied it. This wasn't the Red Cross pin that she had always wanted, but it did have a pin on the back and a red cross was part of its design. So for now, it was perfect.

CHAPTER
EIGHTEEN

December 1, 1915

Ever since Sergeant Baum left the train, Kara had tried to keep a good attitude, she truly had. But for nearly three months, she had been confined to her closet of a compartment or to the dining car, all the while knowing that on the other side of the transom were hundreds of soldiers in desperate need of help. She was miserable.

Not everything was awful, of course. For now, the fighting had quieted down, so the train held no wounded. And this afternoon, she had received a letter from Sergeant Baum. After leaving the train, he had been sent to a base hospital but had written to say that he was finally well enough to be released.

"I had expected to be sent to a prison camp by now," his letter had read, "but I am lucky to have the friendship of Major Dressler, who supervises some German prison camps. I believe this war may have softened him because he bent a few rules to arrange a prisoner exchange for me. I will soon go to Vienna to be with my family."

Kara smiled. That was the best possible news. Even if he was on the wrong side of the war, she still wanted him to be happy.

She set the letter on her bed, then tidied up her dress to go into the dining car to help prepare supper. It wasn't the kind of work she enjoyed, but it was far better than doing nothing, and it gave her a reason to remain on this train.

Kara was about to leave when Mother opened the door to the compartment. "Good news!" she said. "We have been given permission to go into Verdun for a few hours. Want to—"

"Yes!" Kara's coat was on before Mother had the chance to finish her sentence.

The train had begun making Verdun a part of its regular stops lately, but this was the first time the women had been allowed to go into the city for fun, and Kara intended to make the most of it. Christmas would be coming soon, and she hoped to shop for some items as gifts for the other nurses. Maybe even something for Captain Stout. It couldn't hurt.

Verdun was a lovely town of old thatch-roof homes and buildings that had probably stood for hundreds of years. Kara walked beside her mother along a snowy cobblestone road toward the center of town and drew in a deep breath. "Even the air smells lovely, don't you think?"

Mother smiled. "It does not smell like war, and that will always be lovely." She paused, then added, "I confess that I brought you out here this evening to give you some news."

"Oh?"

"I received a letter today from your granny and grandad. They asked that I send you to live with them until the war's end. They say that the ambulance train is no place for a child, and I believe I must agree with them."

"No, Mum, don't send me there!" Kara loved her grandparents, but their house was musty and their food stale. "Let me stay with you."

"There's so little for you to do each day."

"Yes, but if Captain Stout sees that I'm trying to help and obeying the rules, I hope he'll return my apron."

Mother shook her head. "I don't think that will happen, Kara. And I really can't find a reason for you to stay. But for now, cheer up. Let's have some holiday shopping and enjoy the evening."

By then, they had arrived at the center of town, though it was hardly what either of them expected, considering it was so close to Christmas. "Where are all the shoppers?" Kara asked.

The market square was nearly empty, and most of the shops were closed, with snow piled up at their doorways. Just ahead of them stood a pretty girl with light brown hair who might've been only a year or two younger than Kara. She wore a gray coat and carried a small suitcase in her hand. In French, Kara asked her about the shoppers.

The girl's smile back was warm and friendly. She said, "There are rumors that the Germans will attack Verdun. Many families have already left, but not my family. We're still working out some place we might go. My name is Juliette."

Mother asked, "What are you doing out here on such a cold night, Juliette?"

"Selling items for Christmas gifts. Please, madame, have a look." Juliette knelt down and opened her suitcase, revealing several pieces of jewelry, a pocket watch, and a knitted red hat. "We are selling what we can to raise money to help my father."

Kara tilted her head. "What help does he need?"

"Oh!" Juliette hesitated a moment, then said, "We used to live in Lille, farther north. When the Germans invaded, they took control of that entire area. My father worked for the Mayor. The Germans arrested him and many other city leaders. My mother hopes we can raise enough money for a bribe to set my father free."

Kara caught a look in Mother's eye and knew she was going to help as much as possible. She picked up a necklace with a gold pendant. "How much is this one?"

Juliette shrugged. "I'll accept whatever you can pay for it."

Mother reached into her pocketbook and pulled out several francs, far more than the necklace was worth. Kara loved that about her mother.

Juliette's eyes widened when Mother offered it to her. "Oh no, madame, that's too much. Choose a second item, please."

"Very well." Mother looked over at Kara. "Will you choose something?"

Kara crouched down and as she did, she looked directly at Juliette. The tip of her nose was red and she was shivering slightly. Kara wondered how long she had been out here, trying to sell valuables on a street that looked nearly abandoned.

Kara picked up the knitted red hat. "I like this very much."

Juliette's smile changed, ever so slightly. It was still there, but she was making herself smile now. Something was wrong.

"Will this money be enough for both items now?" Mother asked.

Juliette blinked, then accepted the francs. "Yes, thank you very much."

Kara waited while Juliette fastened her suitcase, but when they stood, she held out the hat.

Juliette's eyes narrowed, obviously confused. "You changed your mind?"

"I bought this hat for you."

"But . . . I just sold it."

Kara smiled. "I have no use for it on the ambulance train. This hat is for you."

Now those same eyes filled with tears, though Juliette quickly blinked them away. "Why would you do that?"

"It was already your hat, I think," Kara said. "But you needed to sell it. Now you have, so it should be no problem to return to wearing it."

Juliette smiled, a real smile this time. "Thank you . . ."

"Kara. And this is my mum, Mrs. Webb."

Juliette dipped her head with a respectful nod. "My family thanks you, on behalf of my father. He's been in their prison for a little more than a year."

Kara lowered her eyes, thinking of her own father. It had also been about a year since his loss. Then far behind them, a train whistle sounded, the call for all Red Cross workers to return. Kara wished they didn't have to go. She would have loved to stay and talk more with Juliette.

Mother put her arm around Kara's shoulders. "We should get back to the train, darling." She turned to Juliette. "If you ever need anything, our train passes by here quite often."

"Thank you." Juliette tugged her hat lower on her head. "I'm so glad we met."

"Me too." Kara began to walk away but turned back to wave one last time.

They waited there, watching Juliette linger, looking in shop windows. Mother said, "I believe I will tell Granny that you must stay with me a little longer."

Kara's spirits brightened. "What changed your mind?"

"You have a special way with people, to make them feel happier. Even if you are not allowed near the patients, you are still good for the staff."

Feeling quite relieved, Kara hugged her mother. "Thank you!"

"If only we could have done more for Juliette," Mother said. "She is nearly out of time."

Kara turned to her. "What do you mean?"

"Captain Stout warned us that the city might be abandoned. The rumors Juliette heard are true. The Germans are coming here."

Kara looked toward Juliette, who had begun to walk away. "How soon?"

"Probably early in the new year, when the weather improves. The Germans desperately want control of this part of France, which means the next time we return, it may be to carry the wounded out of Verdun." Mother sounded tired when she said that.

Kara was quiet for a while, then said, "Juliette's family had to leave Lille because of the Germans. Now they will have to leave Verdun too? I wonder where they'll go."

"If the Allies don't turn this war around soon, there will be nowhere for any of us to go," Mother said. "Austria-Hungary is no longer a threat to us, but Germany . . . well, they have become a very dangerous enemy indeed."

Kara frowned and glanced back at where Juliette was, farther down the street, staring in another shop window. "There's no time for that," she said, wishing Juliette could hear her. "Go home, get your family, and leave."

For if she didn't, Kara feared when she saw Juliette again, it might be inside an ambulance ward.

1916

JULIETTE

FRANCE

It wouldn't take anything, just a slightly harder blow, for

everything to collapse.

—*Anonymous French soldier (1916)*

CHAPTER
NINETEEN

February 20, 1916

Juliette stared at the knitted red hat in her hands before pulling it onto her head. This at least was one thing she didn't have to pack. Her bag was already too full.

"Hurry, children, please!"

"Coming soon, Maman!" Juliette gave a quick glance out the window, watching French soldiers march up the road toward their home. The evacuation order was official now; every civilian was to leave at once. No one would be permitted to remain, even if they had to be removed by force. This wasn't out of cruelty; everyone understood that. The soldiers had come to save lives. A large battalion of Germans had already begun gathering just outside of Verdun and an attack could come at any time. The few civilians still in Verdun might have days left to evacuate, or perhaps only hours.

Juliette wouldn't be allowed to bring much with her, but she hoped for a quick battle, one in which Germany lost, and then her family could return in a month or so. Anything else was too unfair for her to imagine. They'd already lost their home in Lille when the Germans took over that area. Now they had to leave Verdun too?

With some luck, the Germans would leave this home untouched. It simply had to be that way, for there was so much here that she loved but could not be carried.

Juliette stuffed the few clothes she could bring into her bag, wishing there was room for the notebook that she loved to draw in, or a small game to entertain her brothers. Instead, she filled the rest of the bag with anything of value. Maman had no idea how much the bribe would need to be for the Germans to release Papa from the prison, so every item was needed, no matter how small.

Maman was downstairs preparing a wagon for the family's departure, but it was already full of larger items they had yet to sell. Sadly, it wasn't much, but Maman believed if they were careful, they would eventually get enough money.

"Your father is no criminal. He's a hostage," Maman often said. "So we pay his ransom and they will set him free."

Juliette doubted it would be that simple, but it was the only plan they had. They just needed a little more money, and they could bring Papa home.

The rest of the wagon was filled with journals and blankets, and what food the family might need until they found a safe place to stay. Most likely, the wagon would end up carrying six-year-old Marcel before the journey ended. Claude could walk for a longer distance, if he had to. He was nine, and both he and Juliette had tried to take on more responsibility since Papa's arrest. Maman had enough trouble already without them being a burden.

"Hurry, children," Maman called from downstairs. "Other families are already leaving. If we are too far behind, we shall be on our own!"

Juliette tied up her bag and slung it over her shoulder, then ran into her brothers' shared room. Claude had done a good job selecting his clothes. He was lacing up his boots but tilted his head toward Marcel, who was sitting on the floor, staring between an old baby blanket he still slept with each night and a book of fairy tales. His bag remained empty.

"Marcel, you should have been finished by now," Juliette scolded. "We can only bring clothes to keep you warm."

"I only want this one book and I need my blanket to sleep," he said. "I would rather be cold than go without them."

Juliette opened the drawer for Marcel's clothes and began pulling out a few items he might need. She stuffed them into the bag and realized how quickly it was filling. Marcel noticed too. Tears began spilling onto his plump cheeks.

"I don't want to leave again," he cried. "Why must we go this time?"

"You don't remember when we had to leave before," Juliette said.

But she certainly remembered. Papa had insisted the family go south as the Germans entered Lille from the north. Maman had begged him to come along, but he couldn't.

"I cannot leave when the Mayor asked all his counselors

to stay and defend Lille," Papa had said. "When this is over, I promise that I will find you."

That had been sixteen months ago, soon after the war had started.

Papa knew that they had fled to Verdun, and maybe this was what bothered Juliette most about leaving. After he was released from prison, Papa would come here, but they would be gone. Juliette couldn't imagine anything worse than to think of Papa not being able to find them again. They couldn't even leave a note behind now, because they still didn't know where they were going next.

In the distance, another round of explosions split the silence. On the road outside, the soldiers shouted with more urgency, *"Tous le monde doit quitter!"*

Everyone must leave.

Juliette crouched beside Marcel and slipped the book into his bag, then fastened it again. He started to protest, but she opened her own bag and removed a sweater, then replaced it with Marcel's blanket. Juliette's heart broke to do so, but one look at Marcel's smile convinced her that she had done the right thing.

"Now come," Juliette said to her brothers. "We must go."

By the time they were downstairs, Maman was outside again, tying up the wagon with twine so that nothing would fall out. Claude stayed behind to help Marcel with his boots while she helped Maman outside. It was a bitterly cold day. Within seconds, she was already shivering.

Maman turned to her. "Juliette, I must ask you for a special favor. If for any reason we are stopped and searched, they will find all the money we have saved. But I do not think they will search you."

Juliette only nodded back. Of course that made her nervous, but she also knew how important that money was. She held out her hand for the bundle of francs, then said, "I can carry it, and I'll keep it safe." Juliette stuffed the money deep inside her bag, folding it into some other clothes to protect it even if she was searched.

"There is no more time," a soldier said, stopping on the road beside them. "Leave now, or you will be in the middle of the fighting."

"I have just a few more things," Maman protested.

"No, now! Get your children and leave!"

Maman called to Marcel and Claude, who ran from the house. She closed the door, then paused and lowered her head, whispering words Juliette could not hear, but which were surely some sort of prayer. Maybe for their safety in leaving. Maybe that they would find a safe refuge. Or, as she noticed Maman look over the contents of the wagon once again, Juliette thought maybe it had been a prayer of hope; hope that they had taken enough with them for a bribe. If it wasn't enough, it would never be enough. They would have no way of gaining anything else of value to sell.

"Now, remember our plan," Maman said as they began walking. "We must stay together, but if there are any problems, as soon as this battle ends, we will meet again right here at home."

"We won't be separated," Claude said. "The plan is to walk straight out of Verdun. If we do, we'll stay together."

"Plans don't always work that way," Juliette said. "It was never the plan to leave Papa behind in a prison in Lille."

"I don't remember him anymore," Marcel mumbled. "Maybe he doesn't remember us either."

"Nonsense," Mama said. "When you love someone as much as he loves us, you cannot forget them. He has four of us to love, so he has four times the memories of each of you."

Juliette wasn't sure if love worked that way, but it did make her feel better. So she pulled her knitted hat down tighter over her ears and took Marcel's hand. The hat had been fine as it was, but she often tugged at it, as a reminder of the way Papa had pulled it down onto her head the day he had given it to her.

Juliette thought back a couple of months to the moment when she had believed that British girl—Kara—was going to buy the hat for herself. Her heart had thudded against her chest in utter despair. She would have sold the hat—anything for more money—but nothing she'd ever owned would have been harder to part with.

At another urging of the soldiers, Maman ducked beneath the bar of the wagon to pull it faster.

"You must watch Marcel at all times," Maman said to Juliette. "Make sure he doesn't get lost, no matter what."

She gripped Marcel's hand tighter. "I promise, Maman. Claude, can you help Maman with the wagon?"

The warnings that Maman had given before were true: Most of the families had already left, so their family was alone, following in the snowy footsteps and wagon ruts of those who were ahead, and hoping if they stayed in that direction, eventually they would at least be with their community. They would fare better in a group than alone.

Juliette took one last look at her home before leaving. She had left her drawing notebook on Claude's bed. Would it be there in that very same place when they returned?

"How far are we going, Maman?" Marcel asked.

"Not far. We will stay close to Verdun until we have enough money to return to Lille. You all have your papers, yes?"

They all did. It was an absolute rule for everyone in France to keep their identification papers with them at all times. Not having them could get a person accused of being a spy or from one of the enemy countries.

Maman continued pushing them forward, the fastest way out of Verdun, then suddenly stopped. The road forked, and they would have to choose to go straight ahead or to take the fork, which curved to the left. Maman started forward, but Juliette wasn't so sure.

"We should go left, Maman," she said.

Maman shook her head. "This is the fastest way."

"But it isn't the best way. If the soldiers come—"

"If the soldiers come, we want to be as far from here as possible. Come, children, we must go faster."

So Juliette followed along behind her mother, and for another half kilometer, it felt like that had been the right decision.

Until they heard noises in the distance. Juliette walked out from behind the wagon and caught her breath in her throat. Maman stopped the wagon and breathed out a soft, "Oh no." An entire company of German soldiers was on the road ahead, marching directly toward them.

Maman's tense voice betrayed her fear. "Hurry, children, we must get off the road."

Marcel practically leapt into Juliette's arms, already crying, but she could only shush him and begin running into the field, though carrying him was slowing them down. Maman and Claude were pushing the wagon through the snow-covered field. Juliette would not be able to keep up this way for long.

"Stay in here," she said to Marcel, placing him in the back of the wagon. Then she leaned low and dug her boots into the ground to help push it.

The wagon went into the field, but the soldiers were approaching faster than Juliette had expected. They needed to move faster and get into the trees ahead.

Suddenly, the wagon lurched to a halt.

"Maman?" Claude called.

"The wagon is stuck!" Maman said. "What is it caught on?"

Juliette had already seen the problem. The wheel had slid into a low point on the ground and now was trapped in thick mud.

"Push harder!" Maman cried.

While Maman pulled the wagon from ahead, Claude and Juliette bent low to push, but it would not budge.

"We need something to pry it out!" Juliette pointed to the woods ahead. "I'll find a stick there!"

"Hurry!" Maman said.

Juliette went running but hadn't expected the snow to be so thick in this dense grove of trees. She began kicking at the ground, but nothing she found looked strong enough to pry out the wagon.

Finally, her foot connected with something solid, and she pulled out a stick of the perfect length and thickness. She held it close as she started back toward the wagon, but when she was nearly at the edge of the woods, she stopped to sink down into the shadows.

The Germans had arrived, and several soldiers already surrounded her family. They were pulling items off the wagon, laughing as they stole the last of their treasures for themselves.

Juliette darted behind a tree, horrified and unsure of what to do. If she showed herself, the Germans would take her bag too, with all their money in it.

She had to hide, just for a few minutes until the Germans moved on. Then she'd return to the road and catch up to her family. The road they would take went straight. It would be easy to find them again. But for now, she had to hide.

Juliette turned, but noticed her own footprints were everywhere in the snow. They would surely give her away. So she stepped into a small brook running through the woods. Icy water flooded into her boots, but she forced herself to continue moving downstream, all the while looking for a good place to hide.

And she'd have to hurry. The soldiers had already moved on from her family, but rather than return to the road, they had entered the patch of woods where she'd found the stick.

Some of them even seemed to have noticed her footprints and were calling, *"Mädchen! Mädchen!"*

Juliette looked around, finally locating a patch of under-brush covered by snow. It wasn't as thick as she wanted, but it would have to do. Already shivering from the water in her boots, Juliette slid beneath the underbrush. Surely the soldiers wouldn't be here long.

But to her dismay, more and more of them came. None of them ventured as far downstream as she was, but if she attempted to get out, they would see her. Orders were shouted, none of which she understood, but the meaning quickly became clear. The Germans were setting up camp. They intended to remain here at least for the rest of the night.

Juliette pulled her coat tighter around her body as the shivering became worse. It would be a very long night.

CHAPTER
TWENTY

February 21, 1916

Juliette's first thought when she awoke was that she was on a bed. Not her own bed, not nearly so comfortable, but it was a bed.

But . . . where was she?

Her confusion only got worse. The bed was . . . rumbling, vibrating in a way that gently rolled her side to side.

This wasn't how things were supposed to be. Something was terribly wrong.

She opened her eyes and sat up straight, her heart racing.

"You're all right, you're safe!" The words were in French.

Until hearing the voice, Juliette hadn't realized someone else was in this small room with her. She turned toward the voice, and to her surprise saw the British girl she had met before Christmas.

"Kara?"

Kara had a cup of water that she offered, but Juliette barely noticed it.

"I don't understand." A shiver ran through Juliette, a reminder that her last memory was of shivering to the point that all she had wanted was to sleep. She must have fallen asleep, but in a forest occupied by German soldiers, hidden by dense underbrush. Panic began to swell in her chest as the awful memories flooded back. "How did I get here? What happened?"

"Our train stopped near Verdun yesterday. One of the orderlies happened to see your red hat and went over to look more carefully. He found you unconscious beneath a bush. Another hour and you—"

"Where's my mother?"

Kara's brows pressed together, confused. "What?"

Juliette's breaths began coming faster and sharper. "My mother, and Claude and Marcel. Where are they?"

"You were alone."

Juliette shook her head, though that brought on a fierce ache. "No, they would have waited for me on the road. We were leaving Verdun together!" She closed her eyes and tried to sort out her thoughts. What did she remember? Maman and the boys had been in the field. She was supposed to find a stick to pry out the wagon. The Germans had come. "I had to hide," she said. "I thought it might be only for a few minutes, but then they set up camp for the night. I didn't dare to leave. But I was so cold, I couldn't stay awake. I must have fallen asleep there."

"Thank goodness we found you when we did," Kara said. "The Germans moved on very early in the morning, closer to Verdun. Our orderlies went out to see if any families still remained in need of help."

"Then you found my mother?"

Kara's eyes softened. "No, we didn't find anyone other than you."

"What about my brother Marcel?" Juliette tried to remember that small detail. She was supposed to hold Marcel's hand at all times, but she had let him go to run into the woods. What had she done with Marcel?

She looked up at Kara, almost yelling, "When they found me, did they look for Marcel?"

Kara took her hand, trying to calm her. "They looked for anyone else. I know they did, because it surprised them to see you out there alone—"

"But I wasn't alone. I was with my family!"

Kara squeezed her hand. "Let's talk this through together. Tell me about Marcel."

Juliette's breaths came sharper as her panic grew. "The Germans were coming, we had to get off the road. Maman needed help pushing the wagon. Did I put Marcel into the wagon when I helped push? I don't remember!"

Kara kept her tone low and soft. "Take three deep breaths, Juliette. Count them."

Juliette did. One . . . two . . . and on the third breath, she finally remembered. "I put him in the wagon. He must be with Maman. I'm the one who's lost."

Tears began to fall in steady streams down her cheeks. Kara sat beside her and wrapped her arms around Juliette's shoulders, but nothing could make her feel better. Nothing could make any of this better.

"There are refugee camps all over France," Kara said. "Villagers bring families in and they post lists of names around town so that people can find each other again. Your family will be on one of those lists."

Juliette sniffed. "Do you think so?"

"Of course! Your mother will be trying to find you as much as you want to find her. Did she say where she was going after she left Verdun?"

"She'll stay close to Verdun, especially now. If any of us became separated, the plan was to return home after the battle ends."

Kara gave her another comforting squeeze. "Then we already know where to look. I'm sure we'll find your family soon."

"Me too." Juliette felt a little better already, and it did make sense. Someone would have seen her family. Someone would know where they were.

Her knitted hat was on the pillow beside her. Juliette picked it up and pulled it close to her, as if that would bring her some comfort.

Kara offered Juliette the cup of water again, and this time she accepted. While she took sips, Kara said, "You are lucky to be alive, you know."

"I am lucky that someone from this train spotted me." Juliette finished the water, then wiped her tears again. She felt miserable and alone and her heart was empty without Maman, but Kara would help find her. So with a deep breath, Juliette asked, "When is the next stop? I want to begin looking as soon as possible."

CHAPTER
TWENTY-ONE

March 3, 1916

Juliette hadn't expected to see her name on the list at the train's first stop. The train was moving away from Verdun, already farther than her family could have come in such a short time. She knew that, but she still looked and still felt the pinch in her heart when her name wasn't there. She borrowed a fountain pen from Kara to scrawl Maman's name onto the bottom of the list, and returned to the train, disappointed but hopeful.

The next stop was even farther from Verdun, so Juliette knew Maman could not be there. But she wrote her mother's name on the posted list anyway. It could do no harm.

Juliette didn't even bother to write her name on the list at the third stop.

However, when the train began to circle back toward Verdun, her hopes lifted again. Most of the time, the train was only at the station long enough to load the wounded on board, but occasionally, it stopped long enough that she could venture into the nearby villages.

At those times, Juliette ran through the square, checking every list she could find. She stopped locals and gave descriptions of her brothers, and of Maman. When there was time, she even walked through some of the refugee camps.

But no one had seen her family, or heard of them. Juliette's name was not on any of the lists, which meant no one had reported her missing. Maman and Claude and Marcel seemed to have simply vanished.

Or, more likely, she was the one who had vanished.

"There must be a reason my name isn't on a list," Juliette told Kara one afternoon as they were returning to the train. "Maybe they aren't looking for me."

"Nonsense!" Kara said. "Of course they're looking."

"They aren't looking here, or in the last village, or the one before that!" Juliette's tone sounded harsh and she didn't intend it to be that way, but her heart had so many cracks in it now, it was nearly shattered to pieces.

"Look up," Kara said.

Juliette did, and there saw an enormous balloon floating high overhead. Hanging from it was a basket with two or three men in it.

"What are they doing?" Juliette asked.

"Looking." Kara smiled. "Yes, maybe they are looking for Germans, or for any other dangers, but just imagine if your mother could get into a balloon like that. She'd be up there scanning every centimeter of the ground below, all to find you. She is looking for you, Juliette."

Juliette stared at the balloon a while longer, suddenly nervous. "Are you sure that balloon is on our side? Could it be German?"

Kara reached for her hand, and now there was tension in her voice. "Yes, it could be. Let's get back inside the train."

"*Les boches,*" Juliette muttered.

Kara turned back with widened eyes, though Juliette couldn't tell if she was truly shocked by those words or if she was only playing. But her tone sounded friendly when she said, "Perhaps it's a good thing your mother isn't here."

Juliette couldn't help but smile. "If she was, my mother would have far worse to say about the Germans."

The girls laughed as they hurried back toward the train. Juliette appreciated Kara's friendship, more than she might ever know. Kara watched out for her, comforted her, let her talk endlessly about Claude's bookish nature or Marcel's innocent giggle. It helped, it likely even saved her in those first few weeks, but even Kara's good nature could not dull the constant ache inside her.

Kara's mother was waiting for the girls when they reached the train. "You two were gone longer than expected," she said.

"But sooner than the train needed to leave," Kara said. "No one had to wait for us."

"No, but Captain Stout had hoped to speak to Juliette. He's been called away now for a patient."

Juliette didn't like the tone in Madame Webb's voice. She had always been kind to Juliette, and maybe that was the problem now. She sounded too kind, too sympathetic. Her heart began to pound. There was a problem, but she didn't know what it could be. She had broken no rules and, indeed, had kept Kara from breaking a few of them. What could Captain Stout want with her?

Kara's mother said, "Sweet Juliette, you came to the train in such a delicate condition, Captain Stout thought you should stay until you were fully recovered and, he hoped, until you found your family. But now—"

"He wouldn't send her away," Kara said. "Mother, she has nowhere to go!"

"This is a hospital train," her mother said. "We're picking up a new nurse at our next stop and she will need Juliette's bunk. Beyond that, our work often takes us into areas that are not safe—"

"Her home was not safe!" Kara protested. "She has no home now."

Juliette blinked hard. It was obvious what was about to happen.

Madame Webb turned to Juliette. "I'm so deeply sorry, but Captain Stout has given his orders. Your bag has been packed. The kitchen staff included as much food as they thought you could carry, and I've written a letter for you to give the refugee camp here in town. They'll take you in and watch over you until your family can be found."

"Captain Stout can't do this!" Kara said.

"No, it's all right," Juliette said. "I can't find my family while I'm on this train." She drew in a deep breath and tried to believe her own words. Even if she didn't, Maman would want her to show dignity now, and to remember her manners. "Thank you for your kindness."

While Kara's mother returned to the train for Juliette's bags, Kara said, "Let me speak to Captain Stout myself—"

"Try that and he'll likely send you from the train too." Juliette made herself smile, hoping to convince Kara that she was happier than she felt. "Besides, I've been thinking of a plan. The train will be near my old hometown today. This is good news."

Kara shook her head. "You can't go back to Lille. The Germans control that entire area now."

"Yes, I know. My father is in prison there. But I have with me all the money we raised. Maman's plan was to go to Lille this spring anyway, so I should go there too. Whether I find Maman or not, at least I can set Papa free. Then together, Papa and I can find the rest of our family."

Kara hadn't stopped shaking her head the entire time that Juliette had spoken, and she was even more insistent now. "You've shown me the money you raised. It won't be enough, Juliette. The Germans will never accept it as a bribe."

"You don't know that."

"I do! They'll take your money and then chase you away, or arrest you too. This plan is too dangerous!"

Juliette didn't want to hear that, especially not now. "What other choice do I have? I can't stay here, so I must go somewhere.

I don't know where my mother is, or my brothers, but I do know where Papa is! If I can help him, then I've got to try!"

Kara frowned, pressing her lips tightly together, but finally she said, "Very well. If you are going to do this, let's give you the best possible chance to succeed."

Juliette paused. "What do you mean?"

Kara reached into her coat pocket and withdrew a gold medal with a large red cross imprinted on it, hanging from a bright red ribbon.

"That's beautiful!" Juliette said.

"I never go anywhere without it. It's called the Golden Cross of Merit, given for exceptional courage on the battlefield." Kara shrugged. "That Austrian soldier gave me this in gratitude." She held it out. "I want you to have it."

Juliette backed away. "No, I couldn't! That is far too valuable."

"Yes, it is valuable, that's my point." Kara took her hand and gave her the medal. "This is probably worth a great deal of money, especially to a German. I don't know if it will be enough for a bribe, but if it can help, then I want you to have it."

Juliette's eyes were growing hot, but she didn't want to cry, not now. Yet as she stared down at the medal, the tears flowed anyway. The truth was that she had doubted whether they had enough money for the bribe. Now it seemed like this almost might work.

She quickly wiped her tears as Kara's mother returned with her bag. It was very heavy because of the food inside, but Juliette was grateful for that.

"If you'd like, I'll have an orderly escort you to the refugee camp."

"No, but thank you," Juliette said. "I'm going in a different direction." She hugged them both, then hoisted the bag higher on her shoulder and began to walk away.

Much as she wanted to turn back, she took one step forward, then another and another. "This is for the best," she whispered. Maybe her plan would work, maybe not. But she felt a new spark of hope, and for now, that was enough.

TWENTY-TWO

March 5, 1916

Getting into Lille had been easier than Juliette had expected. Her papers still identified her as living in the area, so passing through the German checkpoints only required a few lies. Young as Juliette was, her excuses were believed. Walking into Lille was the easy part.

Far more difficult was actually being in Lille again, in the city where she had lived her entire life until the Germans invaded a year and a half ago, forcing her family away. Now Juliette was here, in a city she knew so well but barely recognized.

The soldier at the checkpoint had instructed Juliette to speak in German because she was in their territory now. Juliette knew almost no German, so she hardly dared to speak to anyone at all.

Nor did anyone show the slightest interest in speaking to her. Lille had once been a friendly place, where people waved and where women gathered in the squares to laugh and to gossip, but no longer. A hush had fallen over the city. People hurried through the streets, heads down, avoiding having to look at anyone else. The feeling of fear was so real that Juliette felt it pressing in around her.

She hurried along too, headed to her former home. It had always been admired as one of the finer houses in the city, so much that Maman had cried when they had to leave. It was built of brick and had a full second level with large windows in every room and a long yard lined with tall trees leading to the entrance.

Yet as Juliette came nearer to it, she stopped. German flags hung from the roof and an automobile was in front. Her breath caught in her throat as she tried to absorb what this meant. It wasn't enough that the Germans had taken over her city. Now they had taken her family's home too?

Maybe by now, they had taken over her family's home in Verdun as well. That was all the Germans ever seemed to do, was to take. Take, then destroy, then take some more.

A fierce anger welled up in Juliette, something different than she'd ever felt before. She had never expected life to be fair, but this war had kicked her family without mercy. Every time, Juliette had forced herself back to her feet, only to be knocked down again and again and again. She truly didn't know if she could get up anymore.

The front door opened and a soldier exited. Juliette lowered her eyes and began backing away. The last thing she wanted was to draw attention from any Germans in town. She was so close to setting her father free. Nothing else mattered, not even this house. She whispered those words until they were locked in her mind. Only Papa mattered.

She returned to the center of town, on the way passing very near to what had once been Lille's police headquarters. German flags hung there too. Juliette paused to stare at the building. Was that where Papa was being held? She didn't know, and that bothered her. Who exactly was she supposed to bribe?

Her hand slid inside the bag slung from her shoulder, digging past Marcel's blanket until she found the money that Maman had given her. Would it be enough?

Kara's medal was inside a pocket of Juliette's coat, and she intended to keep it there, ready to give to a soldier if it completed the bribe.

But for now, Juliette had an even bigger problem, which was where to sleep tonight. She had planned to stay at her old house, but that was a foolish idea, she realized that now. Of course the Germans would have taken over her home. Of course things would have changed here.

She just hadn't realized how much.

As Juliette continued walking, every sign she passed was printed in a language she did not know. What she could decipher from the pictures on them suggested that the only accepted money was the German mark. The French were required to leave the sidewalk if a German soldier was on it. And one sign seemed to indicate that breaking any of the new rules could result in a prison sentence.

"More prisoners," Juliette mumbled. Would they eventually have to imprison the entire city? Because eventually, everyone would break at least one of their many rules.

There was another rule too, this one clearly spelled out by a clock drawn on the sign. Curfew would be enforced, which meant she was running out of time to find a place to sleep. But where? She had no German marks to pay for a room, no family nearby, and her closest friends had also left when the Germans invaded.

Then Juliette glanced across the square and saw a familiar face, a girl named Monique. She was at least five years older and probably wouldn't even remember Juliette's name, but Juliette had always admired Monique. She was smart and cheerful and, above all else, kind.

Like Papa, Monique's father was also a city counselor, which probably meant he was in prison too.

When Monique began walking out of the square, Juliette followed. Finally, Monique entered a small and humble house, which made little sense. Monique's family had been very wealthy. So who lived here?

Juliette waited for Monique to leave, but as the sun dipped below the horizon, she realized she had no choice left. With a deep breath, she walked to the front door and knocked.

No answer came, but from the corner of her eye, Juliette saw a curtain move at the window. Seconds later, a bolt was unlatched and the door opened.

Monique had curly brown hair, and she had always smiled

easily when she spoke. But now, she peered around the door with caution. "Yes?"

Juliette stared back at her, realizing she should have planned out what to say. She stumbled over her words at first but finally managed to say, "My name is Juliette Caron. We've met a few times. My father knew your—"

"Our fathers are both in prison now, thanks to the Germans." Monique's eyes darted, as if assuring herself that no one had overheard them. "I remember you. But I thought your family left."

"I came back. I've become separated from my mother and my brothers, and—"

"You'd better come in." Monique widened the door, looked for anyone who might be around, then quickly ushered Juliette inside. Once the door was closed, Monique bolted it tight, then turned to face Juliette. "You're welcome to remove your coat and set your bag down."

Juliette wasn't ready for that yet, and only drew her bag closer. They stood in a small kitchen with bread and cheese on the table, but not much of either. The house felt quiet, almost too quiet.

Monique seemed to know what Juliette was thinking. "I live alone here. They arrested my mother a month ago for failing to pay their war tax. Imagine that! Taxing us for the privilege of being forced to live under their command. We can barely breathe without it being a violation of some rule."

"I didn't realize it had become so awful here."

"*Awful* is the kindest word anyone might use for our lives these days." Monique pressed her lips together. "Most people here in Lille would leave if they could. Why did you come back?"

"I hoped . . ." Juliette felt foolish to speak the words aloud. "I hoped there might be a way to gain my father's release. Perhaps through a bribe."

Monique's laugh was so stiff, she nearly snorted it. "It won't work."

"I could try."

"No, I'm telling you they will not accept bribes. Do you think you are the first with that idea? Do you know how my family lost our home? They took it and there was nothing we could do. Why would the Germans need a bribe when they can simply take what they want, whenever they want? If they find out you have something of value, they will simply take that too."

"Oh." Juliette lowered her eyes and tried not to cry. "Then there is no way to get him out of the prison?"

"Our fathers aren't prisoners, Juliette. They are hostages. They are the reason that people here don't set fire to the German supply buildings or refuse their stupid orders. They are using our fathers and many others to keep us under control. So they won't care about your money. They want control."

"I see." Kara had told her nearly the same thing.

Monique stared at Juliette for a moment. "You do make me curious though. How much money do you have to offer them?"

"More than five hundred francs."

Monique arched a brow. "Impressive, but not nearly enough for a bribe, even if they would consider it."

"I have something else." Juliette reached into her pocket and pulled out the medal. "I think this must be worth a great deal of money."

Rather than admire it or ask about its value, Monique grabbed it and shoved it back at Juliette. With widened eyes, she said, "Show them that, and they will arrest you for having a medal that should belong to them, or the Austrians. Get rid of it, or keep it hidden, but you must not let the Germans see that, ever."

Juliette stuffed it back in her pocket, feeling her heart break apart once again. If she did not have enough money on her own, and if she could not supplement it by offering the medal, then she had nothing at all.

Monique sighed. "I assume you have nowhere else to go and that is why you are here, no?" When Juliette nodded, she said, "Please stay here for as long as you'd like. Tomorrow I can show you the Citadel, where they are holding your father. You won't see him, but at least you will know where he is."

"I'd like that," Juliette said. "Thank you."

"You may sleep in my mother's bedroom, if you don't mind that."

Juliette nodded. Truthfully, she would have accepted any offer to stay here, even if it was in a corner of a cold room. Getting a bed was more than she had expected.

Thirty minutes later, Monique wished Juliette a good

night and closed the door of the bedroom, leaving her alone to wonder how she had gotten herself into this situation.

She opened her bag and, for the first time, pulled out Marcel's old blanket. She pressed it to her face and drew in a deep breath. The blanket still smelled like him. Then, despite knowing how childish it must be, she folded the blanket into a thin pillow and fell asleep.

CHAPTER
TWENTY-THREE

April 22, 1916

Juliette's father and the other hostages were held in the Citadel, a walled military fort that had defended Lille for more than two hundred years.

Now it was a stronghold for the Germans, and a prison for dozens of people whose only crime was that they had once worked for the French government.

Monique had taken Juliette there after her first night in Lille, but refused to go with her again.

"Do you want the German soldiers to become used to seeing you there?" Monique had asked. "That is not wise."

"Then I won't let them see me," Juliette had said. But she did go, every single day. If the chance came to offer her bribe, she wanted to be ready.

"That is even more foolish," Monique warned. "Do not do it."

"What harm could it do?" It was a question that Juliette had asked more than once.

Each time, the response was the same. "They could arrest you for trying. They could take offense at your offer and punish the rest of us for it."

"Or they could accept it and set my father free!"

That's where the conversation ended, every single time.

Then came a morning in late April when Juliette did not ask, because Monique brought up the question first. "How far would you go to set your father free?" she asked over breakfast.

Juliette looked at her. "What do you mean?"

"Would you work for the Germans? Spend a day in their factories building their weapons or harvesting their food, if it meant your father was released a day earlier?"

That wasn't a difficult question. "Yes, I would."

"Would you sacrifice a friendship if that was the only way to get him back?"

Juliette didn't see how that would ever be necessary, but after a moment, she nodded. "I suppose so." She missed her father so much, more than she had ever missed a friend.

"Would you steal? If you needed another five hundred francs to free your father, would you steal that money?"

Juliette hesitated. "I don't know. Maybe. Why are you asking?"

Monique shrugged. "You must know these things before the moment comes to decide. And it may come soon. The war is not going well for us."

"What do you mean?"

"I saw an underground newspaper yesterday. Our own general said that if French soldiers continue to fall as fast as they have in the last two months, by May, there will be no French army left. I wonder what will happen to Lille if the Germans never leave."

Juliette stared down at her hands, mumbling, "I would risk nearly anything to set my father free."

It was a bigger statement than Monique might have guessed. For when Monique announced that she was going to the market, Juliette picked up her bag and headed directly to the Citadel. She had meant exactly what she'd said. She was willing to risk arrest, or a few offended Germans, if it set her father free.

The Citadel gates were at the end of a long bridge. Juliette knew from when they'd passed by before that one of the higher-ranking officers, a German named Major Dressler, left the Citadel from this bridge each day at eleven to make rounds in the city.

At exactly eleven, she was waiting by that bridge.

"Herr Dressler," she began when he approached.

"*Major* Dressler," he corrected her. "*Was möchten sie?*"

"I don't speak German, I'm sorry," she said.

He sighed and switched to French. "What do you want?"

Juliette straightened up, utterly terrified, but she knew this was her chance, probably her one chance ever, to do what she had come to do. She had rehearsed the words in her mind a thousand times. Now she had to say them.

Her voice trembled as she began. "My name is Juliette Caron. My father is in the prison in the Citadel."

He arched a brow and suddenly seemed genuinely interested in her. "Monsieur Caron is your father?"

"Yes. My family has sold everything we have, saved all the money we could. I will give it to you if—"

Major Dressler squared himself to her. "Are you attempting to bribe a German officer?"

"No!" Monique ran up behind Juliette. "No, sir, she is not. She would not."

"That is a serious offense," Dressler said.

Monique's voice rose in pitch. "Sir, it could not be a bribe because she has nothing to bribe you with."

Confused, Juliette opened her bag. Maybe Monique was trying to keep her out of trouble, but if the Major chose to search her bag, he would know how serious she—

Juliette froze. Marcel's blanket was in her bag, and her hairbrush and some food, but no money. The money was gone.

Monique widened Juliette's bag to show Major Dressler. "You see, this was a misunderstanding."

"I am glad to hear it," Major Dressler said. "Now you girls should hurry back home."

He walked on, but Juliette was still so horrified, she couldn't move. She patted the pockets of her coat. No money. What had happened to it?

"We should go," Monique said.

Monique.

Juliette turned to her, almost ill from the anger rising in her. "Where is it?"

Monique lowered her head, refusing to look up.

Juliette took a step toward her. "This morning, when you asked me those questions, had you already taken my money?"

The answer came in little more than a whisper. "Yes."

"I want it back."

"It's gone. I'm sorry, Juliette."

Sorry wasn't enough. Sorry wasn't anything at all. Between gritted teeth, Juliette said, "Why would you do this?"

Now Monique looked up. "Everyone says that France will lose the war. My mother and I must leave Lille, just as your family did. So I needed to pay the war tax to set my mother free. I'm deeply sorry, Juliette, I need you to know that. But I've been two months without my mother—"

"So have I."

Barely controlling her anger, Juliette turned on one heel and marched toward Monique's house. She was already halfway packed when Monique entered the house as well.

Monique stood in the doorway. "This morning, you said that you might steal to release your father. You said that you would lose a friendship to get him back."

"And that's just what you've done," Juliette snapped. "How long until your mother goes free?"

"Tomorrow," Monique whispered. "Of course, you're still welcome to stay with us."

Juliette only shook her head, knowing how badly this would end if she tried to speak right now. She pushed past Monique and started toward the front door when someone knocked.

Juliette stopped there and looked over at Monique, who put a finger to her lips, a warning not to make a sound.

Monique crept to the window and parted the curtain

just enough to look out, then immediately backed away. "Germans," she mouthed.

Juliette's heart pounded. Was she in trouble for having gone to the Citadel? Or was Monique the one in trouble? Did they know she had paid the war tax with stolen money?

A knock came again, this one stronger than before.

Monique took a deep breath and straightened her hair, then began walking to the door.

"Let's run out the back!" Juliette said.

But it was too late. The door was shoved open and two Germans entered.

"*Kennkarte!*" one of them demanded.

Juliette knew what they wanted. She reached into her coat pocket for her identification paper and passed it to the man, as did Monique.

While he looked over the papers, the other soldier said to Juliette, "Why are you wearing that coat and hat? It's a warm day."

Juliette felt flushed as her mind emptied of any excuse she might use to answer him. She always wore the hat, and the medal was pinned to the inside of her dress. She wore the coat to cover where its weight pulled down on the fabric. It was a good thing she had it pinned there; otherwise, Monique probably would have stolen that too.

"I . . . I . . ."

"Hunger makes my friend feel cold," Monique said, offering an explanation Juliette could not come up with on her own.

The first soldier returned the identification papers to each girl. "We can help with the hunger. Do either of you have any health problems?"

Juliette glanced over at Monique, wondering why he would ask such a question. "No," Monique said. "We are healthy."

"Good. Then you will both come with us."

Come with them? What was he talking about?

Monique shook her head. "Where are we going?"

"That will be explained to you. Now come, or we will drag you outside."

Juliette's hands began shaking, but she put her bag over her shoulder and followed Monique out the door. A wagon was waiting outside, one with a roof and a barred door, such as would be used for the transport of prisoners.

Juliette stopped. "What is this? I've done nothing wrong!"

Though she had. She had attempted to bribe a German officer.

Juliette pulled her bag close, but Monique wasn't allowed the time to take anything with her as they were escorted toward the wagon. A soldier outside opened the door and both girls were pushed inside, then the door slammed shut.

Other girls were also here in the wagon, none of them older than nineteen or twenty, and all of them packed tightly together on the bench surrounding the inside of the wagon.

"What is this?" Juliette called out through the barred door, but no one answered. She knelt on the floor of the wagon, too terrified to breathe.

"Juliette—" Monique began but stopped in the heat of Juliette's glare.

"Do not speak to me," Juliette said. "We are not friends."

She found a place to sit as far from Monique as possible, then lowered her head again.

"Does anyone know where they are taking us?" Monique asked. "Or why?"

But no one answered.

No one knew.

TWENTY-FOUR

April 22, 1916

Sometime during the ride away from Lille, Juliette had fallen into a shallow sleep, filled with awful dreams. It wasn't much better when the wagon stopped and she awoke shivering. At first she thought it must be from the cold—she'd been cold often enough over the past two months that shivering had become normal for her. But this was different. This was an emotion she well remembered from the moment she first realized her mother was gone.

This was terror.

A quick glance around the wagon told Juliette that she wasn't the only one who looked afraid. All the girls in the cart had wrapped arms around each other or held hands, whispering words of comfort that they clearly didn't believe in for themselves.

Monique was the only one who seemed calm. With a stern ce, she said, "Do you forget that we are French? We must be stronger than this. We have faced harder times than this before. Wipe your tears. If we do what they say, we will be fine."

Her eyes lingered on Juliette as she finished speaking, but Juliette turned away. She hoped Monique was right about the Germans, but that did nothing to dull her anger.

The barred door opened to a wide yard filled with rows of girls and more Germans than Juliette had ever seen together in one place. The girls from her wagon were ordered outside, and one by one they climbed out. Once on the ground, Juliette stretched her tired legs, then stood and tried to get a sense of where they were.

The wagon had stopped in front of a large house, except that it didn't appear to be used as a home any longer. Or at least, not for civilians. German soldiers stood watch on either side of the door, and Juliette was sure that dozens more were inside.

She absolutely did not want to go into that house, but she had no choice. The soldiers corralled her and the other girls through the front door where a former front room had been converted into a sort of office space.

A young German soldier at a small wooden desk looked up at them. *"Ja?"*

The soldiers with the girls spoke to him with words Juliette didn't understand, and he nodded and disappeared into a back room, then returned a minute later with another soldier. This one had a round face and round glasses, and a rounder belly than most others in the military. Obviously not a field officer.

He walked a circle around them, and they pushed in even closer together to keep as far as possible from him. If Juliette could have, she would have shrunk away to nothing. How much better that would be than to stay here, being scrutinized by this round man. He was the most dislikable person she had ever met.

The round man gestured for the girls to follow him, which they did through a back door and across a path to a building that looked as if it had been converted from a barn.

Before opening that door, he turned and said, "You work for Germany now. At sunrise tomorrow, you will see a large farm. This is one of several farms in the area that will be cared for by the young women of Lille. Do as you're told, work hard, and you will be returned home at the end of the harvest. Now go inside and find a bed for yourself. Sleep well and be ready to work at dawn."

Some of the girls cried out, only to be silenced by glares and threats of lost meals for everyone. The barn door opened and a few lanterns illuminated a large room filled with canvas cots. Each one had a small blanket on it, but no pillows.

Monique said to Juliette, "Go to the center of the room. It will be warmest there."

Juliette ignored her and looked around. Much as she hated to admit it, Monique was right. Monique had already walked on ahead so by the time Juliette got there, she gestured to a cot beside hers. Other girls were already claiming their places nearby. Reluctantly, Juliette set her bag on the cot Monique had chosen for her, but turned her back to sit down while the other girls got settled.

No sooner had Juliette done so than the barn door shut

and the rustling sound of a chain outside confirmed that they had just been locked inside. Juliette was a prisoner now, as her father was a prisoner.

Monique's mother would go free tomorrow. Juliette tried to feel happy for her—she knew the prisons had to be awful. But she still couldn't forgive Monique for what she had done.

"My mother won't even know what's happened to me," Monique mumbled.

Juliette heard her, but she didn't turn around.

Monique continued, "Though I suppose with so many young women of Lille being taken, word will get around of what's happened to us."

"It's not just us," a girl a few cots away said. "When we passed through the house, I heard one German say to another that thousands of us had been taken, from all over the German-occupied zones."

"Then we must act now." Monique stood and raised her arms, calling for attention. "You see how many more beds are here, so we know other girls will be coming. We must be strong so that we can help them, and give them comfort. The Germans want us to be afraid, so we must fight them by refusing to give in to our fears. Tomorrow morning, we will plant seeds and we will do so with a smile and a song."

"How can you say that?" a girl in the far corner asked. "Look at where we are!"

Monique hesitated only for a moment before replying, "Did you ever ask your parents for permission to sleep over at the home of a friend?"

"Y-yes."

"Then let us think of it that way now." Monique smiled, and whether she truly felt that way or not, the mood in the room really did seem to lift. "Here we are, at a sleepover for all of our dearest friends. Now, let us sing!"

She started a tune and slowly the other girls joined in. Everyone but Juliette. She only glanced back once at Monique, long enough to communicate that she was at a sleepover for all her dearest friends, and with one girl who had destroyed their friendship forever.

CHAPTER
TWENTY-FIVE

July 15, 1916

Juliette had pulled so many weeds over the past three months that her hands had become rough and full of calluses. Today's work was in the cornfields. The corn had another few weeks before it would be ready, but her mouth watered for it every time she was in this area. Back at home, nothing had ever tasted better than fresh corn in Maman's churned butter.

As always, a single thought of Maman sent Juliette's heart to her and her brothers. Did they think about her as often as she thought about them? Did they know she was alive?

Was she alive, truly? Was this her life now?

Monique was working in the same row but was in a conversation with another girl. "France must have had a few victories, or this war would be over by now, don't you think?"

The girl shrugged. "If you listen to the German guards, the war has been over for months, and it's only a matter of time before the Allies figure that out and surrender."

"That's their foolish propaganda," Monique said. "We must be near the front lines. If you listen carefully at night, you can hear it. Our soldiers are still fighting, as strong as ever."

"If the war did end, would they let us go home?"

"It's a nice thought, but I don't think the war is ending anytime soon." Monique caught Juliette watching her and added, "Of course, Juliette has lost more than any of us. We will return to Lille in another month or two. Juliette has no home to return to."

"I'll go back to Verdun," Juliette said flatly.

She had to say something, but of course she wouldn't return to Verdun. From what she had heard, the battle there was still raging on. Monique was right; she had nowhere to go once the harvest had ended.

Besides, maybe it didn't matter where she went. Without the bribe money, her father would remain in prison in Lille. And she had no idea where to look for her mother and brothers, especially after all this time. She brushed a work-roughened hand over her dress, where the medal was still pinned. She'd kept it hidden so long, but it would do her father no good.

The girl who was talking with Monique looked over at Juliette. "If you can go faster, we'll all finish earlier."

Every night upon returning to the barn, the girls all gathered in close as Monique shared stories that she would make up as she worked in the day, stories about the Germans that made all the girls laugh.

"And what story has Monique promised us for tonight?" Juliette asked.

"A story about two friends . . . or they used to be friends," Monique said. "But one of them needs forgiveness. She has a plan—"

Juliette huffed and spoke to no one in particular. "Nobody wants to hear that one. Monique should tell her funny stories instead."

Monique frowned back at her. "Juliette, I couldn't let my mother remain in prison. If you knew how awful it was inside—"

"We were friends." Juliette picked up her weed bucket to move on. "Didn't that mean anything to you? Or were you never really my friend?"

Before Monique could answer, a horn blared from the office building, signaling that they needed to stop working and come in for an announcement.

Juliette found that strange. Suppertime was still hours away. Why would they be called in now?

She spotted the round officer who ran this camp, but today, a different soldier stood on a crate beside him. Major Dressler. The officer who ran the prison at the Citadel in Lille.

"What is he doing here?" a girl behind Juliette asked.

Monique answered, "He must be in charge of all the prisons in this area."

Dressler waved his arms for the girls to gather in closer. "You are all to go and wash up as quickly as possible, gather any personal items you may have, and line up again here within the hour to prepare for transport elsewhere."

"Are we going home?" one girl asked.

Dressler shook his head. "No, you are being reassigned to another area."

"All of us?" another girl asked. "Why?"

Now he cleared his throat. "We believe a battle is coming here, perhaps very soon. We have spotted British troops headed in this direction. As a result, we are bringing some of our soldiers from Verdun up this way."

Juliette's ears perked up. Verdun?

"Is the battle in Verdun over, then?" another girl asked.

He shook his head. "I doubt the battle will ever end there. Verdun is a death trap, for both sides, and there is no sign of it ending. Now, you all have thirty minutes. If you are not here when the train leaves, you will be caught in the middle of something that will make Verdun look like a children's game."

The girls began hurrying back to the washbasins or to their bunks. Juliette went first to the barn to grab her bag, then washed up afterward while other girls retrieved their clothes or any small items they had brought with them from home. Some girls were already standing in line to wait for the trains. Juliette caught a glimpse of Monique, who was standing alone as the other girls hurried around her. She had been taken away so quickly, she had brought nothing with her.

Finally, she saw Juliette and asked, "Did you mean what you said in the fields, that you want to go back to Verdun?"

Juliette huffed. "I always say that, Monique. Today is no different."

"But today is different. So is that what you want?"

"What do you mean?"

"I know we're not friends anymore. I know I ruined everything. But I'm asking you to give me another chance, if you can."

"I'm not angry with you anymore," Juliette said. "I've thought a lot about what you did, and maybe you were right, that I would have done the same."

Monique hugged her, and at first, Juliette thought it was to seal the apology, but instead, Monique whispered, "There's a wire fence at the end of these fields. On the other side is an old house. How long would it take you to run that far?"

"What?"

Monique tried again. "Do you want to work in the fields, or do you want to escape?"

Juliette squinted, trying to put together the plan that Monique seemed to have in mind for her. "I want to escape, but—"

"Then in five minutes, I will prove myself as your friend. Be ready."

Juliette wasn't sure what that meant, but she went one way and Monique went the other. She began walking past the barn, the only girl walking in that direction. In the distance, she heard a train approaching. The tracks ran directly past the office, so she was used to the sound of the trains. One came and went nearly every day to collect whatever food had been harvested. But until now, it had never taken on passengers.

How Juliette wished it would be Kara's ambulance train instead, but she knew better. This would be a German train, and wherever it took the girls, on the other end of its journey would be more forced labor, more hunger. More calluses on their hands.

With the approaching train, the soldiers who stood watch over the girls began corralling them forward to prepare to board. But two soldiers still remained in the field, ensuring that no one would be left behind. They would see her.

"I demand to know where we are going!"

Juliette paused, recognizing Monique's voice. Monique never raised her voice, and certainly never caused trouble so openly. Why would she do this?

"We've completed enough of your harvest. Send us home!"

Soldiers began hurrying over to where Monique must have been standing, including the two who had stayed in the field. This was the chance for escape that Monique had promised! For the moment, no one was watching the fields.

Juliette quietly slipped inside the field of corn. Its tall husks were still green and growing, but she continued to hurry forward until she was deep inside. Then she crouched low and waited with her arms tight around her bag, as if to protect it. As if it could protect her.

Much as she wanted to run deeper into the field, she heard Major Dressler calling for anyone who remained outside to come on the train now. She froze, unwilling to even breathe until she had to.

After a while, the soldier continued on, but that didn't mean he was gone. Refusing to be tricked, Juliette waited and waited a while longer until finally she heard the train leave. Even then, she crawled forward, moving slowly and staying in the areas that gave her the thickest cover. She continued crawling at an angle that steadily took her farther from any Germans who had been left behind. The edge of the field was near a forest. It had been fenced, but she had worked back there once and had spotted a small hole in the fence. If she could squeeze through it, she wouldn't have to climb over the top where the soldiers might see her. Maybe it was a good thing they had fed her so little lately.

When Juliette reached the hole, she pushed her bag through first, then she waited to see if anyone on the other side of the field reacted. When no one did, she put her arms through and then her head, then tried to narrow herself as much as possible to fit her shoulders through. She scraped one shoulder and the sleeve of her dress tore, but she did push through. Her hips were the trickiest part, and she had a horrible thought of getting stuck right there, unable to escape in either direction. How miserable that would be! Not only would the Germans find her but they would laugh for hours at her failed escape. That alone was enough to give her extra strength to push the rest of her body through.

Finally, she did, then she stood and ran.

However, she hadn't gone far before she was forced to change direction. A wide empty field was ahead, but German soldiers had already begun to arrive and were digging trenches to set up their camps.

She turned to run in the opposite direction, but so many soldiers were beginning to fill the area, she had no idea where to go. Not far away was the small house Monique had mentioned to her. It wouldn't offer much protection when the shelling started, but it was certainly better than remaining out in the open. Juliette ran inside, then climbed the stairs and slid under a bed in what appeared to have once been a girl's bedroom, and there she waited.

She remained in that very spot all night, trapped between a German army ahead and the Germans who had guarded her work camp behind her. Maybe she'd been in difficult situations before, but never anything like this. This was a disaster!

But it would only get worse. Sometime in the early morning hours, the British anthem played in the distance. Soon after, the first shell whistled through the air. The battle had begun.

TWENTY-SIX

July 16, 1916

A shell landed very nearby the house, ripping Juliette away from any hopes that she would be safe as long as she stayed inside. But where could she go if she left? Somehow she had become trapped in the middle of a battle. How could she have been so foolish to think escape would be as simple as a sprint across a field?

Maybe Monique had thought suggesting this plan was an act of friendship, but she couldn't have been more wrong. Juliette had never been in such a dangerous position before.

That first shell was only a prelude for the symphony of destruction that followed, and in its own way, that's exactly what it was. In one trench was the German orchestra, with the British in the other. Their generals were the conductors who waved their arms, directing the soldiers to create the battlefield melody.

Every explosion was the crash of cymbals separated by the

rhythm of rifle fire. Orders were shouted in trumpeted waves, and the calls and cries of soldiers completed this tragic tune of war.

The song seemed to continue on endlessly, just as this war seemed to have become endless. But it suddenly went silent in Juliette's ears as a new noise grabbed her attention: footsteps. Somebody else was in the home.

Every muscle of her body froze while she listened for any clue as to who might have entered, or how many people were here. No matter how loud the battle was outside, all Juliette heard were the footsteps walking up the stairs, cautious and slow. Someone was checking the house, looking for their enemies.

Such as Juliette.

Then, in German, *"Leer."*

More German followed, faster than Juliette could follow, and so many voices all at once, some laughing, others calling out what seemed to be orders exchanged. She had to get out of here, and fast. But how?

The window! The window of this room had been broken out. If Juliette could get to the window, she could crawl through it just as she had crawled through that gap in the fence. From her position, Juliette could see the jagged edges of glass. It was worth a few deep scratches to escape.

She slid one hand out from beneath the bed and shifted her body toward the edge, then quickly pulled her hand in again as tall black boots entered the room. Whoever wore those boots must have told some sort of joke because when he finished, others out in the hallway were laughing. The soldier quietly repeated the joke to himself as he walked over to the bed and set something down on it. Juliette heard a rustling sound and then what appeared to be the cooing of birds. Why would he bring birds inside a home?

Whatever his reasons, he opened some sort of container, then wings flapped as the bird tried to get free. This made no sense at all.

The soldier stood where he was for a minute while the wings continued to flap, then walked over to the same open window where Juliette had planned to escape. She angled her head enough to catch a quick look at the bird, a pigeon. A round piece of red metal was strapped to its leg, but she couldn't quite see what it was before the soldier released the pigeon. He stared at it for a few seconds, then chuckled some more and walked back to the bed.

He started to lift whatever was on the bed, then the boots paused again and he stepped back. Juliette's breath caught in her throat. Why was he stopping? After a moment of silence, the soldier knelt on all fours and looked under the bed, his eyes immediately connecting with hers.

Before Juliette could think better of it, her fist shot out and hit the man in the eye. Juliette had never hit anyone before, not even in play, but the fear inside her must have created enough force to make him recoil in pain.

She squeezed out from the opposite side of the bed, then raced to the door and down the steps. Another soldier at the bottom saw her coming and turned to grab her, but only got a hand on her coat. She wiggled free of it, but when she did, her bag with Marcel's blanket inside fell to the floor. She briefly turned back to look at it, then kept running.

The front door was just ahead. She even got one hand on the doorknob, but not before two more Germans grabbed her and dropped her onto the floor.

Juliette gathered herself into a ball and lowered her head while both men yelled in a language she barely understood. Then someone yelled at those two men, and they stopped and stepped aside for the German whom she had just punched.

"*Jawohl*, Major Dressler," one of them said.

Major Dressler?

Juliette looked up, and sure enough, it was he, pushing his blond hair back, then putting on his helmet again. Over one arm was the coat Juliette had lost. When he offered it to her, she grabbed it and pulled it close, almost as if it might offer her some protection. But that was foolish too. She knew it wouldn't.

"I remember you," Major Dressler said. "If bribing a German officer is a serious offense, imagine the consequences for striking one."

"I didn't mean to."

"You did. No one accidentally punches like that." Now he smiled. "Was this revenge for refusing your bribe, or would you have hit any German who poked his face under that bed?"

Juliette wasn't in the mood for friendly banter, especially not with the enemy.

"She clearly escaped from the work camp," one of the soldiers behind Major Dressler said. "We should return her at once."

196

"Please don't," Juliette said. "I can't waste any more time pulling weeds for you."

"Waste time?" Major Dressler arched a brow, clearly amused. "You have something more important to do?"

Juliette lowered her eyes again. Of course they were going to return her to the work camp. The round man with the round glasses would mete out a serious punishment for this.

Dressler said, "I think you are someone who has already seen far too much of the war. Is this true?"

Juliette had no idea how to answer that, so instead, she simply asked, "Can I please leave, sir?"

Dressler crouched down to be on her level. "War changes a person, you know. Some will grow angry and bitter. Others will find courage and compassion. Your father is worried about you."

Juliette sat up straighter. "You've spoken to my father?"

"I believe you told me he is a prisoner in Lille. You also said your name is Juliette Caron, did you not?"

"Yes."

"After you tried to bribe me, I reported the incident to your father. He told me about you, smiling whenever he said your name. You gave him happiness, even if just for those few minutes."

For the first time, Juliette looked directly at Major Dressler. "Papa is worried about me?"

"He wondered why you were in Lille without your mother and brothers."

"I was separated from them . . . because of Germans just like you."

Dressler tilted his head. "Like me? You think you know me, then?"

"I think you are like all other Germans, uncaring and coldhearted."

"Ah. So we are all the same?" He stood. "Do you know what we Germans think of the French? That you are weak and unfriendly, and that all you care about is food and fashion. Is that true?"

Juliette rolled her eyes. That was ridiculous.

"That was what I thought of your father when I first met him. He and I have shared many conversations, and I now consider him a friend. He has changed my mind on many ideas I had before the war."

"What ideas?"

Major Dressler stared at her, then turned to reach for Juliette's bag, in the hands of another soldier. He held it out for Juliette. "I assume this is yours."

Juliette took the bag but only held it in her arms, still facing the Major directly. She had no idea what would happen next, nor what she would do about it.

Finally, he said, "I made your father a promise, which now requires me to take you someplace safer." He gestured at her coat. "It is much too warm outside to wear that."

"This month, yes. But soon, it will be cold again." She shifted her weight. "Where are you going to take me?"

"Off this battlefield." Major Dressler held out a hand to help her to her feet. "The rest is up to you."

He glanced back at the other soldiers and spoke to them in

German. One of them went outside, closing the door behind him. Now the Major sighed. "Are you willing to trust a German?"

Juliette hesitated. No, of course she did not trust him. She could never trust any German. She ignored his hand and stood up on her own.

Major Dressler clearly noticed, but he still opened the front door and gestured for her to walk. "You go first," he said. "If it makes you feel any better, I do not trust you either, not after the way you hit my eye."

In a strange way, that did make her feel a little better. Juliette walked outside to where a beautiful brown horse was still saddled, its reins tied to a wood post. Major Dressler helped her into the saddle, then climbed on in front of her. Before leaving, he turned his head back enough to say, "My orders are to bring in any Frenchman caught behind enemy lines. But I have no wish to be captured by your side either, so keep your head down. We are going to ride fast."

And instantly, they were off.

Juliette's thoughts became as jumbled as the ride itself, and she didn't entirely understand where he was taking her, or why. Had he told her the truth, that he was taking her somewhere safe? If so, why would he risk his life for her, a girl of his enemy's country?

Whatever his reasons, gradually, the worst of the battle was left behind, though the echoes of it still played endlessly in the background.

Another noise was ahead too, a train whistle somewhere in the distance. At first Juliette thought it must be the train for the food harvest, come to search for her. But then she caught a glimpse of it through the trees and was sure the train was marked with a red cross on it. Kara's train sometimes came this far north. Could that be hers? It was much too far away to be sure.

And maybe she'd never find out, not before the train left, anyway. Between her and the train was a wide river, one that looked deep and strong. They passed the remnants of a bridge she could have used to cross, but it was in pieces now. Another casualty of the war. Probably every bridge in this area had been collapsed too, keeping enemy troops from sneaking up behind the Germans.

Major Dressler didn't seem surprised to see the ambulance train, so he must have already known it was here. Finally, he stopped at the edge of the river. "You will have to get your-self to that train. That is Allied territory, so I cannot take you across the river."

Juliette shook her head, worried that she had come all this way for nothing. "Sir, when you said that war changes a person, has it changed you?"

He grunted. "It is your father who changed me. I owe him a great debt."

"What did he say?"

"Nothing I wish to speak about here. Now you need to hurry across the river."

Juliette's shoulders slumped. Another question was heavy in her mind, one she had wanted to ask since they had begun riding. Finally, she forced out the words. "Major Dressler, if I had bribed you, would you have accepted it?"

"Why? Are you offering again?"

"I have an old war medal. It's probably valuable, and I will give it to you if you take me across the river."

He frowned back at her. "Is the medal worth my freedom? I have a daughter, Elsa. I promised her that I would come home again."

"Just as my father promised me. You are the reason he cannot keep that promise."

Her words left their mark on Major Dressler's expression, and he didn't cover it well. "Your father said you always got your way. I understand that now." After a heavy sigh, he urged his horse forward into the river. Now that they were in the current, Juliette realized the water was deeper and swifter than she had thought. She would have been swept downriver before she was even halfway across.

It didn't seem much easier for the horse, but Major Dressler continued forward until the water had risen above the horse's belly. Gradually, as they made their way across, the water became more shallow again. Major Dressler lowered Juliette into the water when it came only to her knees. She immediately began reaching for the medal.

He held up one hand. "I do not want your medal."

"But I told you—"

"You asked how your father changed me? He simply challenged me to do what was right rather than to do as I'm told, and I promised him that I would." He looked back across the river again, then with a sadder tone to his voice, added, "The truth is that I no longer believe that Germany is on the right side of this war. I will do my duty to my country, but I will not harm an innocent. So I cannot take your medal."

Juliette stared at him a moment longer. "Sir, if that was your promise to my father, may I ask one more question?"

"Yes."

"Isn't my father an innocent as well? You must let him go."

Dressler blinked hard and said nothing for several moments before he finally tipped his helmet at her. "Farewell, and be safe. I'll press my thumbs for you."

Juliette paused. "You'll . . . what?"

His smile was warm, even as he remained cautious. "It means good luck. Now go and find your mother. Do not give up hope." Then he turned, quickly riding back across the river.

Juliette remained where she was, watching him leave, her feet still immersed in the cold water but barely aware of it. He had been a kind man. But he was still on the wrong side of the war.

When she could no longer see him, she hoisted her bag over her shoulder and began the long walk toward the Red Cross train, though it was much farther away than she had realized at first. Orderlies were exiting the train to pick up wounded soldiers from ambulance wagons, but as the last wagon drove away, it occurred to her that she would not make it there in time.

Juliette began running, waving her arms and calling out to the orderlies, but they seemed too focused on their work to notice her.

"Need help?"

In her hurry, Juliette hadn't noticed an ambulance wagon

had been coming up behind her. She nodded and the driver motioned for her to climb inside. Two wounded soldiers were in the back of the wagon, one British, the other German.

Juliette sat beside them, her eyes shifting from one man to the other. Both were bandaged, both clearly in pain. Both looked afraid for their fates if they didn't get help in time.

"I think I know someone on this train," she finally said. "You'll be fine." Now she smiled over at the German soldier. "You'll *both* be fine."

Minutes later, the wagon stopped and Juliette was the first to jump out.

"Juliette?" Kara ducked out from the train, then ran outside and pulled Juliette into a warm hug. "What are you doing here? You've become far too thin."

With those words, Juliette suddenly felt her exhaustion and hunger, though it was nothing compared to the relief flowing inside her. She said, "If my old bed is still available, I would very much like to have it back."

Kara wrapped an arm around her. "Of course we'll find a spot for you. Are you hungry?"

That simple question seemed to double the ache in her stomach. "Yes, please, I'll eat anything. But I'd love it if . . ."

"If what?"

"Do you have any fresh corn?"

TWENTY-SEVEN

September 22, 1916

Captain Stout had been more than generous with Juliette. On the condition that she helped in the kitchen and laundry, he had allowed her to stay on the train for the past two months.

Two months of a warm bed and hot meals, and with Kara always at her side as the best friend Juliette ever could have imagined.

But it was two months that had to come to an end.

This was going to be a hard day, even harder than the last time she'd left. Juliette was determined to put on a smile and make Kara believe that this was the right thing to do.

"Must you leave?" Kara was seated across from Juliette in the dining car. She'd only taken a few bites of her eggs before she pushed her plate away. If it wouldn't have been rude, Juliette would still have eaten them. She'd been hungry too many times to ever waste a bite of food.

"We always knew I would have to leave once another nurse

arrived." Juliette shrugged. "There's only so many beds, and I daresay a nurse will be far more valuable on this train than I am."

"They let me stay and I'm of no value whatsoever," Kara said.

"Yes, but your mother is here," Juliette reminded her. "Mine is not."

"Where will you go now? Not back to Lille, I hope. And not Verdun. The fighting there is worse than ever."

"I'll go west from here, I think. I'll make my way to the coast and try to get on a ship to Britain, or even to America."

Kara frowned. "I wish I could have helped you more."

"But you have helped me!" Juliette took her hand and squeezed it. "Nobody has done more for me this year, nobody has cared more or tried harder to make me happy. One day, you will make a wonderful nurse. Or even a doctor."

"How? I'm not even allowed to pour a cup of water for a soldier." Kara glanced in the direction of the patient wards. "I wish they understood that my heart is there."

The two girls fell silent after that. Juliette wanted to smile and tell her that she knew everything would get better soon, but she couldn't. She only wished Kara didn't look so sad.

Finally, Juliette released her hand, then picked up her bag, once again filled with food and clothing and supplies that Kara thought might be needed. Juliette lifted the bag over her shoulder, then said, "I suppose this is goodbye."

"Not yet. I have one more gift for you." Kara reached into a pocket, then pulled out a folded paper. "I spoke to Captain Stout and he wrote this letter for you to keep. It says that you've spent time on an ambulance train and that if any other train ever needs help, they should choose you."

Juliette looked down at the paper. "I have no training as a nurse."

"No, but there are many other jobs to be done. You could use this letter to stay in France, somewhere safe, while you're looking for your family."

Juliette lowered her eyes. "I've looked everywhere for them already. I don't know if I can keep trying." But she folded the letter again and put it in her pocket. "Captain Stout is strict, but he's a fair man."

Kara shrugged. "He's a good man, but if he was fair, he'd return my apron and let me go back to work."

"What's this I hear?" Captain Stout walked through the transom with Kara's mother right behind him. He looked down at Kara. "Do you think I have been unfair to you?"

Kara jumped at the sound of his voice and stammered, "I . . . er . . . no, sir. I agreed to this punishment. You've treated me fairly."

Stout pointed to Juliette. "Your friend doesn't think so."

Juliette felt Kara's eyes shift to her, which made it even harder not to smile. "What did you say to him?" Kara asked. When Juliette didn't answer, Kara looked back at Stout. "I never asked her to speak to you, sir."

"Miss Caron assured me of that herself. In fact, she insisted that our conversation remain a secret until I had made my decision."

Kara tilted her head. "What decision?"

"I haven't made it yet. I wish to know whether you regret saving that Austrian soldier's life last year."

"Sergeant Baum?" Kara added, "It was the right thing to save his life, but I should have asked your permission first."

"Agreed." Now he gestured toward Juliette. "Twice you have brought this French girl onto the train. I don't recall you asking my permission either time."

"I thought you'd say no," Kara mumbled.

"Indeed I would have." He paused. "But that would have been the wrong decision. Miss Caron has worked hard while on this train. She earned a place here. So have you."

Juliette watched as Kara lowered her eyes. Juliette didn't mind working in the kitchens and laundry, but she knew Kara only worked there to keep her place on the train. She also knew what Kara wanted most.

Captain Stout continued, "Over the past two months, I have learned two things about Miss Caron. First is that she does not give up on anyone she believes in. Second is that she believes in you, Miss Webb."

Juliette kept her head low, avoiding Kara's glance over at her. It was becoming harder every second not to smile.

Stout said, "Miss Webb, you are headstrong, disrespectful of authority, and you insert yourself into places where you do not belong. However, you have shown courage on the field that equals the finest of any British soldier; you have proven yourself to have excellent skills as a nurse-in-training; and it is plain to see that your heart is full of compassion, both through your care of Miss Caron behind you, and even with your concern for an enemy soldier when none of the rest of us would tend to him." He stood aside, and Kara's mother walked forward.

"Congratulations." Kara's mother held out her hand. In it was the Red Cross apron.

Kara's eyes widened. "I can work as an orderly again?"

"You are not part of the Red Cross, but you can return to your former position, provided that you agree to follow the rules of the Red Cross."

"Yes, of course!" Kara began tying the apron around herself but turned to Juliette with the widest smile Juliette had ever seen. "You did this for me?"

"You've done far greater for me," Juliette said.

Stout said, "Your official title will be nurse-in-training. When you are not needed for other duties, you will work closely with the other nurses on board to learn the skills necessary to one day save as many of our fine soldiers as possible. Do you accept this position?"

Kara's face almost seemed to glow with excitement. "Yes, of course! It's all I've ever wanted."

"Then say goodbye to your friend. Our train is departing and you are needed in the wards."

Just like that, the best part of Juliette's day—or even the best part of her year—was over. Now would come one of the hardest parts. Juliette lifted her bag again, readying to leave.

"Miss Caron, wait." Captain Stout reached out to shake her hand. "Miss Webb gave you my note, correct?"

"Yes, sir. Thank you, sir."

"I sincerely hope you find your family, but if you do not,

any ambulance train in the Allied fleet would be pleased to help you with any need you may have."

"Thank you, sir." Juliette slung her bag over her shoulder, then gave Kara a warm hug.

"I never knew I could be so happy and so sad at the same time," Kara said.

"I will write you when I've found somewhere to settle." Juliette shrugged. "Who knows? Maybe you'll find me back in Britain, living in the flat next to yours!"

Kara took her hands. "I would love that, but . . . please don't give up on your family, Juliette. Please have hope for them."

"I do have hope," Juliette said. "Just not much of it. But I still have my life, and I'm certain that better days are ahead."

Juliette didn't know if she meant those words, but she had said them, and that had to be enough. With a parting wave, she stepped off the train. Seconds later, its doors closed. The new wounded soldiers had been loaded and it had to continue with its mission.

Juliette pulled her knitted hat lower on her head, then turned to begin walking west. She had a new mission too: to be happy, no matter what lay ahead.

TWENTY-EIGHT

November 18–30, 1916

The rains had begun soon after Juliette left the ambulance train, and rarely let up long enough for her clothes to dry before it began again. Winter had arrived early and threatened to be a cold one.

Still, she pressed on from one village to the next, walking through every refugee camp she found along the way. She wasn't looking, of course, because there was no point in it. But *if* Maman happened to be there, then at least she wanted to be seen.

And as expected, Maman wasn't anywhere.

Juliette was near Reims now, about one hundred kilometers east of Verdun. She stared at the list of names and backed away without recording her own name. After dozens of lists, all of them for nothing, she simply couldn't make herself try again. Not anymore.

Behind her, crowds had braved the cold to wave and cheer

for a band of Russian soldiers marching through the town. As they came closer, Juliette joined the crowd. She'd never seen a Russian before, but people around her were saying they'd come to save France, so she thought they must be stronger and mightier than the other Allied soldiers she'd seen.

Juliette pressed deeper into the crowd until she caught her first look at them. They wore the same grayish-green uniforms as soldiers from most other countries, with breeches tucked inside their tall black boots and with a rolled-up haversack over one shoulder and tied on the opposite side of their waist.

"They look so strong, so proud," a woman nearby remarked. "Great victories are ahead!"

Juliette wasn't so sure. There were many soldiers here, which was impressive, but a large number of them marched without rifles, and several looked quite young.

"They are here to help France?" Juliette asked. "Will they go to Verdun, to end the fighting there?"

"I don't know where they'll go," the woman replied, "but the fighting in Verdun may finally be burning itself out. From what I hear, the Germans are retreating. What a terrible battle that has been. Perhaps nowhere in the world has been as awful as Verdun."

"But we are winning?"

"It's better to say that we are no longer losing." The woman tilted her head. "Do you live here?"

"No, I'm from Verdun."

"Oh, I'm so sorry." The woman studied her a moment. "Here in Reims, when the battles come too close, we can take shelter in the caves. We have our schools underground, our church, our markets and hospitals. It isn't ideal, but it's safer than being up here."

"People are living in the caves?" A weight seemed to lift from Juliette's shoulders. "Are there caves near Verdun?"

"I couldn't say, though France does have its share of caves, so it's possible."

Juliette found herself smiling, something she had not done for some time. What if Maman had found a cave near Verdun for shelter? That was certainly possible. If she had, that would explain why Juliette's name wasn't on any of the lists or why Juliette had never been able to find Maman, no matter where she looked. If Maman found a cave she believed was safe enough for her and Claude and Marcel, they had no reason to leave.

The more Juliette thought about this, the more sense it made. Maman had no money, no family nearby, and she had wanted to stay as close to Verdun as possible. Maman must have taken them to the caves!

"Why are you so curious about the caves?" the woman asked. "Do you need—"

If she finished the question, Juliette wasn't there to hear it. She was already on a run out of town, headed west.

After five days of walking through frosty fields and sleeping in drafty barns, Juliette stared across the barren landscape toward Verdun, almost unable to breathe. This wasn't France, it couldn't be. Instead, this place looked closer to what she imagined the moon would look like: endless kilometers of gray dust. In any direction she looked, Juliette saw a thousand small hills and valleys where the bombs had exploded earth in one place, and where the earth had landed in another.

If the city was anything like this, her home would be very damaged indeed.

While walking, she had done the math. The Germans had first attacked this region three hundred and two days ago. According to the newspapers, it was the longest single battle in history. One article said that this land had been beaten upon by every possible weapon of war, and it would take much longer than another three hundred and two days to heal. Something this awful would take years, even decades to recover from.

Perhaps she would live long enough to see this area become green again, to hear birds return once more with their songs.

But maybe not. Why would birds return to air that reeked of poison gas, where land mines surely lay unexploded only millimeters below the gray soil? This was a graveyard now. It was no longer Juliette's home.

And from what she heard and saw in the distance, the fighting still continued as the Germans were chased northward out of Verdun. Left behind were their trenches, long open tunnels carved into the earth, extending in crooked lines as far as she could see.

Juliette walked alongside one until she found a ladder into a trench. She hesitated until she saw a metal box half covered in mud and with a thin dusting of snow over it. Curious, Juliette climbed down the ladder and opened the box, then nearly gasped with joy. The box was full of packaged food.

As hungry as she was, she tore open the top package, finding a small tin of canned beef and a crisp biscuit. She devoured the beef immediately, then followed it with the biscuit. She didn't know what the soldiers might think of this food, but to her, it was just about the finest meal she'd ever eaten.

When she was finished, Juliette picked up the box and continued to walk the trench, eventually gathering a muddy sock and a comb. There were other treasures too, more than she would have expected, but this was all she could carry for now.

Whenever possible, she walked in the very center of the trench, wary of the high dirt walls on both sides, often braced by rough wood slats. She couldn't see more than a few meters ahead before the trench angled. If anyone was hiding, they could be around the next bend, and it always felt like someone would be there. No one ever was, but the feeling remained. Maybe the soldiers who died here had never really left the trench.

Despite that, Juliette felt some comfort here. Up on ground level, anyone might easily see her, so she was far more protected than had she been in the open. Of course, because of these high walls, she couldn't see anyone either.

That made her nervous enough that when she spotted a ladder ahead, she climbed it, peeking up enough to look around, but as before, there was nothing to be seen anywhere, only gray mud with the occasional patch of new-fallen snow. No-man's-land. This was deadened ground, every spark of life that had once been here exploded or trampled or burned.

After nearly half a kilometer, Juliette's efforts were

rewarded. No-man's-land stretched out endlessly to her right, but on her left, she noticed a narrow hole in the rock wall. A cave! She peeked inside and discovered a large room just inside the entrance. Evidence of a fire having been used was in one corner of the room and it even had a small pile of wood against the cave wall.

Silently, she slipped inside, listening carefully with every step for any sign of others being in there with her, even the slightest hint that something wasn't right. But as carefully as she listened, only silence was returned to her. No enemies, which was a relief.

But there was also no sign of her mother, and that was awful. Juliette leaned against the cave wall and shook her head. She couldn't keep doing this, having hope and losing it again.

Yet Juliette reminded herself that now was not the time to give up. Of course she couldn't expect to find Maman in the very first cave she explored. For now, it was enough to know that the caves existed. Until she explored them all, she had to keep trying.

And that's what she did, at least as far as she dared, until the light from outside became too faded, or until the cave wall ended, forcing her in another direction. Finally, she decided to settle in near the entrance where the fire had been built, and used a match from a supply box left near the firewood to ignite it again.

When she felt it was safe, she opened the box found in the trench. Inside were four biscuits, a tin of crackers, and more canned beef. Juliette ate two crackers right away, then wiped tears from her eyes. For tonight, she had light and warmth and food, a rare combination of luxuries since leaving the ambulance train.

At last, she felt a little hope.

Although the plan was to immediately begin searching for other caves, Juliette spent the next several days continuing to explore the trench. On every outing, she always returned with her arms full of useful items. She found food, a few blankets, a pencil, and even a notepad to draw in, and slowly built up a supply of items she could use as she needed them. That was a great comfort because the snow was falling more steadily now, and staying longer on the ground.

After several nights, Juliette was finally becoming more comfortable in the caves as well. She'd fashioned herself a bed with the blankets and cuddled into them with Marcel's blanket in her arms and the knitted hat her father had given her on her head, beside a softly glowing fire.

Nothing in her life was good, but it wasn't awful either.

That is, until one afternoon when Juliette was entertaining herself by building stacks of twigs as high as she could before they toppled. A stack crumbled, and in the same instant she froze, hearing a noise from an area of the caves she had not yet explored.

How did voices get in here? Could there be another entrance to these caves?

Juliette grabbed her bag and darted behind a clump of rocks in the corner. Shortly after making these caves a home, she had rolled and stacked the rocks this very way to give her a place to hide, if it ever became necessary. She was glad for that now, because a quick peek from behind the rocks revealed four German soldiers passing through the caves.

Juliette didn't understand everything they were saying, but by now, she knew enough German to pick out a few words.

"*Familie.*" Family.

"*Versteckt.*" Hiding.

"*Verdun.*"

That could mean a lot of different things, and how she wished she knew more of the language, to stitch the words together in a sentence.

Juliette leaned forward, hoping to hear more, but a rock crunched into the dirt beneath her knee. What a foolish mistake—she never should have moved.

The soldiers stopped walking. One of them said, "*Was ist das?*"

Juliette clamped a hand over her mouth and pressed even tighter against the rocks.

The soldiers came closer. Someone must have kicked over the twigs she had been playing with, and then it sounded as if someone else kicked at the embers of her fire, stirring up the flames once more.

"*Hier ist jemand.*"

Juliette understood that too. The soldier knew someone else was here in the caves; they just didn't know where.

She heard the sound of weapons being drawn and saw black boots stepping closer. They were going to find her, and she had nowhere else to run.

Then from outside, someone shouted in words she couldn't understand, but it sounded like some kind of order. The soldiers responded, quickly lowering their weapons and running outside.

Juliette listened carefully to additional orders being given, and the marching sounds that slowly faded into the distance. They were gone.

Her head fell against her knees, pulled up tight against her chest. By now her hands were shaking so much, she could barely hold them together, but there she sat, unable to make herself move.

Gradually, Juliette began to calm, but she still remained in hiding with nothing to do but to repeat in her mind the words that soldier had spoken.

Family.

Hiding.

Verdun.

He could have been speaking of any one of hundreds of families. Just as likely, she could have misunderstood one of the words.

But what if they had been coming through the caves and found a family hiding near Verdun, somewhere nearby?

What if that was her family?

It was possible.

Which meant it was also reason enough to begin packing up her things and go exploring again. Those soldiers had to have come from somewhere. Juliette needed to go in the way they had just come out.

TWENTY-NINE

November 30, 1916

Juliette knew exactly which tunnel the Germans had used to come through here. At least a dozen times already, she'd stood right there in the entrance and even walked to the first bend before she lost her courage and retreated. After that, she told herself that it was a path to nowhere. For as long and dark as it seemed, what else could it have been?

Now she knew. It was a tunnel to another cave.

Carefully, and making as little noise as possible, Juliette walked forward, pausing every few seconds to listen, then walking again.

Family.

Hiding.

Verdun.

Soon the light grew too dim. This was where Juliette had always turned back before, but not this time. She summoned her courage and put her hands on the cave wall, feeling for any hazards ahead; a low-hanging rock or an uneven floor. The tunnel curved, enough that she began to wonder if she was going in circles, or if she had missed her chance to get out and now would be wandering aimlessly down here forever.

That was possible. Besides, wasn't that the story of her entire life lately, wandering in circles, always moving, but going nowhere?

After nearly an hour of this, Juliette paused, certain she'd heard voices again. She flattened herself against the tunnel wall and listened. The first thing that caught her attention was the sound of a child's laughter, quickly followed by a hissed scolding, a reminder that they must be quiet.

The reminder was in French!

Juliette closed her eyes and tried to remember the sound of Marcel's laugh. Did he sound that young? It had been nine long months since she had heard his voice. The memory of it had faded a little, but that voice was the only clue she had. She couldn't tell anything from the mother's whisper.

More whispering continued, now too low for Juliette to pick out any words. It could be her family. The longer she listened, the more she was sure it must be. Who else could it possibly be? What a laugh they would all share one day, to realize that they had been hiding so close to each other!

Juliette tightened her grip on her bag. Marcel's blanket sat on top, but how would she explain why she no longer had the money that Maman had trusted her to hold? Still, her mother would be happy to see her. The money would mean nothing in comparison. At last, her search was nearly over.

Juliette walked forward, but, in hopes of not startling her family, just before leaving the cave, she said, "Don't worry, it's just"—she stepped out—"me."

The surprise turned out to be on her. A young mother stood in the center of a small cave room, clutching a baby close to her chest. She seemed frozen in place, caught between running with her children and staying to defend them. A girl about eight or nine was pressed against her leg, and a boy who could not have been older than four was seated on the dirt digging with a stick, indifferent to Juliette's arrival.

This was a French family. But it was not Juliette's family.

She stared at the mother, with no idea of what to say. "I . . . uh . . . I'm sorry. I thought—"

"Who else is with you?" The mother was clearly alarmed.

"No one." Juliette glanced behind her. "The soldiers who passed this way have left."

The mother exhaled a sigh of relief. "What are you doing here?"

"I thought . . . I thought you might be my family. My mother is about your height and—" Juliette gave up there. This family had made every effort to avoid being around anyone else. They would not be of any help to her.

"You are from Verdun?" the mother asked.

"Yes. I thought the fighting would be finished by now."

"It nearly is, I think. The Germans are retreating as quickly as they can."

They stared at each other for a moment, then Juliette crouched down and dug into her bag for some of the food she had found in the trench. She pulled out a tin of cookies that someone must have sent a soldier from home and held it out to the mother. "Would you like this?"

The mother received the tin as if it were a most precious gift. She opened it and brought out a half cookie for each of her children. Their eyes widened, but they took the cookies and began nibbling on them as slowly as possible.

"They want to make the moment last," the mother explained. "Who knows when we will get more to eat?" She closed up the tin and offered it back to Juliette.

But Juliette waved her hands, signaling that she did not want the cookies returned. The mother smiled gratefully while the young girl pointed up at Juliette's knitted red hat and smiled.

Juliette smiled back and realized that the girl looked a bit cold. She wanted to offer her the hat, and knew she should, but this hat had come from Papa and she couldn't bear to part with it. Perhaps one day she would be less selfish.

After a moment of silence, the mother gestured around them at a cavern with blankets in one corner and a small area for a fire near the door. A large piece of luggage seemed to carry all the clothing and food they had, which wasn't much. Yet she said, "My name is Hélène. We have little to offer, but you may stay with us, if you would like."

The offer came as a surprise to Juliette. This was not her mother and those were not her siblings, but they were a family and they seemed kind and decent. Juliette stared at Hélène, missing Maman in a way she never had before. Would she ever have the chance to look at her own mother again? Every passing day, it seemed less likely.

She smiled at Hélène. "Thank you, I'd like to stay."

The next several weeks were a happy time. Juliette had missed playing with her brothers, and the children here were delighted by any game Juliette could make up for them. She drew them pictures on her notepad or let them draw pictures with her.

One day, the daughter presented Juliette with a drawing of her family, with Juliette at the center. "For you," she said.

Juliette almost couldn't stop staring at it. Here she was, in a family that loved one another and had grown to love her. She loved them too, she truly did.

Yet deep in her heart, she knew she did not belong here.

Which was why only a few days later, when Juliette stepped out of the caves to scavenge for more food, she knew it was time to make another change.

Because everything outside was silent.

Every day before this one, the sounds of war were always there. But not today. Today there was . . . nothing.

No shells, no gunfire, no marching soldiers. Simply nothing.

Juliette immediately returned to the young family and explained her plan as she began to pack up her bag.

Hélène sat beside her as she worked. "Juliette, I know you want to see them again, but they won't be there."

"They will," Juliette insisted. "Maman said that as soon as the fighting ended, she would go home."

"Your home won't be there! Verdun will be awful, so much worse than you can imagine."

Juliette had seen a lot of awful over the past ten months, so she could handle that. Besides, nothing would keep her from going back now.

So with a hug goodbye to each of the children, she left the caves, hoping that wherever Maman was, she was on her way home too.

CHAPTER
THIRTY

December 15, 1916

"Verdun will be awful, so much worse than you can imagine."
Those had been Hélène's words. They could not have been more true.

Juliette stood on the outskirts of Verdun, gazing at what had once been a beautiful city. Now, it was like staring at a nightmare, one that only grew worse when she walked inside the city's limits.

Only ten months ago, Juliette had called this place home. She already understood that Verdun would be damaged. But nothing could ever have prepared her for *this*.

What had once been a vibrant town filled with tall trees, flowers of every color, and buildings that had stood for over a hundred years now looked as though giants had marched through the streets, crushing everything in their path.

Perhaps that's exactly what had happened. Except Verdun's giants were enormous cannons and artillery guns, aiming their rage toward an enemy they could barely see in the distance. Those were the giants of her world.

Juliette took a deep breath and began to walk deeper into the city, trudging through snow halfway to her knees. Somewhere not far away, she heard soldiers marching, but the orders being shouted were in French, so she doubted she was in any danger.

No danger from soldiers, anyway. Most of the few buildings still standing looked ready to topple over with the next gust of wind. Half of them had at least one wall stripped away. Any memories that might have been preserved for the families who'd lived there once were now open for anyone to view, or they had been long ago scattered about.

Juliette paused at a bit of color beneath a pile of snow and shattered concrete. She moved the lighter pieces aside, then gave a tug on the fabric, finally pulling out a rag doll half scorched by fire.

She stared at the doll for a long minute. "Were you always alone?" she asked it. "Or does anyone out there wonder where you are?"

Finally, she tucked the doll under one arm. It didn't seem right to leave it behind.

Juliette continued to wander the streets. Was her home down this road, or that one? It was hard to be sure. Half the streets were too destroyed to allow her to pass, so she had to choose unfamiliar side roads, and more than once she thought she was lost. Nothing was familiar. Even now, fires still burned in some places, fueled by lingering gasses or debris left behind when the soldiers had moved on to their next battle.

At last she turned onto a road that was familiar. There, not far ahead, stood a house that she recognized, left nearly intact. Her home would be across the road and thirty steps down.

Yet thirty steps later, she stood facing a pile of rubble, rocks and plaster and brick jumbled up with items she vaguely recognized as having belonged to her family once.

This could not have been her home, not this terrible pile of broken dreams. But it was.

Juliette didn't cry or scream or beg fate to change any of it: She knew from experience that it wouldn't work. She merely dropped the rag doll on top of the rubble, then stepped back, finally sitting on the stoop of the home across the road.

Her mind slipped through the past ten months. Through all the good, all the bad, all the exhaustion of looking and hoping and waiting, she had held on to one single thought: She could eventually go home to Verdun.

But Verdun was gone.

Her home was gone.

Her family was . . . gone.

"Maybe they are really . . . gone." Kara had tried to tell her that once, but Juliette had become so angry, she hadn't spoken to Kara for three days.

"Are you sure your family got out of Verdun?" Kara had asked. "The last thing you know is they were surrounded by Germans. What if they haven't found you . . . because they *can't* find you?"

Even now, Juliette winced at the possibility that she might be right. If her family was alive, surely she would have found them by now.

Juliette didn't want to think that way, but now it was time that she did. At the very least, she had to accept that Maman was nowhere near Verdun. Her family had no reason to return here because Verdun was nowhere now.

"What are you doing here, Mademoiselle?"

Juliette stood again, startled. She pulled her bag closer to her and merely stared at the man who had spoken, an older gentleman with a beard as white as any ghost might wear. He leaned heavily on a cane and his hand that held it shook.

He gestured toward the ruins of her home. "Did you used to live here?"

Juliette nodded. "But there's nothing left."

The man stared up at the skies. "They dug the trenches first, long jagged lines for our side, long jagged lines for theirs. Eventually, those trenches were filled in by the explosions. The shelling never stopped, not in the day or night, not for anything or anyone. Whatever home once stood here would've been destroyed again and again until all that was left was the dust you now see. Whole villages here have died for France, likely never to return."

"Oh." That was all Juliette could say. Her heart ached too much to breathe out anything more.

"You shouldn't have come back here, Mademoiselle, there's nothing here for you."

Juliette shook her head. "Before we left Verdun, Maman told

us that if we became separated, we were to return here, and this is where she'd find us. I followed the plan, and it didn't work!"

"But of course it did not work," the man said. "Life is never so simple as that. So what will you do now?"

Juliette shrugged. "I really don't know."

"Yes, I see the problem now. But I can help, if you follow *my* plan." The man gave Juliette his cane, then stepped back, standing in the center of the road. "Use my cane to draw a line from where you are now to where the front door of your home should be."

"Why does this matter?"

"Do you have anything better to do?"

Juliette sighed, then stood and pressed the cane in the snow to create a line toward her home. But she hadn't gone far before she had to stop. The man was standing in her way.

"Would you please move, Monsieur?"

"No, I will not."

"You told me to draw this line. This was your plan!"

"Yes, and now you have a problem because something is in your way. So the plan clearly does not work."

Juliette rolled her eyes, then began pulling the cane around the man. She had just started to circle back toward her home when he stepped in front of her again. She adjusted for that, though it required her to cross over a line she had already made. He continued moving, constantly in her way, but she continued moving too, faster, and trying to trick him long enough to get past him. Finally, almost before she knew it, Juliette's line ended exactly where her front door would have been.

"I did it!" But her excitement quickly faded as she turned and saw the line itself. The man stepped aside, revealing a series of circles and bends and starts that pushed backward through the snow before continuing on again. "No, that's a terrible line."

"How is it terrible? That line got you to where you wanted to go."

"It would have been straight, had you not been in my way."

"Yes, because that is life. Mademoiselle, something will always be in your way. So draw your line around it and keep going. You will find your family again, but it will come at the end of a long and crooked path."

Juliette smiled, finally understanding. She leaned down to pick up the doll and, from that angle, caught a reflection against the sun. She pushed aside a few crumbled bricks and chunks of plaster and pulled out her mother's old stew pot. It took a little more digging, but beneath that were two spoons and a fork.

"Monsieur, will you help me?" she asked. "I see something, but this rock is too heavy."

He walked back and knelt beside her, and together they rolled aside a larger chunk of brick. There, beneath it, was Juliette's art notebook.

She stared at it for a very long time before saying, "I've walked a crooked line for months now. I can do that a little while longer."

He reached down and pulled out the notebook, then placed it in her hands. "Until you do, have courage, Mademoiselle. You are going to be all right."

THIRTY-ONE

December 31, 1916

With nowhere else to go, Juliette eventually returned to the first cave she had discovered outside of Verdun. Her plan had been to stay with the young family who was hiding here, but they were gone now.

Even though they weren't her family, and even though they had no idea she would ever return here, she still felt a little as if they had abandoned her too. That wasn't what had happened, she knew that, but it still hurt.

Especially tonight, this final night of a terrible year. On past New Year's Eves, her parents would invite over friends and coworkers—Monique's family among them—and they would celebrate until dawn.

But tonight, she was alone, and every part of her felt it. Even with the fire and plenty of wood, a howling wind kept whistling into the cave and nearly blowing the flames to nothing. Juliette couldn't allow that. She had only one match left and it couldn't be wasted by wind.

Finally, she went back out into the bitter-cold trenches, hoping to find a large piece of wood or anything she might use to block the cave entrance and protect her fire. Juliette began wandering farther and farther along the trench, feeling the snow and ice creep steadily into what little was left of her shoes, but finding nothing large enough to block the wind.

Juliette started up a ladder to have a look around no-man's-land, then quickly ducked back down. Several meters ahead of her, a soldier was standing alone in a field. She gave a panicked glance behind her. Could she make it back inside the cave without being spotted? Was that the right thing to do, or should she return for her bag, then leave this entire area?

More cautiously this time, Juliette climbed the ladder just enough to get a better look at the soldier. His back was turned and he had no weapon, and the posture of his body seemed crooked, but he wasn't moving. Something was wrong.

As quietly as she could, Juliette climbed out of the trench, but he still didn't seem to notice her. Once on top, she crept to an angle to get a better look at him and recognized the uniform from when the Russians had marched in the streets. Had he been with them? He didn't seem to have the build of a grown man. Maybe he was one of the younger ones she had noticed.

Tiptoeing forward a little more, Juliette got a look at his face in the moonlight. Certainly she had seen other soldiers younger than him—some who had come on the ambulance train with Kara couldn't have been older than thirteen or fourteen. But this boy was young, and he was staring forward as if he was lost.

Juliette certainly understood that. But he shouldn't be lost in that particular spot. The orderlies on the train had taught her about land mines buried underground and the dangers of unexploded shells. So she had a set path to walk on in no-man's-land and never left it.

He was deep within the danger zone.

"Hello?" Juliette called, but the boy didn't turn around. She tried to say hello in Russian. It wasn't the proper way, she knew that much, but it was also the only Russian word she knew, so it would have to do. *"Privet?"*

Now the boy turned to look at her. Or rather, he looked in Juliette's direction, though he didn't seem to see her or even to realize that someone else was here.

Juliette waved her arms, gesturing for him to walk toward her. "There are land mines in the area," she called out. "Land mines."

Juliette said the final two words slowly, hoping he would recognize them. He'd been lucky to have gotten so far across, but his next step might literally be his last.

"Land mines," Juliette repeated, gesturing again for him to walk toward her, but the boy only stared blankly back, as if he couldn't understand.

How could he not understand her gestures? She was pulling her arms toward herself over and over. That seemed like something everyone could interpret.

Finally, he nodded and took a step toward Juliette, but his leg collapsed beneath him and he fell to the ground.

Juliette cried out and began looking around for anyone who might know what she should do. Kara would've known. Kara could have helped him.

But Kara wasn't here. Juliette was, and it was becoming clear that if she didn't do something, he would not survive.

Juliette stepped to the edge of the road, searching the ground for any evidence of where a land mine might be buried, but everything was covered with a fresh coat of snow. She'd just have to take her chances.

Juliette closed her eyes, clenching and unclenching her fists in an effort to gather up her courage. She had been through worse than this, done more difficult things than this, hadn't she? The past year had been awful, but it had made her stronger and she needed that strength now. She had to save that boy.

Even with that decision made, it still took several minutes to convince herself to move, and after only a single step, somewhere far to the north, other explosions began. Maybe the battle had ended here, but the danger in Verdun was still very real.

So with a deep breath, Juliette crept forward, carefully testing each footstep on the ground before making another. It probably didn't matter how carefully she set her foot down. Once the mine felt the pressure, it would go off, no matter how cautious she was.

When Juliette finally reached the boy, she poked his arm, hoping that would wake him up, but he didn't even stir. She felt for a pulse on his neck, the way Kara had taught her, and it was there, though not as strong as she would have liked. His head turned and that was when she noticed dried blood on his temple. With another deep breath, Juliette stood and placed her hands under his arms and began dragging him out of the field, careful to take the same route back as she had to enter.

What would Kara do? Juliette ran that question through her mind a dozen times as she continued to drag the boy. Why couldn't Kara be here now?

Once on the road again, Juliette patted his cheeks, and he mumbled but didn't open his eyes. She sighed and hoisted him up again.

Several difficult steps later, Juliette slid him into the trench, then dragged him from beneath his arms toward the wood shelter, and from there into the cave, where the fire was nearly out.

Forgetting about the boy, just for the moment, Juliette raced to add more wood to build up the fire again. Once it brightened, she prepared a dry area near the fire with the blanket that she normally used, wrapping it around him. He had begun shivering by now, so she moved him as close to the fire as she dared, then opened a medical box she had found only two days earlier. Juliette pulled out a long bandage and began wrapping his head the way she had seen the nurses do it on the ambulance train. When that was finished, she warmed some water and did her best to pour a little into his mouth, and did so every fifteen minutes.

He was still alive, but barely. All Juliette could do now was to wait with him and watch, and pray.

DIMITRI

Russia

No man's land under snow is like the face of the

moon: chaotic, crater ridden, uninhabitable,

awful, the abode of madness.

—Lt. Wilfred Owen, in a letter to his mother (1917)

CHAPTER
THIRTY-TWO

December 31, 1916

Looking up through the haze, the stars appeared as colors. Dimitri wondered if he was the only one who ever noticed that.

When the shells exploded, the sky lit with bright shades of red and blue and orange. It might have been beautiful if they weren't the colors of war, because here, those colors were deadly.

Dimitri had never been in a battle as terrible as this. Artillery shells fell like rain around him, destroying everything within their range.

And sending smoke into the air to color the stars.

Until now, the sky was the one thing war had not taken from him. These trenches that he lived in blocked his view of the land, isolating him within a small world of mud, soldiers, and the fetid air they tried not to breathe in. But no matter how bad things were, he could always look up and see sky.

He especially loved the nights, as a reminder that the trenches were barely a dot upon a big world in a universe he could not begin to comprehend.

Somewhere in all that, there had to be a place this war had not yet touched. He wondered how far he would have to go to escape it.

Only a few months ago, Dimitri had stood on his father's farmland, watching these same stars. He barely could remember those simple, peaceful days anymore.

"Descendre!" someone shouted. That was the first French word Dimitri had learned since joining the French in battle, to get down low. It had served him well.

A shell landed near Dimitri's trench, exploding so close that it sprayed snow and mud in all directions, covering him and everyone else nearby. Dimitri wiped what he could from his face, but realized as he did that he couldn't feel his fingers.

Still crouched low, Dimitri stared down at his hands. The early morning air was like ice, biting through every layer of his clothing. Dawn would come soon, but maybe not in time to save his fingers. He tried squeezing them into a fist, but they barely curled. Dimitri cupped his fingers near his mouth and blew warm air on them, hoping that would help. What if the doctor had to amputate?

That would get him out of the trenches, which would likely save his life. But what good was he to his family if he couldn't grip a plow or pull food from the soil? Maybe it hadn't been Dimitri's choice to join this war, but now that he was here, his family needed the extra money he sent them. For their sake, he needed to stay here.

Farther down the trench, their commander, a man named Captain Garinov, was shouting orders for all soldiers to prepare to fight. He may have commanded the Russians here, but he also had to take orders from the French Commandant, and he clearly hated that. Garinov's last command had been in an eastern territory called Lemberg, a city that Russia had controlled early in the war. But Austria-Hungary had taken it back, and so the Captain was sent here.

"What do you think?" Almost as if unaware of the battle around them, Igor was seated across from Dimitri, carving designs into an old shell casing. "The Frenchmen call this trench art."

Dimitri grinned. "It's not the worst art I've seen."

"It keeps my fingers warm."

Igor was a few years older and watched out for Dimitri, especially when they were in active fighting. He was tall, blond, and thinner than most, and also the best friend Dimitri had ever known.

"See Garinov's eye patch?" Igor whispered. "Rumor is that he got that in Lemberg, from some German girl your age."

Dimitri looked from Igor over to the Captain and tried not to laugh. "That can't be true. How?"

Igor shrugged. "Don't know. You want to ask him?"

"No." At best, Dimitri wanted to avoid Garinov. By now, he'd learned that to gain a single meter of ground, the commander would sacrifice as many men as it took. Dimitri didn't want to be one of them.

"The Captain asked to transfer here," Igor added. "He probably wants revenge on that German girl, but he'll have to make do with fighting the entire German army."

"Everyone at the—" Captain Garinov's voice was drowned out by a fresh round of shelling.

The bombardment had gone on all night, and it now appeared the Germans intended to continue into the morning. Every shell launched was answered by Russian and French shells. Dimitri figured that, one day, one side or the other would run out of weapons, and then the war would be over.

Or at least, he wished it worked that way.

Captain Garinov began walking through the trench, shaking hands with each soldier as he passed by. "Before dawn, we are going to take that German trench and show everyone what a Russian victory looks like."

Dimitri stared at him, wondering if Garinov really believed his own words. No doubt, a thousand meters away, on the other side of no-man's-land, the German commander was telling his soldiers the very same thing: That today, *they* would take the Russian trench.

When in fact, chances were the sun would rise tomorrow with dozens or even hundreds of casualties on both sides of the war, and not a centimeter of ground gained.

Captain Garinov stopped directly in front of Dimitri and Igor and offered his hand to them. "Names?"

Dimitri stood. His cold fingers barely curled over the

Captain's hand as they shook, but he spoke as boldly as he could. "Dimitri Petrenko, sir."

Igor did the same. "Igor Zolin."

"How long have you been fighting?"

"Three months," Dimitri said, followed by Igor's, "Eight months."

"And neither of you have weapons?"

Dimitri flinched. This was the question he had been dreading because he knew the order that would follow. "No weapons, sir."

Garinov cursed under his breath. "Are you loyal to the Tsar, Dimitri?"

"Yes, sir." He knew Garinov wouldn't like his answer, but Dimitri had given the Tsar his oath of loyalty when he joined the army and he had to honor it.

"And you, Igor?"

"I am a Red, sir."

The Reds were called Bolsheviks and were enemies to the Tsar. Their leader, Vladimir Lenin, had been exiled years ago, but everyone knew he was waiting for the chance to return, to take the Tsar's Winter Palace for himself. Indeed, to take the Tsar's throne.

Garinov smiled. "Perhaps Dimitri can explain to us both why he is loyal to a Tsar who sent him to war without a weapon?"

Dimitri tilted his head, surprised by the order. "Sir, it's not my place . . ." He let his sentence fade from there. It was true that Dimitri had plenty of reasons to be angry with the Tsar, who had seemed indifferent to the hunger and poverty of most Russians for years. But Dimitri's father had warned him not to trust Lenin.

"Be careful of any leader who promises everything," his father had said. "Either they are lying, or they will first take everything away so they can give it back again."

Impatient for Dimitri to answer, Captain Garinov said, "Neither of you are worth anything here until you have a weapon." Then he looked around the trench and called out, "Who else still does not have a weapon?"

The only other man to raise his hand was gray-haired and had joined the company at the same time as the Captain.

A week ago, twelve others would have raised their hands, but since then, all the rest had already taken the rifle of one of the dead or wounded, sometimes from a German, sometimes from another Russian.

Captain Garinov looked over the three of them with disgust. "You will go out to no-man's-land and get a weapon." Then his attention returned to Dimitri. "Why don't you be the first out there, in honor of your Tsar? Don't come back without a rifle."

Dimitri sighed. If he went over the top, it was likely he would not come back at all. But there was no other choice. An order was an order.

THIRTY-THREE

December 31, 1916–January 1, 1917

Dimitri watched Captain Garinov walk away as if the order he had just given was nothing worse than ordering Dimitri to tie his boots.

"Why should he be angry with us?" Dimitri muttered as he headed toward the trench ladder. "It's not our fault we don't have weapons."

Beside him, Igor said, "He was angry before he ever spoke to us. Don't you become like him, no matter what happens in this war. Promise me, Dimitri."

Dimitri glanced back at his friend. He couldn't imagine ever becoming the slightest bit like Captain Garinov. "I promise."

"Then let's go find some weapons." With that, Igor followed Dimitri up, with the older soldier behind them both.

The sun was just peeking over the horizon as they climbed to the top, revealing a soft mist hovering only centimeters above the ground. This land might have been beautiful before the war tore it apart. Now it was simply . . . haunted. Dimitri flattened himself to belly crawl over ice and snow and frozen patches of mud. The mist may have offered some protection from the enemy, but it also gave the enemy protection to sneak closer, unseen. Dimitri fully expected, at any moment, a German soldier would leap out directly in front of him, and there he'd be on his belly, with no way of defending himself.

Dimitri heard a sound to his left and startled, then noticed it was the gray-haired man from his company. That man raised a finger to his lips, then pointed ahead. He had seen the rifle he wanted.

He crouched low to get to it faster. Dimitri shook his head, motioning for the man to get down, but he continued forward, disappearing into the fog.

Seconds later, a machine gun fired from the enemy lines, and Dimitri heard a body fall. He lay even flatter on the ground, covering his head with his hands, then heard Igor whisper, "Without a weapon, we're all as good as dead anyway. Come with me."

That was it. No mourning for the man who had fallen, no time to think about who he had been, who he had left behind. Up here, there was only the base instinct to survive.

Which would be more difficult now. The Germans knew they were here.

Dimitri nodded back at Igor, held his breath, then kept his body as low as possible to belly crawl beside Igor. Any available weapons were somewhere past the barbed wire fence that ran along the trench line. Once they crossed it, they'd be even more exposed.

Igor pointed ahead. "See that mound of earth? That's where we're going. Follow me."

Igor led the way and Dimitri crawled directly behind him. They had to be especially careful in crossing the barbed wire. One good cut and then he'd have to worry about tetanus, a disease that could eventually kill him as effectively as any land mine.

Once they reached the mound, Igor turned to Dimitri. "See any rifles?"

Moving no more than he had to, Dimitri glanced out past the mound. Even if he tried to look beyond the fog, there was still nothing ahead. Sixty meters from where they lay was the German trench. It was quiet there, too quiet. They were watching.

"I see two rifles," Igor said. "One is closer to you, the other is straight ahead of me. This is our chance."

"How far are they?" Dimitri scooted to Igor's side of the mound and glanced over his shoulder until he saw both weapons. "Yours isn't too far, but I'll never get to the other one. It won't be safe."

Igor chuckled. "It's no safer to return to Captain Garinov without a weapon."

Maybe Igor had been making a joke, but the words were still true. Dimitri would have to get that rifle.

"Two minutes for you, one minute for me," Igor said.

Dimitri smiled back. "One minute for us both."

They shook on the agreement, then each crawled out from their sides of the mound. The idea was to move fast and be unpredictable, but Dimitri had no sooner left his side when he knew something was terribly wrong. The ground was vibrating. He knew what that meant.

Hundreds of Germans had gone over the top and were now racing toward the Russian trenches. Toward them.

Now reaching that weapon was not just an order from his commander; it was a matter of life or death.

Dimitri leapt to his feet and began running, but he had taken no more than five steps before a meaty German crossed directly in his path. Dimitri twisted to avoid him but the German raised the butt of his rifle and crashed it down on Dimitri's head. Colored stars filled his vision. Dimitri fell to the ground and everything faded to darkness.

The last thing he remembered was the pounding boots of soldiers around him. German boots. Russian boots. Then nothing.

When he opened his eyes again, the sun was higher in the eastern sky, and the area around him was still and silent. Dimitri's head ached terribly, so, moving as little as possible, he looked around enough to see fallen bodies littering the landscape. However, there was no shelling, and no sounds from either trench. The battle must have moved on.

They'd be back today, one side or the other, to bury the dead. If Dimitri had been left here, then either they believed he was among them, or else his comrades had retreated with no time to look for the wounded.

At first, he wondered if he was wounded, or worse. Then Dimitri sat up and was hit with a wave of nausea that settled that question. He touched the side of his head and felt blood. A German had clubbed him there, or at least Dimitri thought that's what he remembered. If he was still here when the Germans returned, a head wound would be the least of his problems.

Dimitri had to find his company again, though he had no idea which way they had gone. Finally, he decided that walking anywhere was better than staying here, so he began stumbling forward.

That was all he did for the next several hours, just walk. Igor had once told him that's what he'd have to do if he got a head wound, to keep moving and not fall asleep. Igor's voice was in his mind now, the only sound he was aware of. Over and over, Igor repeated the same words: "If you go to sleep, you'll sleep forever, my friend. Keep walking."

So he did. Dimitri stayed in one straight line as far as it was possible. One foot landed in front of the other, while the world on either side blurred in his vision. Whatever was on his right or left didn't matter. Nothing mattered.

For the entire day, Igor remained in his mind, warning him of hazards in his path, repeating stories he often told Dimitri when the trenches grew too quiet. And every time Dimitri closed his eyes, Igor seemed to be there, insisting that he find a way to wake himself up.

Gradually, the daylight began to fade, and Igor's voice faded with it. Everything was fading.

Somewhere behind him, a new voice took Igor's place, the voice of a girl. Dimitri didn't know the words she was speaking, and it didn't matter because he was certain he was imagining her. All of the women and children had long ago fled the battle sites.

The voice came again. *"Privet!"*

That was a Russian word, so he did understand it, though it seemed like an odd place for someone to simply say hello.

Dimitri turned to see a girl in a gray coat and a knitted red hat speaking other words he couldn't make sense of, and waving her arms at him.

But why?

Nothing made sense. She didn't make sense, and she was becoming blurry anyway. Dimitri thought maybe she wanted him to walk toward her, so he took a step forward.

Except his leg collapsed beneath him and he fell, so exhausted that he never even felt when he hit the ground.

That was the last thing he remembered before he woke up here. But where exactly was *here*?

CHAPTER
THIRTY-FOUR

January 2, 1917

Dimitri wiggled his fingers. When was the last time they had moved so easily? He hardly could remember. They were finally warm. *He* was warm, thanks to a fire nearby.

Not a fire lit by a mortar shell or the flamethrowers the Germans had recently begun using. But something warm and comforting.

And confusing.

Was he a war prisoner? He didn't think so. His hands weren't bound and from what little he could see around him, he appeared to be in some sort of cave.

He wasn't with the other soldiers from his company, that was obvious, but he didn't think he was alone either. Whoever was in here with him didn't seem to know he was awake, and he wasn't about to let them know it until he had a sense of what was happening.

He closed his eyes once more, trying to piece together the jagged bits of memories that floated through his mind.

Dimitri's company had been sent to France a few months ago, he remembered that. The war here on the western front wasn't going well. The Americans were still refusing to get involved, so the French and British had begged for Russia's help. Dimitri's company was sent to northern France.

Someone stirred behind Dimitri and he froze, listening for any hints that might tell him where he was. Then the sounds went silent again. Were they asleep? He didn't think so, not from the way they had moved.

Dimitri became aware that something was on his head, a bandage maybe? He couldn't remember being injured, but then, there was a lot he couldn't remember.

Somewhere in the fog of his mind, Dimitri recalled being out on no-man's-land with Igor. Something had gone wrong. He shifted, suddenly alarmed. Where was Igor, was he all right?

"Vous êtes en sécurité."

Dimitri's vision still hadn't cleared enough to see who was touching his shoulder, but he felt a kindness in the touch. He didn't think he was in danger.

"Vous êtes en sécurité," the voice repeated. A girl's voice.

This time she moved to where Dimitri could see her, and as his eyes finally focused, he saw a girl staring at him, a cautious smile on her face. She was dirty and much too thin, maybe a couple of years younger than him, but rather pretty.

"Quel est votre nom?" she asked.

Dimitri blinked, trying to make sense of her words. He should know them. His company had fought alongside other French soldiers for the past three months. He had picked up much of their language over that time. He probably used to know what she had just asked, but his brain was still so foggy.

The girl gave up on speaking and reached behind her for a flask that she offered him to drink. Until then, he hadn't realized how desperately thirsty he was, so he accepted the flask and took in water as fast as he could. When it was empty, she reached into a shoulder bag, but he was already becoming tired again, and if she turned back to him, he wouldn't have known. For now, all Dimitri wanted was to sleep.

THIRTY-FIVE

January 2, 1917

Waking up the next time felt easier, though Dimitri was thirsty and desperately hungry. The hunger was enough reason to force his eyes open.

He definitely was in a cave. Before now, he thought he had dreamt that. Then had the girl been real too, or was she part of some strange dream he'd been having?

Dimitri tried to sit up, but gasped and lay back down. His head ached far too much to make a mistake like that again.

As gently as possible, he rolled his head sideways. Yes, this was a cave and a fire was nearby, and he was wrapped in a blanket, making him almost too warm, which was something he never thought he'd feel again. But where were his comrades? Where were the sounds of battle? It was too quiet here.

"*Êtes-vous réveillés?*"

Dimitri turned just enough to see the same girl walking

toward him as he had seen the last time he awoke. How long had that been? Had he slept for hours, or days?

He closed his eyes and tried to concentrate on what she had asked. He knew those words. Maybe she had asked if he was awake. Dimitri nodded back at her.

She held out a flask of water and now he was more certain of what was real. He had seen this flask before, she had offered him water before, and he had accepted it. Dimitri drank again, but this time, when she pulled the flask away, she offered him a cracker.

Dimitri took it and swallowed it in two bites, then was happy to see her offer more.

It wasn't much food. He knew he had not eaten for some time, but for now, it was enough. The girl didn't look like she had much food available. It was better to save it.

"What happened to your head?"

This time, Dimitri understood what she asked and even recalled the proper French words to reply, "I don't know. But it hurts."

She frowned, clearly concerned. Maybe she had no idea what to do for an injury like his. He didn't know either.

"My name is Juliette."

"Dimitri."

"Were you fighting here in Verdun?"

"No." His company had been stationed even farther north, near France's border with Belgium. Dimitri tried to remember the name of the nearest town, but maybe he'd never known it. How was he supposed to return to his company now?

"How . . . did I get here?" Dimitri mumbled.

"Don't you know?" She frowned. "That injury to your head must have been very bad."

Silence fell between them again, until Juliette said, "You awoke a few times . . . screaming. Can you tell me why?"

Dimitri lowered his eyes. He knew exactly why that had happened, but he didn't want to talk about it, or even think about it. Yet she continued to stare, waiting for an answer, so finally he said the least that he had to: "Sometimes, I have bad dreams."

Juliette licked her lips, then asked, "Are they dreams, or memories?"

If the last question was hard to answer, this one was impossible. How could he explain that at night, he couldn't always tell the difference between the two?

Without waiting for his answer, Juliette said, "Shell shock."

Dimitri's brows pressed low. He wasn't sure what those words meant.

"Shell shock," she repeated. "A girl I met last year told me a lot of soldiers leave the battlefield with shell shock, like a part of them is still there, still fighting the worst parts."

She paused and Dimitri let the words soak in. Was that his problem, that a part of him was still on the battlefield? It certainly felt that way.

"Take another drink," Juliette said, bringing the flask to his lips again.

The water helped, and slowly he was beginning to feel better. Dimitri said, "I must return to my company."

"Why? If it was so awful—"

"They'll think I've deserted them. They'll think . . ." His voice drifted off before he realized there was no end to that sentence. How could he know what they'd think, when he didn't even remember leaving?

"You need to take a few days and let your head clear," Juliette said. "I've been hoping that a Red Cross train would come here. My friend Kara is on one of them. But the fighting has ended here in Verdun. The train won't come."

Dimitri was getting tired again, but he still had things he needed to tell Juliette. "Verdun isn't safe," he mumbled.

"I know."

He closed his eyes and tried to think, then opened them again. "When my company went to Belgium, we were ordered to ride as far around Verdun as possible. Captain Garinov said the ground has been poisoned by all the fighting that happened here. There are land mines—"

"I know about them," Juliette said.

"But not only them. There could be unexploded shells. We call them newborns."

Juliette nodded. "The first time I saw you was in a field that might have been full of them. And I know it's not safe, but now that the fighting has ended, my mother and brothers might try to come back here. I need to be here when they come."

"You've lost your family?" Dimitri thought about his family back at home. He missed them terribly, but at least he knew where they would be when he went home, *if* he went home.

"When did . . . ?" He searched his mind for the words he wanted. "When did you last see them?"

"Nearly a year ago." She quickly added, "Losing them felt like a wound of my own, one that no one can see and that refuses to heal."

Dimitri saw that wound in her eyes now, like an injury that had scarred over far too many times. "Shell shock?"

Juliette's smile was full of the same sadness he saw in her eyes. Finally, she shrugged. "I suppose it is. I might not understand the injury on the side of your head, but I do understand your bad dreams very well, and I'm sorry they are happening."

Dimitri turned and stared forward. "When they told me I'd be going to war, I imagined myself returning home with tales of adventure and glory, and a uniform full of medals. Now I doubt I'll ever return home at all. Russia is still in this war only because we have so many soldiers left to lose."

Silence passed between them again until she stood. "More crackers?"

He nodded, and when she gave him one, she asked, "Why would your parents allow you to come to the war when you're so young?"

"They didn't." Dimitri took a bite of his cracker and finished chewing before he added, "Soldiers came to my village one day and said I was recruited. Maybe I look older than my age or maybe they didn't care. Now that I'm here, all I can think about is that maybe this is the best thing for my family. I've seen enough of the world now to understand that there is more for us than the hunger and poverty we have at home. There is free-dom here, real freedom, and I want to be part of it."

Juliette shrugged. "There is only freedom *if* we win."

"That's why I have to go back to my company." Dimitri smiled. "And if I do my best, perhaps I will earn myself a medal. Then I will have my pick of jobs in life. I will have choices that aren't possible for me now."

"So you are fighting for freedom. Ours, and yours?" Juliette opened a bag and began digging inside it. "There is something I want to show you." She pulled out a small blan-ket. "Not this. It was my brother's . . . no, it *is* my brother's." Next, she withdrew a medal hanging from a bright red ribbon. "This! Want to hold it?"

Dimitri took the medal, immediately noticing how heavy it was. It was probably made with gold, except for the large red cross in its center. "This isn't Allied."

Juliette shook her head. "I think it's from the Austro-Hungarian Empire. It must be worth a lot of money."

Dimitri smiled again as he passed it back to her. "If I were to earn a medal like that, I could sell it, then pay for my family to come here to the West."

Juliette turned the medal over in her hands, head down. "This means nothing to me. Money won't bring my family back."

"But you think they will come here, to Verdun?"

Juliette began stuffing her brother's blanket back into her bag. "No, I don't believe that . . . anymore. When spring comes, I'll move on with my life." Now her attention turned to the dwindling fire. "I'd better add another log." Dimitri started to get up, but she shook her head. "Stay there until you feel better."

He did as she suggested for the rest of the day, but the next morning, he felt well enough to walk around the cave. By evening, he even left the cave long enough to help Juliette gather wood for her fire. Dimitri stayed for another few days while he and Juliette explored the area for more supplies. By the fourth day, she had an entire crate of bacon, a half-finished crate of crackers, more matches, and a haversack full of emergency rations. Dimitri didn't know if it would last her through the winter, but he felt better leaving her with more food than what he'd eaten while he stayed here.

And he did have to leave.

The day Dimitri planned to go, Juliette sat across from him with her knitted hat in her hands. "When I had to leave the ambulance train, I promised Kara that I would do everything I could to stay safe. Now I must ask you to make the same promise."

Dimitri grinned. "I promise to do my best."

"If you ever need help again, try to find me."

"Find you?" Now Dimitri chuckled. "Apparently, you are very difficult to find!"

Juliette laughed, maybe just a little, then crouched down and picked up a bag. "I know your haversack was left behind when you were injured, so you should take this one. I put a little food in it for your walk back to your company."

"Thank you," Dimitri said.

He started to leave, but Juliette called, "Wait!" He turned

260

back to face her and saw her deep in thought. Finally, she said, "There's something else." She took a deep breath, then offered him her knitted hat. "I'll be warm here. I think you might need this more than me."

Last night, Juliette had told Dimitri all about her father being imprisoned by the Germans. He couldn't accept this gift. "This hat was from your father."

"My father would want to know that I am the kind of person who helps others. I've never known a colder winter than this one, Dimitri. You need this hat."

After a moment, he nodded, then pulled the hat onto his head. "Perhaps I'll borrow the hat, for now. After the war, I will return it to you with my thanks."

Juliette smiled. "*If* you can find me. As you said, I must be nearly impossible to find."

"But your family is not. Don't give up on them, Juliette. Not entirely."

Now her smile faded. "No, not entirely. And don't you give up until you and your family are free. I already gave you some help for that."

He nodded. "I will try."

Dimitri was several kilometers away before he thought about how strange Juliette's farewell to him had been. He had also begun to realize that his new haversack was heavier than it ought to be if it contained only food.

After a quick search, there at the bottom he found the medal she had shown him several days ago. It was wrapped in a note that read, "This won't bring my family back, but if you sell it at market, it might bring your family to you." Dimitri smiled and clasped it in his hand.

For months, all he had thought about was one day escaping this war, and then finding a way to give his family a better life. For the first time, it seemed possible. However, there was one thing he wanted even more.

He wanted Juliette to find her family again. And until she did, he hoped she would be safe and happy.

If only the same wish could be true for him. Instead, he was headed back into the war, into a reality that could not provide happiness and had never promised him safety.

THIRTY-SIX

April 12, 1917

Dimitri had never liked the trenches, but something about those few days with Juliette had changed him. Now the monotony of the trenches had become pure misery. His whole life had existed in a trench, he realized that now. Back in Russia, there had never been much choice for what he might do or who he might become. You were born into one trench and expected to remain in it, never to wonder what might be possible if only you climbed the ladder to look out.

He would become a farmer because his father was a farmer, as was his grandfather and great-grandfather before that. He would be poor like them, uneducated like them, hungry like them. If any other life existed, then it was happening far beyond these trench walls. Somewhere out there was freedom and hope and the chance to dream of a better future. Down here was a solid line of muck and mud and the barest form of survival.

He had to find a way out.

Dimitri ran to the nearest ladder and put his hands on the rung. This was the life he wanted, to have courage enough to climb out to freedom and build his own future, in any direction he pleased. Anything but this.

"What are you doing there, my friend?" Igor asked, pulling him off the ladder. "Get down, it's not safe."

"One day I'll leave these trenches," Dimitri said. "The whole world is ahead of me. I don't need to live here."

"For now, you do," Igor said, smiling. "I think all you do lately is dream."

Dimitri flinched. The very opposite was true. There were no dreams to be had down here. He spent his days living in mud, fighting off lice and rats, and trying to sleep through exploding shells and men who awoke from their nightmares screaming. Too often, he was the one who screamed.

Igor poked at Juliette's knitted hat, still on Dimitri's head. "Perhaps you want to leave the battlefield again and return to her."

Perhaps he did. The war had been so fierce lately that he had begun to wonder if maybe he had imagined Juliette. Maybe she was just part of the injury he'd suffered in battle.

Her hat was the one piece of evidence he had that she was real. She had wanted him to have the hat for warmth, but it meant so much more to him. What she had really given him was hope.

He needed that. Without this hat, Dimitri might've begun

to believe that *this* horror, this day-to-day survival, was normal.

"What do you suppose Juliette is doing today?" Dimitri asked.

Igor shrugged. "Perhaps she's found her family."

He hoped so. He hoped Juliette was with them, in a place that was warm and safe, and with cupboards full of food. He wondered if she ever thought about him.

"Not answering?" Igor elbowed him in the side. "Do you think she would have helped me too if I had wandered away as confused as you were?"

Dimitri grinned. "Maybe she only helps the most handsome Russians," he teased.

But Igor's face fell. "I saw the hit you took to the head that day. I should have run to help you right then. I even started toward you, but the Germans overwhelmed us. They took our trench and forced us into a quick retreat. I never wanted to leave you behind."

"I know that." This wasn't the first time Igor had explained himself, nor the last time Dimitri would forgive him for something that wasn't his fault.

"The other men said that Baba Yaga got you."

Dimitri chuckled beside his friend. Every Russian knew the story of the witch who appeared as a deformed old woman. If children went missing in the forest, it was because she had eaten them.

Becoming serious again, Igor leaned against the trench wall

beside Dimitri and angled his head upward. "I am a dreamer too, you know."

"Oh?"

He reached into a pocket of his uniform and pulled out an envelope. "I got a letter today with exciting news. The revolution we have dreamt of for so long has finally begun!"

Dimitri's eyes narrowed. "Lenin's revolution?"

"The people's revolution! From city to city throughout Russia, they are refusing to work in the Tsar's factories, refusing to plow his fields or serve at his command. The harder the Tsar fights to keep control, the harder the people push back."

Dimitri still wasn't sure how he felt about this news. "Is the Tsar still in power?"

"For now, but he cannot last much longer. Soon the people will rule and then we shall all be free!"

Dimitri shook his head. "Revolution will not bring us freedom."

"Revolution is our only chance at freedom. Look at this." Igor reached into his envelope and plucked out a stitched red star about the size of a button. "Very soon, you will see these everywhere. This will be our symbol of freedom." His face fell as he looked at Dimitri's frown. "You speak of freedom more than anyone else I know. Why aren't you excited?"

"The Reds preach freedom, but what they really want is power."

"Dimitri, you don't—"

Igor stopped mid-sentence as Captain Garinov walked by.

He nodded at the star between Igor's fingers. "Where did you get that?"

"From home, sir."

"Very good." Garinov turned to Dimitri. "We are all Reds here, are we not?"

Dimitri lowered his eyes, feeling the heat of the Captain's stare. Garinov stepped closer to him. "Why don't you lead us out of the trench again today, Dimitri? Get your gas mask on. We're going to take the Germans' trench if it is the last thing we do."

Garinov moved on, and Igor handed Dimitri his mask. "Don't worry about him. He doesn't like anybody."

"He likes other Reds," Dimitri muttered as he pulled the mask over his head. The French had finally provided the Russians in his company with the weapons and protections their own Tsar had not. The gas mask made fighting far more difficult, but the wind was coming toward them today. There was always a chance of the Germans releasing poison gas. Or if the wind shifted, perhaps one of the Allies would do the same thing. Either way, he didn't want to be in the middle of it.

Captain Garinov blew his whistle, the signal for everyone to move. Every soldier knew to pay attention to that whistle. Each pattern gave different orders: advance, retreat, get down. If Dimitri lived to old age, he would never stop hearing that whistle in his head.

Despite Garinov's orders, Igor was the first onto the ladder. He flashed Dimitri a smile. "You remember your promise to me?"

Not to become bitter and angry, like their Captain? No, he never would.

"I remember." Despite what they were about to walk into, Dimitri couldn't help but return a smile. He'd never have made it this far without Igor's friendship.

As glad as Dimitri was for the warmer weather, springtime had brought rain that created a sticky mud in the trenches and dangerous conditions on top. Dimitri's usual strategy of running at sharp angles to avoid the Germans wouldn't work anymore. Not when the mud grabbed his boots and refused to let go, making it nearly impossible to run at all, much less at the angles he wanted. Today he had no other choice but to set his eye on the German trench and continue to advance as a pinch settled in his gut.

"Faster, my friend," Igor shouted through his mask. "Keep moving!"

Dimitri began to make a joke back to him, but instead, something caught his eye. He immediately began running, yelling through his mask, but Igor couldn't hear him.

Igor didn't know; he hadn't seen the grenade.

"Igor, run!" Dimitri shouted, but his words were lost in the noise of the battle. Mud pulled at his feet, slowing him down.

Finally, Igor looked up to see where Dimitri was pointing, but it was too late.

The grenade exploded. Dimitri crouched low to protect himself, but when he looked up, Igor was flat on the ground.

"No!" Dimitri continued hurrying toward him and fell to his knees at Igor's side. Why was he so still?

This was impossible; it couldn't be happening. Dimitri pulled off his mask to continue yelling his friend's name. He checked Igor's pulse, shook his shoulders, and shouted for Igor to wake up, hoping if he yelled loud enough, Igor's eyes would open again.

But they didn't. And they wouldn't.

No! Only seconds ago, Igor had been fine; he'd been laughing and excited about his letter from home. How could it have changed so fast?

For the months they had fought together, Dimitri had watched Igor dodge the worst attacks, time after time. He always made it out, always got through it. Always.

Until now.

Dimitri realized how deep he had sunk into the mud and cursed at it. If it hadn't been for the mud, he could have gotten to Igor fast enough to save him.

Around him, the chaos continued, but Dimitri hardly cared. None of it mattered. They would take the trench today, or they wouldn't, and tomorrow, the Germans would take it back, or they wouldn't, and this battle would continue on regardless. Because that's all this war ever did. It went on and on and on and on. Nothing stopped it, and nothing ever would. No matter how beautiful the moment, or how tragic, the war was always there, bent on its eternal destruction.

Igor was part of that now.

"Dimitri, start moving or they'll get you too!" Captain Garinov ran past him. "Replace your mask and get on your feet! That is an order!"

Dimitri looked up and saw even more Germans climbing

out from their trenches. He didn't care about fighting any-more, but somewhere in his head he seemed to hear Igor once again insist, "Get up, my friend! The fight is not over!"

Dimitri began digging through Igor's pockets. In his chest pocket he found a drawing Igor had made of a pretty girl back home. Igor thought he might marry her one day. In another pocket he found the envelope Igor had shown him only min-utes ago. As soon as Dimitri got the chance, he would send these back home to Igor's family.

Dimitri also pulled out the stitched star from Igor's chest pocket. Igor's symbol of freedom. Maybe it could be his sym-bol of freedom too.

"Start fighting if you want to live!" Dimitri didn't know if that was Igor's voice or someone else's, but he listened.

With tears still blurring his vision, Dimitri stood and turned to face the first German to reach him.

No matter how bad his nightmares always were, reality was so much worse.

THIRTY-SEVEN

April 16, 1917

Even after four long days without Igor, Dimitri still felt as numb as the moment it had happened. This wasn't the numbness that came from the cold, or that which came from fear—those were temporary discomforts he had learned to deal with long ago. This was different. He was truly numb, as in, he simply felt nothing. There was no fear, no despair or pain. He just stared forward as if he were only a puppet controlled by something bigger than him, outside of him.

Igor's star was in his palm. He wasn't looking at it, he couldn't, but his thumb rubbed over the stitching, the tiny bumps of thread being the only thing he actually was aware of feeling.

Dimitri scanned the rows of soldiers in the trench, some writing letters home, others eating or talking in groups. Some of them stared back at him with the same emptiness in their eyes. One of the men here had stayed near him on the battlefield four days ago, helped him get back into the trench when Captain Garinov called for a retreat, but he couldn't pick out who it was. Maybe it wasn't anyone here. Maybe the man who saved his life had lost his own life to a German grenade, just like Igor.

Dimitri didn't know.

But he felt nothing about that too.

"Everyone, gather close!" Captain Garinov had entered the area and in his hand was an envelope.

Dimitri thought about the envelope he had taken from Igor. It was still in his pocket. He should have already sent Igor's mother a note by now, telling her what a good friend Igor had been, what a heroic soldier he had been. Dimitri needed her to know, but how could he put into words what he still couldn't comprehend himself?

He'd write the letter later.

Dimitri looked up as Captain Garinov pulled out the letter from the envelope. "It's happened, my friends! Two months ago, it happened, only we are just learning about it now."

The area began buzzing with anticipation about what the news might be. Dimitri barely managed to keep his head up.

"What has happened?" a man called. "Tell us!"

Captain Garinov nodded and then a smile broke out on his face. "The revolution has begun. There were strikes in St. Petersburg, the entire city shut down. Finally, the Tsar was forced to abandon the throne. He is gone!"

A cheer rose up among the soldiers, or most of them, anyway. Dimitri sat up taller. Had he heard that correctly? Igor had told him about the strikes, but he might not have known the news about the Tsar. The Tsar was gone?

Someone asked, "Who leads Russia now?"

Garinov shrugged. "What does it matter? Lenin is returning from Switzerland, and soon he will lead us all! My friends, my comrades, we are only at the beginning! When Lenin rules, we will all learn to think the same; we will all work toward one common goal, the greatness of Russia!"

Dimitri tilted his head. How was that any kind of freedom? Weren't they only exchanging one bad ruler for another?

The soldiers cheered at the Captain's news, something that jarred Dimitri back to attention. He looked around and saw only one or two other soldiers who seemed to be as equally alarmed as he. The rest were clapping one another on the back or exchanging hugs or reaching for a canteen to raise in a toast of celebration.

"Captain! What is this?" Commandant LeBlanc marched into the area. He was the French officer in charge of all the Russians here, including Captain Garinov. "You Russkies are so loud, you'll draw every German to us within a hundred kilometers."

"We don't care if we do," Captain Garinov said. "Every Russian in this trench is finished with this war."

Commandant LeBlanc folded his arms. "You may command your Russian soldiers, Captain Garinov, but I am in command of *you*. And you are not finished with this war until the Tsar says otherwise."

Garinov turned to face him. "There is no Tsar, not

anymore. There is no *us* anymore. I will gather my soldiers and we will return to Russia."

"Not until I give you permission."

Garinov shook his head, clearly losing patience. "You do not understand, Commandant. We are not asking your permission because we no longer need it. My soldiers will no longer fight for the Allies. It is time for us to go home and fight for Russia."

The Commandant's face reddened. He gestured at two other soldiers near him. "Arrest that man."

But the two soldiers were both Russian. They glanced at each other, then with a nod, they straightened up and folded their arms, making it clear they were refusing to act.

Dimitri looked from one man to the other, wondering exactly what was happening, and what he should do about it. He had seen soldiers so exhausted that they could barely pull themselves off the ground, but when the order was given, they did it. He'd seen soldiers too terrified to fight when they were ordered over the top, but they did that too.

Never once had he seen a soldier refuse a direct order from his commander, and he certainly had never seen an entire unit refuse orders before.

Finally, Commandant LeBlanc said, "When I return, any man who continues to refuse my orders will be arrested for mutiny. That includes you, Captain Garinov."

The soldiers only laughed as he stomped away, but once he did, Captain Garinov became serious again. "We need a symbol, to show that we are uniting for revolution at home!"

His eyes fell on Dimitri. "What happened to that red star your friend had?"

Dimitri closed his fist tight around it. "Sir, we gave our oaths to fight this war to its end."

Captain Garinov stuffed his letter into his pocket, then crossed over to Dimitri. "Our oaths were to a Tsar who no longer exists. The only war that matters now is the war for Russia. We must return and fight for Lenin, fight for power to the people!" His eyes fell to Dimitri's closed fist.

Before Dimitri could act, Garinov grabbed his arm and forced his hand open, revealing Igor's star. "So you are with us after all!"

Dimitri closed his fist around the star and yanked his hand away. "I am not with you, Captain."

Garinov's face reddened. "You will join us, or you will leave this trench."

Leaving the trench was not an option. He'd be charged with desertion, and that was only if he survived, which he likely wouldn't. So he wiggled free of the Captain, then reached down to grab a rock and held it up, ready to throw it at anyone who came closer.

Captain Garinov chuckled. "Do you think you can win against me? This is mutiny, Dimitri."

"No, this is *your* rebellion against the Commandant! I will not follow you any longer."

"Do you think you have a choice?" Garinov asked. "Once Lenin is in power, you will not be allowed to oppose him. No one will." Dimitri didn't move and finally, Captain Garinov said, "Very well. Give me that star, then you will leave this trench."

Dimitri straightened up, knowing things were about to get worse for him. "No, Captain. I will not."

Garinov motioned with one hand and immediately three other Russians pounced on Dimitri. While two men held him back, the third picked up his haversack and passed it to the Captain.

"Let me show you how the Reds work, Dimitri." Captain Garinov pulled out the notepad Dimitri used to write letters home, then looked around at the others. "Is it fair for this boy to have an entire notebook while none of us has even a single piece of paper? It is not." And he opened the notebook and tore out every sheet but one, which he tossed at Dimitri's feet.

He looked inside the haversack again. "So many useful items!" He began pulling out items, tossing them to various men. "Socks for you, gloves for you, this knitted hat—"

"Not that!"

Captain Garinov looked up. "What's so special about this hat?"

Dimitri swallowed hard, terrified that his answer might bring on something worse. But he couldn't allow the Captain to give that hat away. He said, "It belonged to a friend of mine. I promised myself I'd give it back to her one day."

"Of course, Comrade!" Captain Garinov brought the hat over to Dimitri and placed it on his head. "The Reds are fair to all." He reached for the haversack again, and now Dimitri was truly nervous. Still in there was the medal from Juliette.

He needed that to have any hope of getting enough money to bring his family out of Russia. Dimitri stretched out his hand. "Give me my haversack."

"Not until I'm finished," Garinov snarled, reaching his hand inside once more.

"Captain Garinov, you will drop what you are holding and step back!" Commandant LeBlanc ordered. He had returned, this time with a dozen French soldiers at his side.

Captain Garinov glared down at Dimitri. "If I ever see you again, we will finish this."

"I ordered you to step back!" the Commandant repeated.

Captain Garinov dropped the haversack and did as he was told. "For us, the war is over. But to avoid a fight, we'll go our way, you go yours."

Dimitri scrambled to his feet, gathered what still remained of his things, and began to stuff them back into his haversack. This time, he tucked Juliette's medal into his pocket for safekeeping.

"If you wish to leave, I will not stop you," LeBlanc told Captain Garinov. "But if you stay, you will follow my orders."

Captain Garinov smiled. "Very well. Then we will leave."

He gestured for the other Russians to follow him. Each soldier picked up his own haversack and weapon, then gave a salute to Commandant LeBlanc as he walked away.

Dimitri was left alone.

After the last of the Russians was gone, LeBlanc turned his attention to Dimitri. "How old are you?"

He hesitated. "Fourteen."

"Fourteen? You have no business being in this war. Why did you volunteer?"

"Sir, I didn't." Dimitri thought that was enough of an explanation, and the Commandant seemed to agree.

"I'm going to begin the paperwork to send you home."

"No, sir, please don't." Dimitri hesitated again. "Let me stay here, at least until I figure out my plans."

"What about your family?"

"That's why I must stay. I send my pay home to help them."

"Fourteen years old." The Commandant's sigh was heavy. "You should not have to manage so much on your own."

Dimitri immediately thought of Juliette, and how much more she had lost than he had. "My problems are not as great as what others have, sir."

"No indeed. Well, it just so happens that our company has received orders to move farther into Belgium. If you will stay, then you will come with us. Dismissed."

But there was one more question, one Dimitri hardly dared to ask. "What will happen to the other members of my company, sir?"

Commandant LeBlanc frowned. "This area is crawling with Germans. I daresay that if your Russian friends survive the next few hours, then it's only because they are on their way to a German prison camp."

Dimitri blinked hard and looked off in the direction in which his company had gone. That was the answer he'd come up with too. He'd heard the prison camps in Germany weren't good. Even for mutiny, Dimitri wondered if a prison camp was far more punishment than Captain Garinov deserved.

"Get some sleep tonight and pray the Germans don't hear that half our company just walked off the lines," LeBlanc added. "If they do, they will attack, and it might only be you and my men to defend this trench."

Dimitri frowned and took up a position in the trench where he could be ready in case the Germans came over the top.

His worst fears had just come true. This day had turned into a nightmare far worse than anything he had ever dreamt.

Dimitri wished he was back near Juliette. Back there, where his dreams felt normal, where his life had felt normal.

Back where thinking of home had been a good thing.

As far as Dimitri was concerned, if revolution had come to Russia, then he no longer had a home.

THIRTY-EIGHT

June 7, 1917

Dimitri had gone with the Commandant's company to fight in Belgium, though by now, everyone had heard of the mutiny of the Russian soldiers all throughout Europe. Dimitri saw the suspicion in the eyes of the French soldiers. They were waiting for his mutiny too.

Because they kept him at a distance, Dimitri never knew what any day's fighting would bring. Normally, he didn't mind that, but today was different. He had overheard a few French soldiers talking—the British were here on the front lines, too, and had a major operation planned for today. All he could gather was that a couple of days ago, several of them had been assigned to run cable lines across what would soon become no-man's-land. Now they were waiting for the Germans to come.

And last night, they did. Whatever the Allies were planning, a strange energy was in the air. Something big was going to happen today.

Dimitri stood watch from his position in the trench, nervous and curious. He heard movement behind him and turned to see Commandant LeBlanc standing there.

"The war is finally turning in our favor," LeBlanc said.

"But is it? I heard—" Dimitri hardly dared to ask because it wasn't something he should know, but rumors flew through the trenches every day and he had little to do but listen. "I heard the French are building a fake Paris."

His eyes narrowed. "Where did you hear about that?"

"Lots of people are talking about it. A false city just outside Paris, to fool the German bombers."

LeBlanc *humphed*. "Well, if we are, that is certainly not information a Russian foot soldier needs to know."

"Yes, sir."

"However . . ." LeBlanc was smiling when Dimitri looked up again. The Commandant added, "In the next few minutes, you will want to keep your eyes ahead. Turn at the wrong moment and you will miss one of the great turning points of this war."

"Sir?"

"Do you see those cables?"

"Yes."

"For the past four years, the Germans have shot their bees at us and we have been stung without mercy. Today, we will sting back. On the other end of those cables are more than four hundred and fifty thousand kilograms of explosives."

Dimitri peered over the trench. "Where is it all?" If it was that much, the Germans should have seen it by now.

"Just you wait and watch." Then, with a slight chuckle, the Commandant moved on.

As had become the routine, the shelling began with the sunrise, though today, it only seemed to be coming from the German lines. Their bombardment continued for nearly an hour, while the Allies did nothing in response. No one gave orders to fire, or to attack, or to do anything at all. Dimitri couldn't understand that. Why weren't they responding?

He glanced farther down the trench and saw Commandant LeBlanc with a British captain taking turns looking through a periscope that allowed them to see over the trench without poking their heads up. A soldier waited nearby with a telephone. LeBlanc took the call, said something to the British captain with him, then they both smiled.

But why?

His curiosity rising, Dimitri turned toward the German trench again. He had no idea how many men were inside it, but he saw the tops of what had to be hundreds of helmets, and that was only what he could see from his position. For all he knew, thousands of German soldiers were stretched out along their trench line.

"Attention!" Commandant LeBlanc ordered. "Be at the ready, and if you have the courage to do so, look over the top."

Dimitri did look, but it was from curiosity more than any form of courage. He dipped his helmet low and stepped up a single rung of the nearby ladder to peer out across no-man's-land.

Then it happened. An enormous boom coming from the German lines. Earth was thrown up so high into the air, it rained down on Dimitri even this far across no-man's-land. The ground shook violently and hadn't ceased to shake when a second explosion happened, immediately followed by a third, fourth, and continuing on until he had counted nineteen explosions in total.

When it was finally finished, dust and smoke rose from what was left of the German trenches, mostly craters now. From the British lines, Dimitri heard wild cheering that gradually flowed toward him as the French began to see the whole of the British plans.

The smoke cleared and Dimitri looked for the rows of German helmets, but he saw nothing. No helmets, no trenches. It was as if the entire enemy army had vanished in less than twenty seconds.

Commandant LeBlanc called out, "That was ten thousand men we no longer need to worry about."

Dimitri turned to him, unable to believe that he had heard the number correctly. Ten thousand?

"But how?" a soldier nearby asked.

Commandant LeBlanc continued, "It took the British two years to dig a tunnel beneath those trenches, and we won't let their efforts go to waste. Over the top, boys!"

They climbed out and began to run across the battle-scarred land. But nobody shot back. If any Germans had survived, they'd be in no condition to fight.

"Oi, Russkie!"

Dimitri turned. A British soldier pointed toward an area off to the far right, beyond where the worst of the explosions had been. Dimitri veered in that direction to search, though it was immediately clear that no one was here. The tents had collapsed, now buried beneath mounds of dirt.

He walked over the top of them, following the direction of where the trench had once been.

Suddenly, he stopped, frozen in place. A wagon was ahead in the distance with two horses still milling about, but their reins were loose. Something was wrong.

After an explosion like that, the horses should have set off in a run and would have been far away by now. If they were still here, then it was because someone had calmed them. Someone who had survived the explosions.

Dimitri's heart pounded, but it was his job to investigate this area, so he began crossing to the right of the wagon. Fallen trees had piled up like an obstacle course. A German easily could have hidden behind or beneath any of them. The sooner he cleared this area, the better.

He continued moving around the wagon when the order came: *"Halt."*

Dimitri stopped and immediately dropped his weapon to raise his hands in surrender. Three Germans stood in front of him. One soldier approached Dimitri and began searching his pockets for any other weapons. He found Igor's stitched red star, frowned at Dimitri, then put it back where it was. In another pocket, he found the medal from Juliette.

"Was ist das?"

Dimitri didn't know enough of his language to reply, so he merely shook his head and held out his hand for the medal.

After another long look at it, the soldier returned it to Dimitri's pocket.

More German was spoken, then Dimitri's hands were bound behind his back and he was led into the wagon.

Seconds later it began to drive away, toward Germany. The Allies may have won the battle, but Dimitri had just lost his own personal war. He had become a prisoner of the Germans.

THIRTY-NINE

November 7, 1917

A s difficult as conditions had been in the trenches, for the past five months, Dimitri had come to understand that things could always get worse.

He'd been sent to a prison camp in Germany, near Freiburg, where he was lucky to find a cot to sleep on at night, and luckier still if he didn't have to share it with a rat or two. Food was scarce and the Germans worked him hard cutting logs in the forest. He'd written numerous letters to his family, but nothing ever arrived for him. Lately, he'd begun to wonder if his family knew he was still alive.

However, after five months, today offered him hope for something better. He and a few other Russians had been ordered onto a prison wagon headed into the city of Freiburg. Apparently, some German officer wanted prisoners brought in to do work on his home. Dimitri resented the forced labor, but anything that offered him a day away from logging trees sounded wonderful.

He peered through the bars of the wagon as it drove through the streets of Freiburg. Women here were shopping or walking the streets with their children. Old men stood on the corners with newspapers in their hands, pointing to the front page and talking with one another about what they were reading. How strange it was to see people carrying on with their lives as if the world was normal. It had been so long since he had been part of this, he no longer felt that he had a place with people like these. For him, life was only war, or dark caves, or a wretched prison camp. Nothing else existed.

Finally, the wagon stopped, but when Dimitri stepped outside, he saw a second prison wagon already here.

"Who came in that wagon?" he asked.

The soldier he'd spoken to said, "Major Dressler brings those prisoners in from another camp every week to do work around the home. The group of you are only here today because there's more work than usual. Start walking."

Dimitri followed the other prisoners onto the property. Set back several meters from the road was a two-story home with brown timber siding over faded yellow plaster. Behind the home was a wide grassy lawn, except for the far corner of the property where a small wooden structure appeared to have been built for pigeons.

Dimitri turned when he heard noises behind them, then saw the other prisoners who had been brought to the home. Instantly, his stomach turned.

"Well, this is an unexpected pleasure." Captain Garinov was at the head of four other Russians who had once been in the trenches with Dimitri. Garinov stepped forward. "Dimitri Petrenko. I'm surprised to see you."

Dimitri straightened up. "You're surprised that I was captured?"

"Surprised that you're still alive. I heard they sent you into Belgium. From fire into flame, was it?"

"I did my duty there," Dimitri answered.

Captain Garinov narrowed his one good eye. "You did your duty, but did you do what is right?"

The soldier who was keeping watch on them stepped forward. "Enough talk. It's time to get to work." He pointed down at the grass on which they stood. "Major Dressler's daughter wants a garden next spring, so you will help her by clearing this grass."

Garinov's group already had the shovels, so Dimitri began picking up the piles of cut grass. For the most part, that allowed him to keep to himself.

As he labored, Dimitri listened to Garinov speak to the other Russians at work. His voice was so low, Dimitri couldn't catch every word, but he certainly heard enough.

"Revenge."

"German."

"Dressler."

Then a minute later, Garinov whispered, "No, I will stay in Freiburg. I have unfinished business here."

Dimitri had seen Major Dressler walk through the prison camp on only a few occasions. He seemed to be a fair man, but

Dimitri had no loyalties to him. If Captain Garinov was planning revenge, that wasn't Dimitri's problem.

"Dimitri!" one of the Germans called. "Go to the back door and ask how large Elsa Dressler wants her garden to be."

Grateful for the excuse to get away, Dimitri ran to the house. He went around a tall hedge to reach the back door and knocked. Seconds later, a girl near his age, with light brown hair that hung in curls around her face, came to the door. She looked at him with some amusement.

"Yes?"

"I was sent here to ask—"

"You're younger than the other prisoners."

He paused, unsure of how to respond to that. Finally, he repeated, "I was sent here to ask—"

"What's your name?"

"Dimitri Petrenko."

"I'm Elsa. Is this your first time working at our home? We've had the most interesting experiences with other prisoners here, but you're the youngest I've seen."

He ignored that. "How large do you want the garden patch?"

"As large as possible. We nearly starved last winter, and this summer hasn't been much better."

He was quickly losing patience. "When you say 'as large as possible'—"

"About double the size of my pigeon house. Did you see that?"

"Yes. Thank you."

After Elsa closed the door, Dimitri turned to leave but almost immediately bumped into Garinov, who grabbed him by his shirt. "They sent me to find out what was taking you so long."

"I wasn't taking long at all." Dimitri tried to push past Garinov, but the man shoved him against the side of the house.

Garinov's lip curled as he leaned toward Dimitri. "I know you were listening in on my conversation back there. Did you say anything to Dressler's daughter?"

"No, of course not." Dimitri tried to spot the German guard on the other side of the hedge. "Let me go or I'll call for help."

"You think he cares if one Russian kills another Russian? Do you still have that stitched star? I want it."

"You can't have it." Dimitri struggled again, only to be pushed harder against the house.

"Turn out your pockets. That's an order."

Dimitri huffed. He didn't have to follow the Captain's orders anymore.

Garinov put one thick arm across Dimitri's chest and began searching his pockets with his other hand. Almost immediately, he found Juliette's medal. Dimitri's heart raced. This, the star, and Juliette's hat on his head were the only three things Dimitri owned in the world, and each was valuable for its own reason.

Garinov held up the medal. "Where did you get this?"

"Give it back!"

"This is Austrian. You must have stolen it!"

"I didn't, I swear!"

"That's what took you so long at the door. You were stealing from Major Dressler!" Garinov put his face close to Dimitri's. "You know what happens to prisoners who violate the rules."

Dimitri did know. At best, he'd be sent to a work detail near the front lines. Few prisoners ever returned alive.

With panic rising in him, Dimitri said, "I did not steal that medal!"

"Where is the star?" When Dimitri didn't answer, Garinov's grip tightened on his arm and he began dragging Dimitri out from behind the hedge. "Sir!" he called to the guard. "I want to report a theft." Then he placed the medal into the guard's hands. "This belongs to someone on your side. He probably stole this from the house just now."

The guard grunted, then raised his rifle and directed Dimitri to return with him to the house. He knocked on the door and once again, Elsa answered. Her eyes went from Dimitri to the soldier with the rifle. "What is wrong?"

"I must see your father," the guard said.

"Both of my parents are busy," Elsa said. "You can talk to me."

"Very well." He held out the medal to Elsa. "The boy has been accused of stealing this from your home just now."

"That isn't from here. We have nothing like . . ." Elsa's eyes suddenly widened. Dimitri's stomach knotted as Elsa flashed him a glare, then took the medal. She turned it over and over again, then let out a gasp and looked up. "Bring him inside. I'll be right back."

The soldier shoved Dimitri ahead of him, into what was surely the finest kitchen he'd ever seen in his life. Elsa must have been exaggerating when she said they were hungry. She couldn't know what real hunger felt like.

"Major Dressler is a fair man," the soldier said. "But mark my words, that medal you stole will be your death sentence."

A wave of fear rushed through Dimitri. Innocent or not, he had every reason to believe the soldier was right. He wasn't likely to live out the rest of this day.

CHAPTER
FORTY

November 7, 1917

Several minutes later, Elsa returned to the kitchen with a small envelope in her hand. While she pulled out the letter inside, she asked Dimitri, "Where did you get this medal?"

"It belongs to a French girl, a friend of mine."

"That's a lie," Elsa said. "This belonged to Felix's family, I'm most certain of it!"

Dimitri squinted back at her. "I don't know anyone named Felix. My friend got it from a British girl who works on a Red Cross train."

Elsa's expression changed, though he wasn't sure what this new expression meant for him. She unfolded the letter and a smile slowly widened across her face. Then she said, "The girl who worked for the Red Cross, was it someone named Kara?"

Dimitri was slow to nod. That was the name Juliette had mentioned once, maybe, but that was a long time ago. Maybe the name was Kara.

Still smiling, Elsa spoke to the soldier in the room. "You may return to the other prisoners. My father will be here any minute, but I want to speak to this boy alone."

The soldier nodded at her, then said to Dimitri, "If you try anything in this home, I'll execute you myself, Russkie."

Dimitri merely lowered his head and waited for him to leave.

When he was gone, Elsa said, "Why did this French girl give you such a valuable medal?" Dimitri shrugged and she asked, "Maybe you saved her life?"

"She saved my life."

"Not really. Not if you ended up in a German prison camp."

Dimitri said nothing. A pitcher of water was on the counter and Elsa poured a cup, which she offered to him. "Go ahead and take it," she said. "You look like you need it."

Dimitri took the cup and swallowed it nearly in a single gulp. "Thank you."

"The prison camps can't be as bad as some people say. My father takes great care—"

"They are worse than you can imagine, despite your father."

Elsa refilled his cup. "You won't be there much longer. Papa says Russia will leave this war soon. Your side has lost."

If that was true, then it was only because Lenin wanted to bring the soldiers home to fight for him. He'd end one war to expand another one, a civil war.

"Every side is losing this war," Dimitri replied. "I've heard the prison guards talk. They are hungry and want to go home.

They know that Germany is collapsing. And now that the Americans have joined the war—"

"Germany is as strong as ever!" Elsa insisted. "We're training elite soldiers, the best of our best. We call them storm troopers. When we're most ready to unleash them, the Allies will have no chance of winning."

"Germany is a house of cards," Dimitri said. "At the next stiff wind—"

"I know about card houses," Elsa said. "But Germany will not fall. Our soldiers sing from the trenches before going into battle."

"What other lies do your German newspapers print? If you want the truth about this war, go and see France for yourself. See what Germany has done to it."

Elsa continued, "I do understand this war. Very often, I can hear the battle from right here in my home. They launch their mortar shells and our homes shake. Then it goes quiet and we know that our side and your side are about to fight."

Dimitri felt a bitterness rise in him, almost like bile in his throat. "And hours later, the hospitals will fill up again, more graves will be dug. You don't understand the war. You don't know what it is to stand in a trench, dreading the orders to join a fight that you might not survive."

"What about being chased from your home at night because British bombers are flying overhead? Do you know why they come here, Dimitri? They've told us in the pamphlets they drop from the sky. They bomb us for revenge."

"And have you ever wondered what the revenge was for?"

Elsa took a deep breath, then lowered her voice. "No," she finally said. "I never have."

Dimitri lowered his voice as well. "One day, someone will claim victory in the war, but no one will have won."

Elsa whispered, "I hate this war, Dimitri. I've never told anyone that, but I hate this war."

"Me too." He met her eyes, and there found someone who looked tired, like he was. Who seemed to feel helpless in the same way he often did.

They were still staring at each other when Elsa's father walked into the room. Major Dressler was tall and trim with lighter hair and a clean-shaven face. He looked from Dimitri to his daughter. "What is going on here? What is a prisoner doing inside my home?"

"Papa, look!" Elsa thrust the medal and the letter she had been holding toward him. "This is a letter Felix Baum wrote to me almost two years ago about a girl from the Red Cross named Kara. She saved his father's life, so his father gave Kara his medal!" She pointed to Dimitri. "I think he has Sergeant Baum's medal."

"How do you know it's the same one?"

"Felix showed it to me that night we were at their house for supper. The fabric on top was torn the very same way as this one."

Major Dressler read the letter, then studied the medal, and when he'd finished, his eyes fell on Dimitri, and he finally asked, "Why are you here?"

Dimitri tilted his head, even more confused than before. "I came on the prison wagon—"

"No, why are you here in the first place? How old are you?"

"Fourteen."

"That's my age," Elsa said. "Papa, we can't allow him to remain a prisoner."

"He's still a Russian soldier, Elsa. And a prisoner of Germany."

"But he shouldn't be! Papa, didn't you tell me that you promised to protect the innocents in this war? That's him, even if he wears an enemy's uniform."

Major Dressler stared at Dimitri for what seemed like a very long time before mumbling, "Wait here, please." Then he stood and left the room.

"We're going to help you," Elsa told Dimitri.

But he only snorted. "You'll help me into a grave. I expect nothing more from a German."

Elsa sighed. "Do you hate all Germans, Dimitri?"

He stared back at her, unable to respond. Did he? Igor was killed by a German grenade. How was he supposed to forget that?

"I feel your anger," she said. "What happened to make you so angry?"

"Please stop." With those words, Dimitri sucked in a harsh breath and couldn't release it. It was impossible for her to know about his promise to Igor, yet she spoke as if she knew every word of it, and knew that he had failed to keep it.

"What's wrong?" Elsa asked.

Dimitri finally exhaled, slowly, while he made a decision. He didn't entirely believe his words, not yet, but it was the way Igor would want him to answer. "I don't hate all Germans," he replied. "I don't hate you or your father."

"I don't hate all Russians either." Elsa laughed. "Only the ones still working out back. Whenever they come, I go somewhere else."

Captain Garinov!

When Major Dressler returned to the room, Dimitri said, "Sir, I don't think you should trust Captain Garinov."

"Why not?"

Dimitri eyed Elsa, not wanting to say too much in front of her. "I just . . . don't."

Major Dressler nodded at Dimitri, then motioned for a soldier behind him to go out the back door. He turned to Dimitri. "An automobile is waiting for you in front of the house. It will take you as far as the French border, but," he added, "this is only on condition that you swear not to return to the war. You're too young for a uniform, and I will not keep an underage boy in a German prison camp."

Dimitri paused to consider the terms he was being offered. He had sworn to fight for Russia until he was released from service. Did he have the right to make this agreement?

Elsa said, "You never should have been here, Dimitri. Accept my father's offer while you still can."

Dimitri nodded and mumbled, "I will not return to the war." With those words came a flood of relief, as if a thousand kilos of weight had just been lifted from his shoulders. Was this real? Would he finally be free, after all this time?

"Where will you go?" Elsa asked. "Back to Russia?"

"Don't go to Russia, Dimitri. It is not safe there." Major Dressler handed Dimitri a paper. "An old friend of mine owns a shop near Verdun, or he did once. If it's still there, you'll find it near the church in Belleray. Tell him my name and he'll give you a job."

Dimitri put the note in his pocket. "Yes, sir. Thank you." He turned to Elsa. "And thank you."

She shrugged. "It's too bad our countries are at war. I think we might've been friends."

Dimitri only smiled back at her. "You and I are not at war."

"You are no longer at war at all," she said.

The soldier who had gone out to check on the prisoners returned and looked directly at Major Dressler. "Sir, Captain Garinov has escaped with your horse. I've sent the other guards out to go look for him. Do we have your permission to shoot him on sight?"

Major Dressler closed his eyes for a moment, then said, "He is an officer, and has no doubt been through far too much. If you find him, he must be treated with respect." Now he turned to Dimitri. "Thank you for the medal. I hope better days are ahead of you."

"Thank you, sir," Dimitri said. "Goodbye, Elsa."

As the soldier began driving him away minutes later, one thought after another passed through Dimitri's mind. He didn't have a single coin to his name. He had no possessions other than a stitched red star and a knitted winter hat, and he was headed toward a country where he would have to build a future on his own.

A smile widened across his face.

None of that mattered. He was finally free.

FORTY-ONE

December 13, 1917

A s Major Dressler had promised, his friend in Belleray offered Dimitri a job in his market. The pay wasn't much, but Dimitri was allowed to sleep on a cot in a back room, and was given a few francs' worth of food to eat each night.

Dimitri worked as much as the market owner allowed, and saved every coin that he could. If he still had the medal, he would've already sold it and sent the money to his family, but now, all he could do was write to them and ask them to be patient. With five younger siblings, it would be months before he saved enough money to pay for their passage west.

Today, that bothered him more than usual. Dimitri straightened a pile of newspapers near the door with the head-line: RUSSIA EXITS THE WAR.

That was it. Lenin was in power now and had fulfilled his promise to end the war for Russia. But as Dimitri read the article, he saw that Lenin had also taken control of all private property. His parents' small farm would now belong to the state. Lenin also controlled Russia's newspapers and had begun to imprison anyone who publicly disagreed with him.

Such was the freedom the Reds had wanted.

"Pardon?"

A woman tapped Dimitri's shoulder as he was restocking a shelf with new supplies. Rations were strict and there was never enough of what people needed for their families, so he was often asked for help.

"Yes?" Dimitri turned and saw a kind-looking woman who somehow seemed familiar, though he was certain he had never seen her before. Maybe it was her eyes, a combination of hope mixed with tragedy. Dimitri had seen someone else with that same expression before.

She smiled. "Your accent . . . is that Russian? Were you in the war?"

Dimitri nodded. "But I'm here now, and I hope to remain in France."

"France is still being torn apart by war," she said. "If you have loved ones with you here, I hope you will all move on *together.*"

Something in the way she said that final word sparked another memory in his mind. But before Dimitri could ask, she continued, "You make me think of someone I lost nearly two years ago, my daughter. She's the reason why I came over to speak to you. She had a knitted red hat very much like the one you are wearing."

Dimitri's heart pounded. "Do you mean Juliette?"

The woman began to visibly tremble, and her eyes filled with tears. "How do you know that name?"

Dimitri pulled off the hat and held it out to her. "A year ago, she saved my life. She gave me this to help me stay warm while on the front."

"My Juliette is alive?" The woman grabbed his arm, clinging to it as if she didn't dare to let him go. "Do you know where she is? I've looked everywhere, been to every place I could find that accepted refugees."

"She's looked for you too." Dimitri was so excited, his words spilled over each other. "I know where she was a year ago, but I don't know if she is still there."

"Will you take me to her?"

Dimitri set down the cans of food he'd been holding, then broke free of the woman long enough to speak to the market owner. Seconds later, he was escorting the woman outside. "We're some distance from her," he said. "It will take most of the day to walk there."

"No, no." Juliette's mother took his hand and began pulling him along with her. "I have a wagon and traded everything else for a horse, to make it easier to search for my daughter. We can go now."

She led Dimitri to the wagon, where two boys sat in the driver's seat, waiting. "Claude, Marcel!" she called. "Hurry to the back. We must leave at once!"

The boys obeyed, though the older one remained standing at first, clearly suspicious of Dimitri.

"You should take the reins," the woman said, placing them in his hands. "Please, just go as fast as you can."

Dimitri immediately began driving them away while Juliette's mother turned to explain to Claude and Marcel who he was and where they were going. The younger one—Marcel—was staring at him as if he didn't entirely understand this new change. The older one—Claude—kept a careful watch on Dimitri until he saw the knitted red hat in his mother's hands. Then he tapped on Dimitri's back. "Can you go faster?"

Dimitri shook the reins again and prayed that Juliette would still be in the caves. He had offered their family hope. It would devastate them if this was all for nothing.

Little was said on their journey. Everyone in the wagon had questions about Juliette, but Dimitri hadn't stayed with her long enough to know many answers, and it had been so long ago now. Whatever was true a year ago might not be true now.

Juliette's mother did explain that for most of the past twenty months, they had stayed in a cave of their own, though she had ventured out whenever possible in hopes of finding Juliette.

Several hours later, as they approached Verdun, Dimitri's gut began churning. The area had changed a great deal from the last time he was here. French soldiers were posted at stations for as far as he could see and the cave and trenches where Juliette had scavenged for supplies were surrounded by barbed wire fencing.

Juliette's mother started to climb down from the wagon, but a soldier instructed her to return to her seat.

"No, I must go in there," she protested.

"I am very sorry," he replied, "but this area is too danger-ous to allow anyone to pass. This is a Red Zone now."

"What does that mean?"

"It means that the ground is littered with unexploded land mines, with the remnants of poison gas and shells. No civilians are allowed to come any farther."

"But my daughter is in there!"

Dimitri pointed past the trenches to a cave opening. "She lived in a cave over there."

"How long ago?"

"Almost a year."

"That's about when we took Verdun back from the Germans. This region is ours again. If someone was living in a cave, she would have been forced to leave months ago."

"Where would she have gone?" Juliette's mother asked.

The soldier only said, "I recommend looking in the Red Cross camps."

She sat back, defeated. "Oh yes, of course. Thank you."

Dimitri shook the reins to drive on but barely had the cour-age to look over at her. When he did, she wasn't crying. He was sure she had heard these same words far too often before, but the hollowness in her eyes was almost worse than tears. The only other time Dimitri had seen that same hollow expression, it had been in Juliette's eyes when she told him she was giving up the search. She had planned to move on in the springtime, once the weather warmed.

Whether Juliette was forced out by the soldiers, or chose to leave on her own, she was still gone.

It would be impossible to find her now.

Or would it? Dimitri had an idea. He wasn't ready to give up yet.

FORTY-TWO

December 13, 1917

Ten minutes into their ride away from Verdun, a train whistle sounded in the distance. It was faint, but it seemed to be coming closer.

Juliette had spoken endlessly of the Red Cross trains. Civilian trains weren't running in this region because of the war. It could be a military train or a supply train, but . . . he knew of a Red Cross train that came to this area often. Juliette had a British friend on the trains. If they found her, maybe she would know where Juliette was.

Dimitri shook the reins and turned the horse in a more direct route to the train station. He knew this was a risk, that if this failed too, it would add even greater heartbreak to the family. And it likely would fail. There were too many ifs with his plan.

But they had to try.

"Where are we going?" Claude asked.

"There's a train stop just ahead," Dimitri said.

"Only ambulance trains come this far now," Juliette's mother said. "If you want passage on a civilian train, you will need to get to Paris."

"Ah yes, that is good advice." Dimitri continued to drive that way, his hopes rising. He saw the train in the distance with the same red cross on it that Juliette had once described. Of course, there had to be several different trains that operated in France, but he guessed each one had its own route. He hoped this was still the route that Kara's train took.

The train had already come to a stop when they arrived, and orderlies were loading injured soldiers on board. Dimitri practically leapt off the wagon, then ran toward the orderly. In his excitement, he sputtered out the first few words of what he wanted in Russian, then switched to French, but the orderly merely stared back at him, confused.

"We're with the American Red Cross," he said.

Dimitri stared at the man. Was that English? If it was, he didn't understand a word of it.

"*Je cherche*—" he began. The man was in France, surely he knew some French!

But it obviously didn't matter. If this was an American train, then Juliette wouldn't be here. She would be on a British train with Kara, and that was only if Kara was still on the trains herself.

It had been too long now. This had been a foolish idea, and one glance back at Juliette's mother told him that she understood why they were here, and her heart had broken yet again.

The man turned and called back to someone inside the train. Again, Dimitri couldn't understand the meaning, but he did recognize the word *French*. Maybe the orderly was asking if anyone inside spoke French.

But that was pointless. He already knew it was the wrong train. He turned to leave when a girl behind him said, "Dimitri?"

Dimitri turned and saw Juliette leaning out the door from the train car. The same bag she always carried was slung over one shoulder. "What are you doing here? Is everything all right?"

He smiled back at her. "Yes, it is." Then he stepped aside so she could see the wagon behind him.

Juliette saw the wagon and began to turn away, then stopped as if time had frozen for her. She squinted and her eyes began to fill with tears. She shook her head. "Dimitri, is that . . ." But her voice trailed off.

Dimitri knew the exact moment she recognized her mother. Juliette's eyes, always with that hint of pain and loneliness, now lit up with a joy beyond anything he had ever seen. "Maman?" she cried. "Maman!"

Juliette's mother let out a similar cry and leapt from the wagon, then they ran toward each other, folding together in a tight embrace. Both were nearly sobbing and each one spoke so fast that Dimitri could no longer keep up with their conversation.

Finally, Dimitri understood one question only, when Juliette asked, "How did you find me?"

Her mother pointed to him. "Your red hat."

"My hat? Oh, and I have this!" Juliette dug into her bag and pulled out a blanket for her younger brother.

Marcel's eyes widened as he reached for it. "Finally, I will be able to sleep!"

Dimitri stood back and watched them embrace again, now joined by her two brothers. For the first time in over a year, he realized he was smiling. Truly smiling.

Overhead, he heard the coo of a pigeon traveling high above them and vaguely wondered if it was one of Elsa's pigeons. If it was carrying a message back to her, then he hoped he could add to it his gratitude for getting him released from that camp.

Dimitri's eyes traveled lower to a brilliant sunset. The warm colors lit up the sky in oranges and reds—this time not the colors of war, but the colors of peace and comfort. The first star of the night was already visible, and it took on the same red tone, so beautiful now.

He reached into his pocket and slid his thumb along Igor's red star. He was finally free. Free from control, free from the war, free from the dreams that had haunted him for so long.

"Thank you," Juliette said, then widened her arms to bring him into their circle.

And Dimitri accepted. If he could not have his own family here, then this was the best ending he ever could have hoped for.

1918

ELSA

GERMANY

With a view to avoiding further bloodshed, the German Government requests the immediate conclusion of an armistice on land and on water and in the air.

—German Prince Maximilian (October 4, 1918)

FORTY-THREE

April 22, 1918

Elsa sighed, staring at the long lines of people still waiting for their daily ration of food. She knew the public kitchens were necessary—thousands of Germans would starve without them—but it was discouraging work.

"Turnip soup *again*?" one woman scowled as she received her cup from Elsa. "That was supposed to have ended last winter, and then again this year. When will we get something other than animal feed to eat?"

When the Allies lift the food blockade, Elsa thought. If they planned to win the war through starving the people of Germany, it seemed to be working.

Listening to the endless complaints might've made for a miserable day of volunteer work, but not today. Papa was here, escorting other German officers through the kitchen. His hope had been to prove that civilians were still in good spirits and supporting the war, but it was in vain. All they saw were people who were tired of war and rations and propaganda. They were especially tired of turnip soup, and Elsa hardly blamed them for that. She disliked it too.

After the other officers had left, Papa signaled that he would wait until she was finished with her service, then they could walk home together. Elsa was glad for that. Her father was leaving again tomorrow on another assignment. Until then, she wanted as much time with him as possible.

Coming up in line was a husband and wife, each with cups ready to receive their soup. "Isn't that Major Dressler in the back of the room?" the woman was saying to her husband. "He's probably here looking for army deserters, waiting to drag them to that prison camp he runs."

Elsa quietly rolled her eyes but said nothing. Russia and Germany had signed a treaty a few weeks ago and all Russian prisoners were released. The camp her father ran was closed now. Besides, he wasn't here to arrest anyone.

"If I wouldn't be arrested myself, I'd tell Dressler what I think of him and everyone else who's been running this war," the man said. "He promised Germany glory and victory. Instead, what did we get? Widows unable to support themselves, mothers to mourn their sons. Our economy is in ruins, our pride is broken, and"—he held out his cup to Elsa—"and they are slowly starving us to death on turnip soup."

Elsa only stared back at him, then flatly stated, "Major Dressler is not responsible for all of that."

"No, but he is part of it," the woman said. "Does he still

have a home after that last round of bombings? Because we don't. Does he still have a family after the last burial of soldiers?" Her eyes welled with tears. "Because we don't."

Elsa pressed her lips together. "I'm most sorry for your loss," she said, filling the woman's cup with soup. "But that is not Major Dressler's fault."

"Of course she'd say that," a woman next in line sneered. "Don't you know? You're speaking to his daughter!"

In a single motion, the wife Elsa had just served reared back her cup and threw the soup directly on Elsa. Elsa stood back and gasped as her father ran forward.

"Who did this?" he demanded, looking around.

Elsa looked too, but the couple was gone. She grabbed a nearby towel and began mopping herself. "It's all right," she said. "They were upset."

Papa held out a hand to her. "Let's go home." He walked her away from the kitchen in silence, but when they were alone, he said, "Was that about me?"

Elsa shrugged. "How did you know?"

"Every eye in the room was glaring my way." He tried to smile, but his sadness showed through. "Every eye but yours. I wish I did not have to leave tomorrow."

"Then don't leave, Papa. How many times have you said you were tired of the war, that you wish it was over?"

"I did say that, and I do wish that, but I have some unfinished business in Lille."

Elsa's heart skipped a beat. "You're going back to Lille?"

Early in the war, her father had been one of the officers to take possession of that region in northern France. It had been under German control ever since, but it was still in enemy territory.

"I asked to go. In many ways, that entire area has become another prison camp, this one for innocent civilians, most of them women and children. Conditions there are not good."

"What is your unfinished business?"

Papa looked around them before answering, then lowered his voice to speak. "Do you remember that French girl I helped a little over a year ago?"

"Juliette Caron?" Elsa said. "Yes, you told me about her and her family."

"But there is something of her story you do not know. On the morning that I took her away from the battlefield, she said something that still bothers me to this day."

"What did she say?"

Papa wrapped an arm around Elsa's shoulders. "I told her that I had promised to come home to you. She said her father had given her the same promise, only I was the one who prevented him from keeping his promise." He shrugged. "She was right."

"You were only following orders, Papa."

"The orders were wrong. I should have challenged them. Instead, I gave orders of my own, and some of them were just as wrong. After speaking with Juliette that day, I decided that I would do my best for Germany, but I would no longer do anything I knew to be wrong."

Elsa glanced down. Even if her father wasn't saying the

words, she knew how serious this was. He had probably broken a great number of rules in the past two years, and likely would break even more after he returned to Lille.

"What if someone reports you?" Elsa whispered. "What if they find out?"

"Then I will accept my fate." Papa stopped walking and turned to her. "When this war began, all I could see was glory and victory for the German Empire. Now, I see the price that millions of innocent people have paid for those foolish ambitions. The Allies have committed their crimes too, but what does it matter? The point is that I cannot be part of it anymore. Elsa, I love Germany, I always will. But I must return to Lille and make some things right again."

Elsa had seen her father's ideas change during the war. Maybe hers had too. She took his hand and they began walking again. "Will you take Wilhelm, my pigeon, with you? If anything happens, you can send him back to me."

"I will take the pigeon if it makes you feel better, though I fear for you more than for myself."

"We'll be fine. We always are."

"But things are not as they always were, not anymore. The people only want peace. They don't care whether it's a peace in victory or a peace in defeat."

"The newspapers say Germany is still winning." Elsa glanced up at her father. "They say we are gaining ground in this latest offensive, and that the Allies have no defense against our storm troopers."

Papa sighed. "The newspapers are not telling the complete

story. Yes, we are gaining ground, but at a terrible price—over two hundred thousand soldiers in only a few weeks. Even if we win this battle, it will not change the outcome of this war."

They continued to walk on in silence until Papa spoke again. "I don't want you to return to the soup kitchen."

"People are hungry, Papa."

"Yes, but—"

Papa stopped speaking as they rounded the corner and saw a large crowd ahead. A man in a long black coat was on a platform and in his hand was a newspaper that he lifted high in the air. "The worst has happened!" he shouted. "The Red Baron is dead!"

Elsa stopped in her tracks. The Red Baron was the most famous fighter pilot in all the world, and the best of them. He had downed at least eighty planes, more than anyone else in the war, and was feared by Allied pilots everywhere.

He couldn't be dead.

Elsa stepped closer, and there at the top of the newspaper, the headline was printed in big, bold letters. Even then, it was impossible to believe. He represented all that was great about Germany, their strength and power and confidence.

The man continued, "Germany has lost this war. It is time that we admit it. We must demand the Kaiser abandon the throne. We will form a new government, a better government."

Papa pulled Elsa along with him. "We should not be here."

But they were almost immediately stopped by a young man with scars on one side of his face who thrust a paper at them. "You're Major Dressler, is that right? We need a man like you on our side. It is time for new leadership in Germany. Don't you agree?"

"I know what kind of leadership you want," Papa said, pushing the paper back at him. "We'll have no part in it. Come, Elsa."

He led her away from the crowd, but Elsa glanced back. "What do they want?"

"A pure empire," he said. "They want a Germany of pure-blood Germans only."

"So Felix's family . . ."

"Would not be welcome here." Farther on, Papa continued, "From now on, I'd like you and your mother to stay home as much as possible. Work on the garden. Then, if this war continues into yet another winter, you will both have the food you need."

"Will it last that long?"

"I hope not, but life will not get easier after peace is declared." Papa glanced back to where the crowd had been. "When people are poor and hungry enough, they will give away freedom to anyone who promises to save them from their problems. If Germany loses the war, our hunger and poverty will only get worse." He sighed. "I want you and your mother to be prepared to leave Germany, if it becomes necessary."

"Leave Germany? No, Papa!" Elsa stared over at her father. "This is our home."

"It is a home we may not recognize over the next few years. Indeed, after some of what I have seen on the battlefields, I am not certain it is a home I wish to claim now."

"We're no worse than what any other country does."

"But we were the first to do it. Germany is about to go through some terrible times. Try to stay away from any trouble you see."

Elsa nodded, but avoiding trouble here seemed to be like asking her to stand out in the rain and not get wet.

She thought back to the houses of cards she had built for Felix so many years ago. Then to a few months ago when that Russian boy—Dimitri—had used the same image to predict Germany's collapse. The winds had turned against Germany now.

All that remained was to wonder how long until the last card fell.

FORTY-FOUR

June 12, 1918

Somehow, Elsa had managed to find three eggs at the market, which was amazing enough, but she had also found them at a reasonable price, which was nearly unheard of. Before leaving the shop, she tucked them at the bottom of her pail, covering them with a sweater, determined not to let anyone around her know.

People were generally polite. Hungry people, however, could not be trusted.

And everyone was hungry.

Mama and Elsa did have one thing to look forward to. Their garden patch had been planted weeks ago and the young plants were finally beginning to shoot up through the soil. Within two or three months, they would have all the food they needed for the winter ahead. Elsa hardly could wait, though for now, at least she had the three eggs.

She had barely stepped outside when a familiar face across

the square caught her eye. He was in a dark suit with a hat pulled low, but it was his square jawline that caught her attention. She squinted, certain that couldn't be right, but yes, it was he. Once he turned enough that she could see his eye patch, her suspicions were confirmed.

That was Captain Garinov, the Russian prisoner who had escaped from her home last fall! After searching everywhere in Freiburg, they had decided he must have returned to Russia. What was he doing here still?

Elsa backed against the wall, turning her back to him, wondering what she should do next. He hadn't seen her, so that gave her some advantage. And it was one she probably needed. If he was still here in Freiburg, then that was for a reason.

Only one possibility came to her mind: He was here for revenge on her father.

What else could it be? Russia had ended its role in the war, so there were no longer any Russians in the prison camps, no one he might want to free. And he had seemed insistent on returning to Russia as soon as possible, to help Lenin win power there.

But he must've thought her father would still be here.

Garinov walked on through the streets, occasionally stopping in front of a window to look at the displays. Cautiously, Elsa followed, irritated by the wood soles of her shoes, which made a clacking sound everywhere she stepped. Hoping he wouldn't notice, she kept herself at a distance and put her head down, but she had to know more about what he was doing here.

Hadn't Papa warned her of this? She thought back to before he'd left, asking her to promise to avoid trouble.

"Sorry, Papa," she mumbled beneath her breath. He would forgive her, if he understood that she was doing this to protect him, to protect Mama and their home. Because Garinov knew exactly where they lived.

When the shops thinned out to houses, Garinov turned on the next street. Elsa took a deep breath. Fewer people were here. She'd have to be even more careful now. At least he was facing forward, so he wouldn't know that she was there.

He made another turn, and this time the street was even quieter. The only other people in the area were a couple walking ahead of Garinov. But at the next corner, they went to the right.

And instantly Garinov turned around to face Elsa.

His good eye locked onto hers. He had known all along that she was there, that she was following him.

Elsa was so startled, she started to back up, then tripped over her own feet and fell onto the cobblestone road.

Garinov glared down at her. "Why are you following me?"

"You escaped from my home. You stole our horse and we need it back!"

He came closer. "Is that all you remember of me? Nothing from four years ago?"

Four years ago? When would she have met a Russian—

Four years ago, when Elsa helped to rescue Felix. She had cut the chain on his wrist and it flipped up and hit a Russian in the eye.

Garinov's eye patch.

It had been dark that night, and Felix never said Garinov's name afterward.

He said, "I recognized you the first time your father brought me from the prison camp to work at your home. You never knew me, but you do now."

Garinov took another step toward her and Elsa twisted around, rose to her feet, and ran. She continued running until she was most of the way home, cursing herself for having followed Garinov. What a mistake that was! But only when she slowed down did she realize that she had made a second mistake.

She had left behind her pail with the eggs inside, and her sweater. That news was almost as awful as seeing Garinov again, but she didn't dare go back.

"What took you so long at the market?" Mama asked when Elsa finally returned home. She was at the stove stirring a pot of what would likely be another meal of thin cabbage soup. "And where's your sweater?"

Elsa finally released the tears she had been holding in the entire way home, then rushed at her mother, wrapping her arms around her waist. "I think we're in danger here!"

Mama set down her spoon, then walked Elsa over to the kitchen table. "Tell me everything."

Mama listened carefully as Elsa explained what had happened and was silent for a long minute afterward. Finally, Mama said, "I will send a letter to your father and ask him what he wants us to do. Until we hear back from him, we must carry on with our lives. There is too much work to be done for us to hide in fear."

Elsa nodded. Mama was a strong woman and she loved that. Until they heard back from Papa, she would have to be strong too.

If she could.

CHAPTER
FORTY-FIVE

August 15, 1918

Two months had passed without any sign of Garinov still being in Freiburg, and Elsa was finally beginning to relax. It wasn't an easy summer, of course, not when every day's news was worse than the day before. With each report, the people became angrier as they waited in lines that were longer to receive a ration of food that was smaller. To preserve coal, the electricity was turned off for an hour at first, then an evening at a time, then an entire day. The public baths were closed, forcing the poor to bathe in the rivers, or not at all. But Elsa also learned to catch fish and once or twice, she and her mother gathered wild mushrooms from the nearby woods. The harvest from their small garden was nearly ready. Perhaps within only a few days, they could finally enjoy it.

Elsa came inside after a morning of weeding to find Mama in the front room holding two envelopes. "I have happy news. These letters just arrived!"

Elsa smiled and hurried closer. "From whom?"

"One is from your father, and the other is from your friend Felix."

"Felix?" They hadn't heard from him in ages, not a word since he had gone off to war himself. However, the first letter they read had to be Papa's, so she reached for that one. He wrote,

> My dearest family,
>   I just received your letter about seeing Captain Garinov in Freiburg. I have sent orders to soldiers stationed in the area to search for him, but be careful. I am still in Lille and have begun making arrangements to send the city leaders home. I will send more details when I can, but in the meantime, be safe. I hear conditions in Germany are not good.

Elsa read over the letter a second time. "I wonder if soldiers would protect our home too. Many of them are angry with Papa."

Mama gave a slight cough. "They would if they were ordered to. Open the second letter."

Elsa did, and began to read aloud:

> Dear Elsa,
>   I am coming to Berlin soon to receive a medal. If I can, I will drive to Freiburg afterward and pay a visit to you and your mother. Or perhaps your family would consider visiting my family in

Vienna after the war ends. There is very little
food here now, but I understand it is not much
better in Germany.
Sincerely,
Felix

Eagerly, Elsa looked over at her mother but instantly knew she would not like the answer. Mama said, "With what little we have, we would be poor hosts if Felix did come to visit."

Trying to hide her disappointment, Elsa replaced the letter in its envelope. "We would find something to feed him. I used to consider him a friend."

"He is still your—" Mama stopped for a longer coughing spell.

Elsa's brows pressed low. Something was wrong. "Are you ill? I've heard you coughing a lot today."

"It's nothing, just a cold. I only meant to say that if you wish to reply, we could trade a carrot from the garden for a stamp."

Elsa shook her head. "No, I believe these days, the carrot is more important!"

They both laughed, which ended in Mama's coughing once again. This time, Elsa took Papa's letter from her. "Why don't you go lie down for a while? I'll bring you some tea."

Mama nodded and looked almost relieved to be able to rest. She went into her room while Elsa warmed some water in the kettle. When it was ready, she walked the tea into her mother's room, only to find her already asleep.

Elsa checked on her mother frequently throughout the rest of the day, though each time she did, Mama seemed to be a little worse. More coughing, paler skin, and by nightfall, what had begun as a mild fever was now heat Elsa could feel even before she touched her mother's forehead.

Elsa sat beside her bed and dipped a cloth in some cool water, then pressed it to her mother's forehead. It wasn't much, but she didn't know what else to do. When Mama awoke, Elsa pleaded, "Let me call a doctor."

Mama shook her head. "It's just a cold."

But it wasn't just that. "I heard some women in the market talk about it. They called it the Spanish flu, and it's spreading all over Germany, maybe beyond. This is a serious illness, Mama."

"I only need to rest. Could you bring me that tea now?"

Elsa hurried back to the kitchen to rewarm some water and returned with a teacup and the day's newspaper. "Perhaps I can read to you while you finish the tea."

"I'd like that," Mama mumbled.

Elsa scanned the headlines. One in particular caught her eye. "Mama, the Russian Tsar was assassinated. He and his whole family are dead! Did you know that?"

With her eyes closed again, Mama said, "It happened about a month ago, a terrible tragedy. Didn't you tell me of a Russian boy you once met? Did he return to Russia after his release?"

"Dimitri? No, I think he wanted to stay in France."

"You must hope that's what he did. It has become very dangerous in Russia."

Elsa wondered if Dimitri had heard that news, and what he thought about it. She wondered about Dimitri often, actually. Papa had given him the name of an old friend near Verdun where he might get a job at a market. The war was as fierce as ever in France, so it was hardly less dangerous than Russia, but this war was ending. According to the newspaper, the fighting was only getting worse in Russia.

Mama touched Elsa's hand. "I am tired now, Elsa. Let me sleep."

Elsa pulled the blankets up around her mother, then left the room. If Mama was to have any hope of recovering from this sickness, she would need more food. Elsa knew that she wasn't supposed to harvest anything from the garden early, but she decided to pull a potato or two and an onion and some carrots. Just enough for a little stew.

She grabbed a basket and went outside, but within only a few steps, her heart slammed against her chest.

Everything in the garden was gone. All of it.

FORTY-SIX

August 16, 1918

Mama seemed a little better the next day, though she still had a fever and she slept most of the time. When she did wake up, it was only long enough to say, "Elsa, I think it would be best if you brought in the food from the garden. I fear that something may happen to it."

Tears filled Elsa's eyes, but she blinked them away. She knew that she should tell her mother the truth, but how could she give her such awful news when she was still so sick?

Mama continued, "Perhaps you could use a little of what you bring in for a stew for us."

"Yes, of course." That was all Elsa could say, and she left Mama's room with no idea what to do next.

At one time, their cupboards had been full and life was simple and exciting. Those days had ended now, for Elsa, perhaps for all of Germany. Months ago, Papa had suggested that they leave Germany. Back then, Elsa would never have thought about leaving, but now . . . she was thinking about it a lot.

Yet those thoughts always ended in the same place: Where could a German possibly go these days and be welcomed?

Their situation was desperate. Everyone in Germany was desperate, of course, but for tonight, the only person Elsa cared about was her mother. To have any chance of getting well again, she needed something more to eat.

Which was why late that night, she found herself sneaking out of the house with one of her mother's pearl necklaces, hoping to trade for some black-market food. At one time, it was easy to purchase food from farmers who came in from the countryside. It was expensive, but a person could usually get what they wanted. Then the government began taking produce from the farms, just to have some way of feeding the people. In protest, the farmers stopped growing it. She had no idea whether she'd be able to find food or not.

Elsa walked to the alleys where the black marketeers used to sell, but no one was there, not on any corner. Sadly, she started back home, with no idea of what she would say to her mother. But her thoughts were disrupted by the sound of shattering glass. Elsa ran toward the sound and saw a group of rioters in front of a Jewish market, fighting one another to see who would get inside first.

"Shame on you!" Elsa bent down to pick up a rock, then raised it in her hand and shouted, "You will all stop this at once!"

Heads turned toward her, most of them with expressions that sent a chill down her spine. "What is it to you?" one man snarled.

"I know her," another man said. "She's the daughter of Major Dressler."

Elsa knew she should have been afraid, and she was, but the anger welling in her was taking over. She'd had enough of this. Enough of the accusations, enough of the blame and violence and greed. "Yes, I am his daughter," she shouted. "And if you don't all leave at once, I will make sure my father knows who robbed this store. Go home and be with your families. There is no food in any of the stores, this one included. Harming this family will do nothing for you." Elsa slowly lowered the rock. "Please, everyone, go home."

Most of the group began to leave, but a few had already been inside the store. They walked out and announced, "Dressler's daughter is correct. There's nothing here."

One rioter pushed past her, saying, "At least the food from your garden tasted good. Tell your father thank you for us."

Elsa closed her eyes as the anger burned even hotter, but she did not react. She could not react because she was alone here and she had already pushed this crowd far enough.

When the last of the rioters was gone, a man with a long beard and in a dark suit covered by a white apron stepped out from the alley beside the market. He must have been hiding there. "Thank you for what you did."

Elsa stared at him a moment. "I only . . . is that your shop?"

He nodded and glanced down the street in the direction the rioters had gone. "It is beginning to feel like the old times again. This is not the last of troubles for the Jews here in Germany."

Elsa nodded sadly. Sad, because she knew far too little of what it meant to speak of the old times. And because he clearly knew too much of such trouble.

"I'm most sorry this happened," she said.

"You tried to help us," he replied. "You have nothing to apologize for. If I had any way to thank you, I would."

"You owe me nothing," Elsa replied. And while that was true, the more selfish part of her had hoped for some reward, a single cracker even. Truly she had never known that hunger like this was possible.

"You should hurry back home now and stay there if you can," he said. "A flu is spreading in Germany, perhaps through all of Europe. They are calling it the Spanish flu." He paused a moment, then added, "I wonder if Spain hates being blamed for this illness, just as we Jews are blamed for people's hunger."

Elsa smiled, just a little, then started toward home. What a failure tonight had been, and a disappointment, and a lot of risk with no reward. At least that family's market had been saved. Perhaps one day, they would have food again. Until then, she had no—

"Please wait!"

Elsa turned to see the man she had just spoken to running after her with a small sack in his hands, which he held out to her.

Elsa didn't understand. "What is this?"

"We did have a little food left at the market, better hidden than a mob would ever find. My wife insisted that we share some of it with you."

Elsa wanted to refuse the offer. That wasn't the reason she had defended the market, and she knew there were others who needed this food just as much. But she was so hungry, so tired of every day being a war of its own just to find something to eat. The weaker part of her finally gave in and with a polite nod of her head, she thanked the man, then accepted the bag, which she pulled close to her chest as she walked the rest of the way home.

Only when she was safely inside did she dare to open the bag. Inside were four eggs, half a loaf of bread, a tin of crackers, and even an apple! Elsa opened the tin and ate two crackers right away, then wiped tears from her eyes.

What she had done for that family was nothing compared to what they had just given her. Mama's sickness still worried her, as did Papa's work for the war. But she now had two pieces of wonderful news. First was that they had a little food again. And second, that at least two people in Freiburg did not consider her family an enemy.

At last, she felt a little hope.

FORTY-SEVEN

November 10, 1918

Even rationed out, the food had been gone within a week, but by the end of that same week, Elsa's mother seemed more like herself again, and they had returned to their usual routine. Elsa fished. She searched the markets for food.

But they never spoke about what had been stolen. The only time Elsa mentioned the garden, Mama's reply was "They must have been very hungry to do such a thing." After a slight pause, she had added, "They should not have taken the food, but if they had asked, we would have told them yes."

Elsa didn't answer. She was fairly certain that if they had asked her, she would have chased them off with a stick. Mama was a good woman, and maybe one day Elsa would be the same. But not right now. Life was too difficult for her to care about being good.

It only worsened as late summer turned to autumn. Another wave of the flu returned, this one far worse than what

Elsa's mother had faced, with dozens of deaths announced each week. Every day, the streets buzzed with rumors that Germany would soon surrender. Protestors marched through Freiburg, shouting out the daily numbers of dead and wounded soldiers, all from battles Germany had no hope of winning. The newspapers began calling for a new government, demanding a replacement for the Kaiser. And since he was a major in the military, Elsa's father was inevitably connected to the unpopular war.

Which was why the growing anger turned toward Elsa and her mother whenever they were in public.

"Your father betrayed us!" some would shout.

"Our boys will never come home!" others would scream. "Your father should not come home either!"

"Do not respond," Elsa's mother said. "That will only make it worse."

At first, Elsa had wondered how it could possibly get worse, but those questions were soon answered.

Even when food was available in the market, the grocers would refuse to sell to them. Mama even tried to sell her jewelry or silverware or her fur coat, but nobody wanted to buy those either. They only replied that the Kaiser, and all those associated with him, must resign, then walked away.

Mama came home one afternoon with the same valuables she had left with that morning. "We can't offer to trade anymore," she said. "I fear that we are advertising to the public what they can steal from us."

Elsa agreed. If they had stolen the food from their garden, it wasn't impossible to believe they would steal from their home, if they had the chance for it.

Mama reached into her pocket and pulled out an envelope. "The news is not all bad. I do have this. It's from your father."

Elsa's hands trembled as she waited for Mama to open the letter. Mama glanced over it, her brows knitting tighter together with every line, then she passed it to Elsa to read.

My dearest wife and daughter,

Germany will ask for peace any day now. There is some concern that the Allies' terms for peace will be harsh, worse than anything we have endured in this war. But we have no choice. Our weapon supplies are depleted, and we have lost the confidence of our soldiers. Some of them are refusing to fight. They want to see a new Germany rise from the ashes we have made of it.

For these reasons, the time has come to leave Germany. I have sent a telegram to Felix's family, asking if we might stay with them until we find a new home. I hope to be released from my duties soon, and then I will join you in Vienna.

I am sending you what little money I have saved. I wish it was more, but Germany has not paid its soldiers for some time.

All my love,
Papa

On the back of Papa's letter was scrawled one final note:

Perhaps on my way home, I will stop and say hello to Dimitri in Belleray, if he is still there. I will tell him hello from you too, Elsa.

Elsa felt herself blushing. "I barely met him," she said. "But he did seem most nice."

Mama hummed, but her attention was on the money Papa had sent, and her disappointment was clear. "This isn't enough for a single train ticket. Even with our savings, we don't have enough to go all the way to Vienna."

Elsa looked at the money. "If the war is ending, perhaps everything will calm down again soon." She tried to sound hopeful but didn't even believe her own words. If the people who were fighting for control of Germany did take power, then more trouble was certainly ahead.

Mama sniffed and looked around the home. "I need you to pack up our belongings and prepare to leave. I'll take the wagon and drive out far from Freiburg, until no one knows your father's name. I'll sell everything I can until we have enough money for two train tickets."

"Yes, Mama." Elsa thought of her own possessions, what few items could be brought in a bag or two on the train, and what must be left behind.

"I may be home very late, so do not worry for me," Mama said as she left.

Though of course Elsa would worry very much. How could she not worry when Germany itself seemed to be falling into its own civil war?

She worked for the rest of the day, packing as much as she could into the few bags they would be allowed to carry on board a train. Eventually, the evening grew dark and Mama still wasn't home.

Elsa was about to go to bed when out back she heard a fluttering sound and a familiar coo pass overhead. Wilhelm?

Elsa ran to the back, and there was her pigeon on his roost. He flapped his wings and Elsa noticed a paper tied around his leg.

It had to be a note from Papa, probably following up from the letter they had received earlier.

Yet when she retrieved the note and unfolded it, Elsa immediately became alarmed. In poorly scrawled handwriting that she barely recognized as her father's, the note read:

Injured on return home. Near Belleray. Send help.

Elsa ran back into the house, almost in a panic wondering what she should do. Her father had many friends here in Freiburg, but she had no idea how to reach them this late at night.

Finally, she determined she would have to save him on her own. She wrote a note to leave for her mother, then went into her room for her coat, and while there, she heard the glass in the front room window shatter. The sound was so familiar, reminding Elsa of just a few months ago when rioters were about to rob that Jewish store. Which meant—

Elsa ran into the front room, feeling cold air rushing in through a hole in a window. Shards of glass had scattered across the floor, and in the center of it was a large rock.

From out on the street, someone shouted, "Down with the Kaiser. Down with those who still serve the Kaiser! We demand to speak with Major Dressler!"

Elsa stuffed her father's note into her pocket and ran back into the kitchen for her mother's largest pan. It was all she had to defend her home, but she fully intended to do it.

Elsa hurried outside to see a group of at least fifty people on the grass in front of her house. She raised the pan and tried a similar threat as she had used before. She shouted, "Leave my home now, or the Kaiser himself will hear of this."

But this time, it didn't work.

"As of yesterday, the Kaiser is gone," a man in front of the group said, then tossed a newspaper at her feet. "Your father must answer to us now."

"My father is not here, and even if he were, he has done nothing wrong."

"Tell us where he is," someone else said. "It's him we want, not you."

As if on an invisible signal, the crowd rushed toward her. Elsa tried to run back inside, but one woman grabbed her sweater by the pocket and ripped it. She clutched at Elsa again but stopped at the sound of a rifle firing into the air. Above its echo came the words, "Leave now!"

In a panic, the rioters quickly scattered. One by one, their layers peeled away until only a single person remained at the back of the group. Captain Garinov. Fear squeezed Elsa's heart. The rioters had been frightening, but to see the cold expression in Garinov's eyes filled her with terror. Without a word, he started toward her.

Elsa backed up, then raised her pan.

"Don't you come any closer."

He stopped, then glanced down at the note that had been in Elsa's sweater pocket before it was torn. He picked it up off the ground, unrolled it, then said, "So your father is near Belleray? I know where that is."

Elsa rushed forward but was too late. Garinov dropped the note, then ran to a familiar brown horse down the road, the one he'd stolen from them a year ago!

Elsa started toward the horse. She needed to reach it first, for her father's sake. But she wasn't fast enough. Garinov mounted the horse and sped away. What was she to do now?

Seconds later, she heard the rumbling sound of an engine as a motorbike rounded the corner. Its driver was a soldier in an Austro-Hungarian uniform, staring directly at her. He stopped in the center of the road and removed his goggles.

Something clicked in Elsa's memory. She knew this boy. Was this . . . could it possibly be Felix? He'd grown older, of course, but she remembered those eyes from many years ago. He said, "Elsa? Is that you?"

Elsa ran toward him. "Felix! I need your help!"

"Is it Captain Garinov?"

"Yes, but . . . how did you know?"

"Get on the motorbike. I'll explain."

Elsa immediately dropped the pan, then slid sideways onto the seat behind him. She wrapped her arms around Felix's waist and closed her eyes as he sped them away.

FORTY-EIGHT

November 10, 1918

Elsa directed Felix to ride near the border, away from the main roads. Because of the battles in this area, she hadn't been here in years. The moonlight cast a haunted glow over the land. It should have been thick with trees, but that was all gone, and the air reeked of chemicals and dust.

"I'm glad it's so dark out here," she said, burying her face against Felix's back. "I don't want to see anything more."

"No, you don't," he replied.

"I met a Russian boy last year. He told me that if I wanted to understand Germany's role in the war, I needed to see what we had done to France."

"I never fought in France," Felix said, "but I know what we did to the land in the east, and it's awful."

Elsa looked at him. "And they gave you a medal for that?"

"No, not for that." Felix glanced back at her. "Did I ever tell you about when I saw the Archduke's assassination?"

"No. I only know that you were there."

"I was right behind the assassin when it happened. I saw the weapon in his hand, I knew what he was going to do . . . and I did nothing." Felix was quiet for a moment. "You have no idea how that's haunted me all these years."

Elsa patted his arm. Of course that would bother him.

"About six months ago, one of our generals came to see us in battle. While we were there, our camp was attacked. I saw a Russian sneaking up on him and . . . well, I saved the general's life." Felix briefly paused. "That doesn't make up for what happened to the Archduke, but at least I know I'm not the same boy that I was back then."

"Yes, you are that boy," Elsa said. "You just needed time to grow into your courage."

Felix gave a shy smile, then said, "Anyway, they gave me the medal in Berlin a few days ago. I decided to come to Freiburg, as I told you in my letter. Once I arrived, I began to ask around for the location of your home, and everyone seemed to know it." He glanced back at Elsa. "Your family isn't very popular right now."

"Yes, because of my father—"

"Actually, I heard more about you. There's a story of you defending a Jewish market last summer, probably the way I just saw you defending your home. Then someone told me about a Russian named Captain Garinov who was causing you trouble. I'm sorry, Elsa. That's probably because you saved me back in Lemberg."

Elsa shook her head. "It's because Captain Garinov is angry at the world and blames my father for it."

"Those who have seen war have every right to be angry," Felix said. "But I've also seen what happens when that anger controls a person. I won't let that happen to me."

Had that happened to Captain Garinov? Elsa wondered. *Did anger control him now?*

She said, "I've seen the anger too, during the riots in Freiburg. But then I began listening to the people there. What looked like anger was really hunger and pain, and this feeling of helplessness in the face of a war that is killing their sons and husbands. This war has ruined so many lives, Felix."

Felix nodded, but his attention was fixed on the road ahead. "What's happened here?" he mumbled.

A small guard post was set up at the center of a bridge crossing the river. A candle was lit inside, but there was no guard and the wooden board meant to keep people from charging across the bridge was on the ground and smashed in half.

"This is the border with France." Elsa pointed to hoof-prints in the mud leading away from the bridge. "Garinov must have come this way."

"If there was a fight, then Garinov won," Felix said. "Let's keep going."

"I know a shortcut," Elsa said. "Turn north. We can still get ahead of him!"

Felix turned onto a dirt trail, littered with abandoned shell casings and helmets. They even passed a small cannon half buried in dried mud. In the distance, a fire was burning.

Before the war, Elsa's family had often come to France to

tour the countryside or to shop in Paris. She knew what this area was supposed to look like, how beautiful it was in every direction.

But now the clouds had parted, and in the moonlight, Elsa saw the landscape more clearly. Everything as far as she could see was gray and desolate. Places that she knew had once been lively villages were now just collections of abandoned houses, torn down to their frames, surrounded by uneven mounds of earth, as if the ground had been scooped up from one place and dropped in another.

"This is horrible," she said.

"This is war." Felix continued driving but began to shake his head. "How much farther to Belleray? Maybe we should wait until dawn, then find someone to give us directions."

"It can't be much farther ahead," Elsa said. "Besides, even if we stopped, nobody in France would help a German and an Austrian."

The next hour passed so slowly that Elsa thought she was going to burst with worry. Her father would have sent his note a long time ago, and she had no idea where to begin looking for him. And what if Garinov found him first?

"Belleray!" Felix pointed to a small roadside sign with the name on it and an arrow pointing to the right.

"That's it!" she said to Felix. "Turn here!"

Felix followed the sign into Belleray, a small village of homes and farmland. A winding dirt road took them directly to the town square, though of course at this hour, it was entirely dark.

"You start knocking on doors on one end and I'll start on the other side," Elsa said.

"Knocking on doors for what?"

"We need to find Dimitri. He'll know this area better than anyone."

As agreed, Elsa ran to the nearest door while Felix started on the opposite side of the square. She pounded on the doors and heard him doing the same, but there was no response; no lights came on. Nobody seemed to be here at all.

Finally, she realized her mistake. These were shops where people worked. She had no idea where Dimitri slept at night.

They would have to find Papa on their own. And in this vast area, he could be anywhere.

Elsa sat on the stoop of the building behind her, utterly discouraged, and hung her head in her hands.

That was the very moment when she heard a familiar voice ask, "What do you want?"

DIMITRI

FORTY-NINE

November 11, 1918

I t must have been very early in the morning when Dimitri heard the pounding on the door of the market. He sat up on his cot, thoroughly irritated. Nobody should be awake at this hour, certainly not him.

Yet the pounding continued, and someone on the other side was shouting. Finally, he threw on some clothes and shuffled to the door, ready to send away whoever was there.

Dimitri flung the door open. "What do you want?"

But he had no sooner gotten the words out than he gasped with surprise and immediately tried closing it again. Maybe he'd expected to see a refugee seeking shelter or a parent needing supplies for a sick child. Anything, really, except a young blond Austro-Hungarian soldier who shoved one foot in the doorway, preventing Dimitri from closing the door entirely. As the soldier pressed on the door, he began rattling off phrases in German faster than Dimitri could follow him. He did catch a few words: *Help. Father. Injured.*

Dimitri wasn't about to fall for any tricks. This boy wasn't injured and he appeared to be alone. And he could have no good reason to be in France.

Finally, between other rants in German, the boy paused and simply said, "Dimitri?"

Dimitri tilted his head. How did this boy know his name? Cautiously, he reopened the door. "Who are you?"

"Dimitri?" a new voice said.

He looked past the soldier to a girl running across the square. It was too dark to see her well, but as she came closer, he thought those curls looked familiar. "Elsa?"

Breathlessly, she said, "My father is somewhere near this village, and he's injured. We need your help to find him."

She looked desperate and was clearly frightened. He was sympathetic, he really was. But he couldn't help her. "I'm sorry, but I've had my share of war, and I won't go looking for it now."

"He released you from a prison camp. He got you this job!"

"I know that, and I'm grateful, but your father could be anywhere. This area is dangerous, especially at night. There are unexploded mines, pits in the ground that you will not see in the darkness. And if the people who injured your father are still in the area, they'll treat me like their enemy too."

"I can pay you." Elsa reached into her pocket, but the Austrian standing beside her grabbed her arm and spoke to her in German. Dimitri caught enough of the words to understand that whatever Elsa was about to offer was the only money her family had left.

Then the Austrian reached into his haversack and withdrew a fistful of money, which he held out to Dimitri. In halting French, he said, "My name is Felix Baum. This is everything I've saved since I joined the fight. It's yours, if you help us find her father." He added, "I saw the battles too, Dimitri. Maybe from the other side of the trenches, but I saw the same things you did. This is one last call, asking you to leave the safety of the trench and come over the top with us."

Dimitri stared at the money and for the first time in months, Igor's voice was in his head again, asking, "Didn't you promise not to become angry and bitter?"

Yes, he had.

Dimitri sighed. "Wait here. I'll get a lantern and borrow a bicycle."

By the time he rode into the square, Elsa and Felix were on their motorbike with the motor running. "Where do we start?" Elsa asked.

"Follow me," Dimitri said. "But stay on the roads or where you see tracks. Don't be the first to go anywhere."

They began by riding slowly up the road leading from Belleray, checking every ditch, pausing with the lantern to chase the shadows away. Elsa called out for her father, though Felix reminded her not to be too loud. Nobody in France wanted to hear a German accent these days.

After crossing the bridge, they followed the main road, which Dimitri considered far more dangerous. Anyone could see them here, even from a distance, and the way they were poking around at the ground definitely looked suspicious.

Elsa had taken to whistling. "It's a song my mother used to sing in the evenings," she explained, "Papa will recognize it."

Dimitri quietly rolled his eyes. The tune was even more German than her accent. Yet within two kilometers of searching, someone whistled back.

"Papa!"

Elsa nearly leapt off the motorbike and raced across the road where her father lay reclined against a tree.

"Elsa?" he mumbled. "I thought you would send help. I never meant for you to come."

"I had to come, Papa. What happened?"

By then Dimitri and Felix had reached his side. Dimitri took one look at the blood soaked through the side of his uniform and knew how bad this was. He eyed Felix and subtly shook his head.

"Did the French—" Elsa began.

"No," Major Dressler said. "Other Germans did this . . ." His voice trailed off.

"But why?"

"We can talk later," Dimitri said, running for his bicycle. "I know someone who can help him. She isn't far and I'll hurry back as fast as I can."

"Please hurry!" Elsa said, then turned back to her father. "Hold on, help is coming."

JULIETTE

November 11, 1918

Juliette sat up in her chair. "Did someone just knock on our door?"

Her father arched a brow. "Do you normally get visitors past midnight?"

Was it already so late? Juliette glanced outside and for the first time realized how dark the night had become. Had they really been talking all night? Her poor father had only been home for less than a day and was clearly worn down from his time in prison. He had to be exhausted.

There, the knock came again.

Papa stood and straightened his tie. "It will take some time to return to the routine of everyday life. Is it now customary in France to call on one's neighbor at two in the morning?"

He walked to the door, and Juliette heard Dimitri say, "Is Juliette—oh. You must be Monsieur Caron."

Juliette ran forward. "Dimitri, what are you doing here at

this hour?" He was still staring at her father, so she added, "Papa came home this afternoon, finally! Can you believe it?"

"Welcome home, sir," Dimitri said. "I need—"

But Juliette had more to tell him. "Do you remember me telling you about that German officer who helped me escape from the work camp? Major Dressler—"

"Major Dressler is injured and not far from here," Dimitri said. "He needs help."

Instantly, Papa reached for his coat. "I'll find us a wagon and follow your tracks, but it will take me some time. Juliette, get some blankets and give Major Dressler any help he needs to survive."

Juliette went running, returning a minute later with two blankets under one arm and her knitted hat on her head for the cold night.

Dimitri was waiting for her at the door. "Your father came home? What wonderful news!"

"Major Dressler arranged it." And after hours of speaking with her father, Juliette understood how important it was for them to help the Major now. She climbed on the back of the bicycle behind Dimitri. "How far away is he?"

While Dimitri pedaled, Juliette explained, "Major Dressler supervised the prison where Papa was held, but over time, he became a friend to the prisoners. My father is alive today because of him." For that matter, *she* was alive because of him.

Several minutes later, Dimitri pointed out where the Major was and as they got closer, Juliette saw two unfamiliar faces, a girl and a boy in an Austro-Hungarian uniform. "Dimitri . . ." she said cautiously.

But she got no further before the girl looked down and spoke to Major Dressler in German.

Juliette slid off the bicycle with the blankets still in her hands and addressed the girl first. "Are you Elsa?" Major Dressler had said he had a daughter by that name.

Elsa nodded. "You must be Juliette."

Together, they wrapped one blanket over her father and put another blanket beneath him, but it wasn't enough.

"He's shivering." Juliette pulled the knitted hat from her head and put it on the Major. His eyes were closed and he stirred slightly, but during her time on the trains, she had seen other soldiers in this condition before. He was very near death.

A glint of moonlight brushed across Elsa's tearstained face as she looked down at her father again. "I don't know what to do for him," she said. "What if we're too late?"

Juliette touched her hand, the best comfort she could offer. "There's a Red Cross train nearby. They've been stationed here for a week. My father is coming with a wagon and we'll take him there."

"No, you won't."

This new voice carried the same Russian accent as Dimitri's, but it sounded older and was sharper in tone. Juliette first looked up at Dimitri, who seemed to have turned to stone. He obviously recognized this voice.

Still in his same rigid posture, Dimitri said, "What are you doing here, Captain Garinov? I thought you'd be in Russia, fighting for Lenin."

"I have unfinished business here."

"Our business is also unfinished." Felix walked forward. "I doubt you remember me."

Garinov laughed. "I remember a small, scrawny boy who vowed one day to stop me."

"This is that day." Felix lunged at Garinov and swiped a fist across his jaw, sending him to the ground.

Felix started forward again, but Garinov raised a hand and shouted, "I came looking for Major Dressler. I'm here to help!"

Elsa stood. "How did you know he needed help?"

"I overheard some soldiers in town talking. They heard he released some prisoners from Lille, so they tried to kill him, but he escaped and hid."

Juliette bit her lip. He'd released her father and paid a dear price for it. She said, "Why would you help a German?"

"The day I escaped from his yard, I snuck back to Dressler's home, planning revenge on him and his daughter. Then I heard him say that if I was caught, I should be treated with respect because I was an officer."

Garinov looked over at Felix. "Although I was an officer, I failed to respect you. I'm sorry for that." His eyes traveled to Elsa. "You only did what was necessary to save your friend. I understand that now." He looked at Dimitri. "You did not deserve the trouble I caused for you. I'm sorry for that too."

Dimitri offered a hand to help the Captain stand again. "You said you came to help?"

Garinov nodded. "When I passed through the border, the guard was called away to help search for any Germans still in the area. They could be here soon. I will try to find them and send them in another direction. I hope that will give you enough time to get Major Dressler to a safer place."

Dimitri reached into his pocket and pulled out Igor's red star. "To me, this means both freedom and friendship. I have my freedom now. And I hope for you, it will mean we part as friends."

Garinov accepted the star and stared down at it, mumbling, "The Reds are fair to all." He turned and brought his horse over to Elsa, putting the reins in her hands. "Get your father the help he needs." He gave one last look at the group. "A new world is beginning. May you all be brave enough to face whatever is still to come."

He walked off in one direction, followed only a minute later by the arrival of Juliette's father in the promised wagon. Together, Felix and Dimitri carried Major Dressler into the back of the wagon and Elsa climbed in after him.

Juliette said, "I know the way to the Red Cross train."

"Getting here in that wagon was hard enough on me," Papa said. "I'm not sure I have the strength yet to go much farther. But I can take that extra horse back home for safekeeping."

Dimitri climbed into the driver's seat beside Juliette. "I can get us to the train."

"Then go quickly. Major Dressler is a better man than any of you may know. Save him," said Monsieur Caron.

Dimitri shook the reins and the wagon began to drive away.

"Please hurry," Elsa said. "He's not doing well."

Juliette turned back, then faced forward again, her expression resolved. Major Dressler had saved her life once. It was her turn to save him now.

KARA

FIFTY-ONE

November 11, 1918

K ara had just finished dressing for the early morning shift when her mother ducked into the nurses' quarters. "Kara, you are needed."

Kara's brows pressed low. "Already?" The train had no wounded and they weren't expecting any. What could she possibly be needed for?

Curious, Kara followed her mother into the nearest ward and was surprised to see Juliette in the aisle. "What's wrong?"

"Dimitri is here with me," Juliette said. "And two . . . friends of his. And a German major who is wounded."

"What?" Kara shook her head. "A German officer is here?"

"He'll die if you won't help him."

Kara's mind instantly retreated to that time so many years ago when she had saved Sergeant Baum's life. She had believed then that it was the right thing to do and still believed it, but she had also lost any chance of earning her Red Cross pin because of it.

She licked her lips. "Mum," she began. "I'm sorry if this breaks any rules, but I hope you'll understand. I need to help that officer."

"If you felt any other way, you wouldn't be a true nurse," Mother said. "Of course you must help."

Kara smiled and reached for a medical bag, then exited the train with her mother right behind her. A wagon was stopped near the train. Dimitri and an Austrian boy in uniform stood beside it. A girl with long brown curls in the back of the wagon quietly climbed out to make room for both Kara and her mother.

Kara lifted the blanket and immediately understood how serious the Major's condition was. "I'll do what I can," she told Juliette. "But I don't understand why this German is so important to you."

"He saved my life," Juliette said. "Now please, try to save his."

"I'll ask Captain Stout to prepare for surgery," Mother said.

"He's lost a lot of blood," Kara said. "He'll need a blood transfusion."

"Yes, but . . ." Mother sighed. "Who could we find out here willing to risk their life for a German?"

"I will." Four voices had spoken.

Kara turned and saw that everyone had raised their hand: Juliette and Dimitri and the boy in the Austrian uniform, and the girl who had been sitting beside him when they came.

The boy in uniform stepped forward. "I think you saved my father's life once. I want to help you save this father's life now."

"You must be Felix Baum." With a wide smile, Kara gestured toward the train. "We will save him, together."

ELSA

FIFTY-TWO

November 11, 1918

For the last three hours, Elsa had paced a solid path along the center of the train aisle, her worries becoming deeper and harder to manage with each passing minute. Finally, Felix was escorted through the transom.

"I did my part for your father," he explained. "Now your father must do his and survive."

Elsa was asleep at a table when the transom door opened again and Kara came through. Elsa immediately stood, too afraid to ask.

"It's too early to be sure of anything," Kara said, "but your father did well and is resting comfortably. He asked to see you as soon as possible . . . to see all of you."

"Did he explain how this happened?" Elsa asked.

Kara nodded. "He had just left Juliette's father with his family and was headed back to Germany. He had been followed by a group of German soldiers. They knew he had released your father and a few other prisoners. They wanted to punish your father for it, and go after the prisoners themselves, but your father stopped them, Elsa. He paid a heavy price for it, but he saved their lives."

"I expect that you have saved many lives too." Elsa noticed a Red Cross pin on Kara's collar and was curious about it. "How did someone your age become part of the Red Cross?"

Kara beamed. "An hour earlier, I wasn't. They gave me this pin only a few minutes ago, to recognize my work in helping your father."

Juliette ran over to her with a hug. "Congratulations!" Then she widened her arms to pull Elsa into the hug as well.

When they separated, Elsa stared at the two girls, and at Dimitri and Felix, who were seated behind them. Never in a million years would she have imagined this. She said, "I can't believe you all helped us in the middle of a war."

"What war?" Kara pulled out a pocket watch, then smiled broadly. "We just received word. As of twenty-three minutes ago, we can officially be friends again. The war ended at exactly eleven o'clock."

Juliette smiled. "And today is the eleventh day, of the eleventh month."

"Ending five years of a terrible war," Dimitri added.

"Ending a story that began the day I watched an assassination that would change the world," Felix finished.

"The world has already changed," Dimitri said. "The Russian Empire has fallen. Somehow, I must get my family out of Russia before it's too late."

"There is no more Austria-Hungary either." Felix shrugged. "I suppose I'm only an Austrian now."

Elsa nodded. "The German Empire is finished as well, though I think many people in Germany will disagree. This war has certainly made a mess of our lives, hasn't it?"

"Life is messy," Juliette said. "It's a line that moves in circles, and weaves itself into the circles that others have created. Our lines should be messy because that's how our lives connect together."

Kara smiled again. "I am so glad it connected us. So what now?"

"Some are calling this the war to end all wars," Felix said. "Let us hope that is true."

As Elsa looked around the room, it was clear that everyone agreed with that.

FELIX

FIFTY-THREE

November 11, 1918

A s the afternoon wore on, the five new friends were invited into the ward to see Major Dressler. Felix was the last to exit, and he grabbed Dimitri's arm to hold him back.

Dimitri turned, his suspicious expression cooling once he saw Felix's smile. Felix said, "We need to talk."

Dimitri relaxed, a little. "About what?"

Felix reached into the pocket of his uniform and pulled out a roll of money. "This is for—"

Dimitri backed up. "No, you don't have to—"

"I promised to pay for your help with Major Dressler."

"I didn't help him for the pay."

"But I still promised." Felix held out the money to Dimitri. "I heard what you said about getting your family out of Russia. You have your freedom. Now give them theirs."

Dimitri pressed his lips together as he accepted the money, though he held it in his cupped hands, staring at it. "Thank you."

After a grateful handshake, they crossed the transom and there found Elsa at her father's side with Kara and Juliette nearby.

Major Dressler looked sleepy and weak, but his eyes first fell on Felix. "You risked your life to bring Elsa to find me."

"Yes, sir," Felix said. "But we wouldn't have succeeded without Dimitri's help."

"I'm only here because you released me from the prison camp." Dimitri smiled at Elsa. "After Elsa told you to do it." Then he added, "And without Juliette, I wouldn't be here either."

Juliette pointed to Kara. "When I had no one else in the world to turn to, Kara saved me."

But Kara only shrugged as she looked back at Felix again. "After helping your father, I was so hopeless, I nearly gave up on the Red Cross. But your father gave me his medal, reminding me to have courage. I wonder what ever happened to that medal? I gave it to Juliette."

"And I gave it to Dimitri."

Dimitri tilted his head at Elsa. "And she took it from me."

"But it was never for me." Elsa turned to Felix. "I heard a story about this medal, that your father tried to give it to you before he went to war. You refused it because you wanted to earn your own medal instead."

"And I did earn it." Felix proudly glanced down at his medal hanging from his uniform. "But where is the old one?"

"I have it." Major Dressler pointed toward his uniform, hanging at the side of his bunk. While Elsa began fishing through the pockets, he said, "I've kept it since the day we took it from Dimitri."

"Here it is!" Elsa pulled out the medal, which she placed into her father's hand. "It should be yours, Papa."

Major Dressler lifted the medal only high enough that he could see it. "Medals are given to those who show exceptional courage. But do you know? Most of the people who receive them will claim they are not courageous at all. They will only say they were in a terrible situation and made the best choice they could."

"That's true for me," Felix said. "I never was very brave."

"No, that's my point," Dressler said. "You always did have courage, Felix. You just needed to look inside yourself to find it."

Elsa said, "You taught me to have courage to stand alone and do what is right."

Now her father smiled. "You've always done what you believed was right. When I saw the harm that Germany had caused in this war, I learned from you."

Dressler next looked at Juliette. "I learned from you as well. I can't imagine the strength it took to face this cold world alone. Or for you, Dimitri, to face the heat of battle."

"All I wanted was freedom, sir, and you gave that to me."

"Yet your heart was always free. I wanted that same freedom for my family. That's when I knew we would have to leave Germany, while we still could."

At last, Major Dressler turned to Kara. "I never had the opportunity of meeting you until now, and I am sorry for that. I understand you broke a serious rule in order to save my friend Sergeant Baum. I think you and I may have that one thing in common, for I broke a few rules myself over the past few years, but always when I believed I was doing what's right."

He lifted the medal again. "This medal belongs to every one of you. At some point, each of you found yourself in a terrible situation, and you responded with courage, with honor, and with kindness. Through your great examples, you saved me."

"That is a most beautiful way to end," Elsa said.

The others quickly agreed, but Felix quietly smiled to himself. This was not an ending. Their lives had only now begun.

AUTHOR'S NOTE

*L*ines of Courage was partly inspired by my own interest in learning more about a war I'd never completely understood. Yet the more I learned, the more I wanted to tell this story from a wider perspective. Hence, the five viewpoints in this book.

Part of the difficulty in understanding World War I is that there is no central issue that all countries were fighting for. Some fought for power, others to support an allied country, and others still for revenge, or for national pride, or to gain land they felt should belong to them.

There is also a challenge in that many of the countries that were involved no longer exist, or now exist with different borders. For example, we no longer have an Austro-Hungarian Empire, nor an Ottoman Empire, nor Prussia. Other countries were created or remade as a result of the war, including Hungary, Czechoslovakia, and Yugoslavia, among others.

It is further important to acknowledge that the world itself was rapidly changing during these years. Many countries were experiencing revolutions or uprisings, a 1918 pandemic began spreading throughout much of the world, and there were major inventions or advances in technology, including communications, transportation, and medical science.

Understanding World War I can be difficult, but it is well worth studying. Here are a few insights into some of the facts referenced in the book.

THE ASSASSINATION OF THE ARCHDUKE FRANZ FERDINAND

Imagine this: Your job is to drive one of the most powerful men in the world through a hostile city. He insists on keeping the top down on the car so that he can wave at the people, hoping this will calm tensions.

This decision only makes you more tense, so you are already on high alert when you see the grenade coming for the car. You react in time to save your passenger, but he insists you continue on with the plan.

You would have preferred that he ask for an enclosed car, or for a military escort. You would have suggested that he cancel the rest of his trip and return to the train station. You would have wanted him to do nearly anything but continue on.

And in fact, he does change plans. He wants to visit the hospital, to see those who were injured in that grenade attack. He told his wife about the change, and the mayor, and the officials with him. He told everyone . . . but you.

So when it's discovered that you're on the wrong road, there's no problem. Just a simple turnaround, right?

Except the place you choose to turn around puts you directly in front of one of the assassins, a Serbian man named Gavrilo Princip. He sees his opportunity and takes it, killing the Archduke and his wife before you even realize what's happening.

One month later, World War I will begin. History will record that it started because a driver made a wrong turn on the road.

THE RED CROSS TRAINS

The Red Cross trains were a vital part of a network designed to save lives. When a soldier was injured on the battlefield, stretcher bearers would carry him to the nearest aid post, which could do little more than treat minor injuries. So if he needed more serious care, then the stretcher bearers would rush him through the trench network to a Casualty Clearing Station behind the front lines, often a tent or an unused building. This is where most combat surgery happened. From there, the soldiers would be taken by ambulance (which, frequently, were just wagons with some basic medical equipment) to the hospital trains, which would carry the wounded to base hospitals for recovery.

Red Cross trains could be up to a half mile in length and were nearly complete hospitals in themselves. The nurses and staff who served had to be incredibly brave. Early designs of the trains allowed no way of passing from one train car to another while in motion, so the staff learned to climb outside and crawl along the sides of the trains until they reached the next car to climb back inside—all while the train was traveling as fast as sixty or seventy miles per hour!

TRENCH WARFARE

World War I introduced soldiers to a very different style of fighting. Each side dug long trenches into the ground, and for weeks or even months, soldiers would live there, always ready to fight. They could endure bombardments from within the trenches, but at some point, a commander would have to order his troops out from the trenches to cross what was known as no-man's-land—the area in between both sides' trenches—in hopes of taking the enemy trench. Because the soldiers in no-man's-land were exposed, this would inevitably result in a high number of casualties.

Yet life within the trenches often wasn't much better. Trenches were often muddy and unsanitary, making it a simple thing for soldiers to get what was known as "trench foot," a serious condition resulting from feet being wet for long periods of time, or other bacterial-related diseases. Since they were right on the front lines, soldiers endured the constant bombardment of shells, which made sleep hard to come by. There was no privacy, no comfortable place to sit, and very little room to lie down. Even if a soldier did find a spot, he probably wasn't there for long before his commander called him back to his feet, ready to fight.

However, sometimes the trenches were built outside entrances to caves, and the soldiers could go inside them for a little rest from the war. Some were so large that soldiers added "street signs" to give directions for traveling from one cavern to another!

THE BATTLE OF VERDUN

The Battle of Verdun was the longest battle of World War I and is the longest single continuous battle in all of history, lasting from February 21, 1916, to December 18, 1916. Over those 302 days, there were over 700,000 casualties—an average of more than 2,300 killed or wounded soldiers every single day.

The exchange of weapons, gasses, and human debris from each side was some of the most fierce the world had ever seen, so awful that by the end of the war, about 460 square miles of Verdun was declared a "Red Zone," meaning it could not be safely inhabited by humans. Although vegetation has now returned and a vibrant population surrounds the Red Zone, the cleanup of weapons and poisons from the soil still continues. In fact, it is estimated that at the current rate, it will still take another three hundred years to restore the area to what it was before the war.

Despite its lasting damage to the environment and high death toll, Verdun was not the most severe battle of World War I. That may have been the Battle of the Somme, which lasted from July to November 1916 and resulted in 1.2 million casualties, including 57,000 British casualties on the first day of battle alone.

THE RUSSIAN REVOLUTION

Russia had by far the largest army in World War I, but it was at a greater disadvantage than many other countries. The Tsar was mistrusted and disliked. The Russian generals openly fought with one another. The Russian understanding of German technologies was outdated, so they didn't know that everyone was listening when they communicated top secret strategies over their radios.

But perhaps worst of all was their disregard for their own soldiers. Nearly a third of all soldiers sent to the front lines went there without a weapon and often without even a helmet. If they wanted a weapon, they would have to scavenge one off the battlefield from a fallen soldier.

The frustration stemming from this didn't improve the Tsar's popularity. Vladimir Lenin, a revolutionary in exile, saw his opportunity to seize power. By 1917, his followers in Russia began to riot and strike, finally forcing the Tsar to abandon his throne. Lenin returned to Russia and took power, assuming control of the press, the military, and other institutions. He pulled Russia out of the war, bringing the soldiers home to fight for him. Very quickly, Russia was transformed from a monarchy into Communist rule. Russia was a significantly different place for the soldiers who returned home from the battlefields of Europe, and would have many difficult years ahead.

THE WEIMAR REPUBLIC

In 1914, perhaps no country was as eager for war as Germany. The Germans had developed weapons and armaments such as the world had never seen before. They were superior in air and were the first country in centuries to pose a threat to the British Navy. They saw the assassination of the Archduke as their chance to expand their borders and emerge as the most powerful empire in all of Europe.

Yet when the tide of war began to turn against Germany, the people felt this loss in personal ways. A blockade of supplies had been enforced in the West, so Germany was unable to import the food and goods their population needed, and long, difficult winters had threatened their own crops. The people were hungry, and their economy was in ruins.

When Germany finally did surrender in November 1918, the terms of the treaty were harsh. Conditions that were already bad turned worse.

From among those ashes, a voice emerged to proclaim that Germany's punishment was far beyond what it deserved, that it was a great country and deserved to be treated as such. Many Germans, who were enduring years of hunger and poverty because of the treaty, began to listen to this man, who was named Adolf Hitler.

Within a few short years, Hitler would begin to amass power in the country and to build a new war machine—not to start a new world war, but to continue the old one.

THE LASTING IMPACT OF WORLD WAR I

By the end of the war, almost forty million people, including civilians and soldiers, had lost their lives, and millions more were wounded, displaced from their homes and villages. The war would redraw world maps, topple empires, and change the trajectory of world history.

Most historians will say that as destructive as World War I was, the real tragedy is that it led to nearly a century of conflict throughout the world.

Certainly there were many reasons why World War I began, but it is a curious thing to wonder how history might have been different, if only a driver in Bosnia had not taken a wrong turn one afternoon in June.

ACKNOWLEDGMENTS

World War I spanned four years, three months, and fourteen terrible days and spread to over one hundred countries worldwide. Most estimates place the casualty numbers at around forty million, making it the third deadliest war in history. The war brought down empires, changed world maps, and introduced a modern form of warfare that did more than scar the landscape—it scarred so many people who were part of it. Verdun, often mentioned in the book, was declared a "Red Zone" after the war, with officials describing it as, "Completely devastated. Damage to properties: 100%. Damage to Agriculture: 100%. Impossible to clean. Human life impossible."

The cleanup continues, but life has returned to Verdun, both in nature and with a healthy population of the area. It returned because nature wants to heal.

Lines of Courage was written during the global pandemic, a time of heightened anxieties, worries about the future, frightening news headlines, and isolation. The First World War could be described in the very same way.

Which is why lines of courage matter; those lines we extend from ourselves to offer strength and encouragement to others. And those that flow toward us, boosting our courage for whatever the future may bring.

I treasure the lines extended to me by my family, who give me happiness and strength, particularly my husband, Jeff—my best friend and the pillar at my side, every single day. I am grateful for the lines of wisdom, friendship, and inspiration that come from my editor, Lisa Sandell, and agent, Ammi-Joan Paquette, both brilliant, accomplished, and highly talented women who have taught me so much.

Many thanks also to the ever gracious Joanne Levy, for her willingness and wisdom when it was needed most.

And readers, I want you to know how much you matter. You are the rising generation, and the books you choose will influence who you become. I am honored that *Lines of Courage* is part of that choice.

World War I was called the "War to End All Wars." That didn't last long, of course, but may you be the generation that ends the conflict, whether on a global scale, or in your community, or within your closest relationships.

May you do so because nature wants to heal.

And with a little courage, we will too.

ABOUT THE AUTHOR

Jennifer A. Nielsen is the acclaimed author of the *New York Times* and *USA Today* bestselling Ascendance Series: *The False Prince*, *The Runaway King*, *The Shadow Throne*, *The Captive Kingdom*, and *The Shattered Castle*. She also wrote the *New York Times* bestseller *The Traitor's Game* and its sequels, *The Deceiver's Heart* and *The Warrior's Curse*; the *New York Times* bestselling Mark of the Thief trilogy: *Mark of the Thief*, *Rise of the Wolf*, and *Wrath of the Storm*; the standalone fantasy *The Scourge*; and the critically acclaimed historical thrillers *A Night Divided*, *Resistance*, *Words on Fire*, and *Rescue*. Jennifer collects old books, loves good theater, and thinks that a quiet afternoon in the mountains makes for a nearly perfect moment. She lives in northern Utah with her family and is probably sneaking in a bite of dark chocolate right now. You can visit her online at jennielsen.com or follow her on Twitter and Instagram at @nielsenwriter.